I0591016

# THE FUCHSIA
# SARI

# THE FUCHSIA SARI

## MERYL DUNTON-ROSE

*North Bank*

North Bank Institute of Independent Studies
PO Box 153, Bellingen, NSW, 2454, Australia
lizardland@bigpond.com

*The Fuchsia Sari*
2025

Copyright © Meryl Dunton-Rose

ISBN 978-0-6457731-2-5

 A catalogue record for this
NATIONAL   book is available from the
LIBRARY   National Library of Australia
OF AUSTRALIA

*The Fuchsia Sari*, a novel
Author: Meryl Dunton-Rose
Cover design: Meryl Dunton-Rose, Ross Macleay

This book is a work of fiction. Any references to historical events, real
people or real places are used fictitiously. Any historical or religious
inaccuracies are the author's. Other names, characters, places and
events are products of the author's imagination.

*For my daughters, all three*

And suddenly we see
That love costs all we are
And will ever be.
—Maya Angelou

I

# One

Mangaldas sat at his father's feet, his skinny legs crossed in the dust. He sorted small shiny stones into piles and then moved them around, adding and subtracting from the different piles until he was satisfied. He tipped the piles over, muddling them with his small hands. Shuffling them made a harsh grating sound and he glanced up at his father, but he did not seem to notice. He counted the stones out again and put them together neatly into different towers. He wasn't sure but this arrangement felt right as well. He was happy with the sums he had made and looked at his father for approval.

His father, also cross-legged, was staring out of the window, sad-eyed and grey-faced. His hair, lank and dirty, fell in damp curls around his ears. Every few minutes he would sigh deeply, but his gaze didn't wander.

Mangaldas could hear his sister's soft murmurings punctured by the whimpers of his mother. Jasleen had been in his mother's room all day and most of yesterday. He didn't know why his Amma wasn't bustling around, sifting lentils and singing to herself as she usually did, her small, round face exuding contentment at even the most trivial task. When he tried to go into his mother's bedroom, his sister had snapped at him to stay out. It wasn't safe. Safe? His

3

mother's quiet, cool room wasn't safe? He was confused; but when his father arrived home from work, questions in his eyes, he pushed past Mangaldas and hurried to the door behind which his wife lay. His sister answered the hesitant knock and whispered to his father. It seemed to be a secret. What were they saying? Fear and terror wrote themselves on his father's face and Mangaldas dropped his gaze. There were his stones. He would play with them. He glanced up. The terror had faded from his father's face but there was a darkness which he had never seen before. An emptiness.

"Mamaaji will be getting up soon, won't she, Pappa?" His father's stare shuddered as he glanced down at his son. Who was this boy interrupting his thoughts? His world was changing and he had no control over it. He needed to stay inside his mind. He shook his head as if covered in flies and stared again out of the window, away from his son.

"Can you read to me, Pappa? I've done my sums."

This was his favourite time of the day as he snuggled under his father's arm and smelt the jasmine soap he used to wash with when he came back from work and changed into a clean *dhoti*. His arm comforted and protected him. But not today. His father had not washed. A rank odour seeped from his pores to where Mangaldas sat and he was astonished to see that grease and dirt from today's toil remained on his father's *dhoti*.

His sister, Jasleen, crept on soft feet out of his parents' room. Her happy face was not on today. Why was everyone he loved wearing those sad faces? Gently, she shook her head at his father who had turned to look at her with a flicker of hope in his eyes. His father looked again out of the window and appeared to shrink. His soul seeped into the floor. His voice when it came was a whisper.

"Do what you have to. We will need to record the death. We will have to burn all her clothes and clean the house so thoroughly it will never need cleaning again," he said bitterly. Mangaldas saw his father's clenched fists and thought it best not to ask about his reading time again.

"Take the boy away. I'll go and speak to the priest while you see to her." He pulled himself heavily to his feet, his slight body swaying as he began to absorb the enormity of his life change.

Jasleen lay a hand on his arm. "Pappa, first you must wash yourself. Put some oil on your hair and prepare for the mourning. I'll have the oil lamp ready for you."

Mangaldas, crouching on the floor amongst his stones, looked from one to the other, at their anxious faces and their dark eyes, behind which lay their still unshed tears threatening release.

"I'm frightened," he said, his lips trembling. "Can I go and see Mamaaji? Where is she?" His tinny voice wavered and sobs shook his tiny body.

"No. You can't," they both said in unison.

"You will be able to soon, once we have washed her with milk and honey and dressed her in her red sari," his sister continued more gently. "Go with Pappa and see he washes himself. You must be a big boy. We'll have to learn to live without our Amma."

Without his Amma; he could not imagine it. But given a job, Mangaldas wiped his eyes on his sleeve and pulled at his father's hand to take him to the washroom. His father, a ghost of a man, followed as he tugged him along.

Half an hour later he heard a wailing. The boy's hands flew to his ears as he raced back towards the large front verandah. Neighbourhood women were seated in a circle, swaying as their voices rose in a strident ululation. It was deafening to him and he turned to his father.

"Why are they doing that?" he asked. "Who are all these people?"

His father's mouth drooped.

"Your mother has gone," he said. "She won't be here again. Not in this life. We must see her into the next one. All our neighbours and family will help us."

More women arrived with plates of betel leaves, nuts and

flowers. They embraced Jasleen in turn, painting her forehead with sandalwood paste. They then set about pulling mattresses onto the floor. Jasleen directed the men who had arrived to put up a canopy in the courtyard so that meals could be cooked and passed out to the mourners. More mattresses were dragged outside for the male friends and relatives who Jasleen told him would soon be arriving. Mangaldas watched in amazement as these preparations were made; his father stood in stupefaction, shepherded around by Jasleen and whispered about by the women as they sat cross-legged, ceasing their chants as they watched the grieving husband.

# Two

*1897 Bombay*

Mangaldas ran along the *wadi's* narrow winding streets, his slate
and book tucked under his arm. He stopped to watch Krishnan
pounding ginger on a stone to add to the boiling can of chai.
Krishnan grinned up at him and nodded. The smell was enticing
but he was anxious to get home. He picked up his heels and turned
the corner, nearly colliding with a cow ambling her way between
food offerings. He gave a reverent bow and slipped down another
alley where his small home was squeezed between others. The statue
of Ganesh nearby was newly anointed in oil, a dot of red powder
on its forehead. He smiled at the marigold garlands; such a cheerful
colour. He wondered if it was his sister's doing. He paused to see
if she was sitting on the verandah in front of the house. The chair
was empty. He raced into the downstairs room under the arched
doorway of faded blue paint and called out to his sister. There was
still no sign of her. He ran back outside and up the staircase at the
side of the house. Surely she would be up there. He was so excited.
His sides were heaving with the news. He revelled in learning and
when his teacher Mr Mistry had called him to one side and told him
he was the most clever boy he had ever taught he nearly burst. He
would tell his sister first and then his father when he came home

from work. He pushed the door open, the fretwork panel shivering as it banged against the wall.

"Jasleen!" he called out. Still nothing. He frowned, raced up the stairs and looked out from the landing into the small back garden where sometimes she sat sifting stones from the lentils. It was quiet and empty.

His shoes clattered against the wooden stairs as he flew down again. He must have missed her. She would be in the kitchen at the back. Once more he raced down the hall and found an empty house. No one in the kitchen. No one in the sitting room. He sat on the front step to wait for her.

Neighbours waved as they saw him sitting there. Mr Roy waggled his head at him.

"Back from school, already, I see."

"Do you know where Jasleen is? She's always here when I come home."

"No, son. But a railway man came and gave something to your sister. Perhaps it was from your father. Be patient. You will find out soon, I'm sure of it."

The sky was fading from dirty blue to black by the time his sister returned to the house.

"Where have you been? I'm hungry and I wanted to tell you what Mr Mistry said."

She threw her arms around him, enveloped him in her soft blue cotton sari and with her head resting on his started to tell him what had happened to his father.

"It can't be true!" he said. "Appa was fine this morning!" His distressed voice caused her to squeeze him more tightly.

"Oh, Mangal," she said, "it is not for us to know how and why these things happen."

She told him his father had collapsed at work and two of his compatriots holding his arms and legs had raced him to the railway doctor. By the time they reached the doctor's office, he was limp and lifeless.

"Keep him away from me," the doctor had said. "You know the plague is coming again. We must cover our mouths and stay away from him."

The plague wallahs picked him up in their cart and before Jasleen could see him he had been taken to the plague pits where bodies were burnt with little ceremony.

"We must bathe in coconut water and milk for protection against the plague," Jasleen said as she ran into the kitchen. "Help me find some fruit. Do we have any lemons left, or even pomegranates?" she demanded. "Any juice will help us as we pray to Hariti."

Mangaldas was distraught. Both his parents had left him. His sister was the only one he had left in the world. He knew she would look after him, but would she read to him at night? Would she be too busy with the household and finding money to keep them to pay him the attention he craved?

Later that evening as they sat in stunned silence, Jasleen remembered to ask him what Mr Mistry had said.

"Nothing," he said, "nothing important."

Jasleen fell back into a reverie, her father's death raising fearful thoughts and memories which raced through her as her stomach clenched. She looked over at Mangaldas and tried to cling on to the fondness with which she held him. The dark memories of his conception threatened to engulf her and she hid her face and sobbed as the blacked-out thoughts she had previously managed to tamp down had free rein.

That night. That horrific night when she had been walking back home from a friend's house, humming, with no cares in the world, and her arm was seized. The unexpectedness of it caused her to freeze, to not cry out as she should have done. Before she could gather any semblance of wits about her, another hand was clamped over her mouth and she was hustled by someone of much greater strength than her own into a dark alleyway, unfrequented by night.

A nasty-tasting gag was thrust into her mouth and her frightened eyes saw very little as the night was dark, the moon not having risen.

When she returned to her house, her sari torn and dirty, her hair falling in her frightened eyes, she was unable to voice her feeling of desecration, of violation. Her pounding heart, the traces of tears on her face, her stunned stupefaction told her mother all she needed to know.

Jasleen had fallen onto her bed, her knees pulled in tight, her clothes awry, her eyes wide and unseeing. She remained like this for several days, her gentle mother soothing her brow; until one day she rose, washed, and pretended nothing had happened.

"Jasleen?" Mangaldas' voice penetrated the weave of recollections that threatened to engulf her. "I'm hungry. Can we have something to eat?"

It was a few months later that she understood from a letter Mr Mistry had sent that Mangaldas really was an exceptional student and that he could benefit from a scholarship. She determined to talk to the teacher without her brother's knowledge. He could not bear another disappointment. Losing two parents was enough.

She, however, knew that he still had a remaining parent. Ten years ago when she had been the victim of that violent assault, Mangaldas was the result. Her parents had kept her safe behind closed doors during the pregnancy and she of course did not return to school. Her mother stayed out of sight, too, and gave credence to the pretence that Mangaldas was her child and Jasleen had been looking after her during a difficult pregnancy. It was a lie which suited them both. Appa had always wanted a boy child and after Jasleen was born Amma had conceived several times but had miscarried each one. Jasleen did not need the responsibility of a child; and if it were known, her parents would never find a suitor for her to marry. Amma had a baby boy to cherish and cuddle. She had finally brought a son to the home. It was a deceit of which Mangaldas had no inkling.

Mangaldas loved his sister deeply but the loss of his parents had struck him hard and his schooling suffered.

"I've seen Mr Mistry," his sister said. "He said if you don't work hard you will never win that scholarship; and I shall be so disappointed."

Mangaldas bowed his head. His heart felt squeezed and his grief was still waking him in the night with a rapid heartbeat and a feeling of dread he couldn't quite pinpoint in his half-awake state. The joy he had felt in the learning and his ability to concentrate had quite deserted him. Many times a day Mr Mistry called out his name to answer a question and he was unable to respond, unable to recall where he was and why he would need to speak. His head was full of fog and it was all he could do to try to focus on Mr Mistry's moustache as it squirmed around on his upper lip, the words lost in the mere shape of his mouth. The look of concern on his kindly teacher's face was lost on him. As this showed no signs of abating, Mr Mistry requested to see his sister.

"It is very worrying, Miss Jasleen. I am not knowing what to do. Perhaps you can talk to him. He is seemingly not interested in the schooling any more. What can you do? I am thinking that he is very upset about his father's demise. It is understandable. But of course after six months he should be living like a young boy, not dwelling in the past. Surely as a Hindu he knows death is part of life? He must accept this, Miss Jasleen. You must be telling him so."

Jasleen nodded in agreement. She responded in Hindi. Her understanding of English, the language of business and education, was good but she felt far more comfortable expressing her emotions in her first language.

"I have tried talking to him, Mr Mistry. I have taken him to the temple and we have walked around the shrines; I have prayed to all the gods I know but he is showing no interest in anything. I am worried too."

"We will have to put our heads together and see what we can

be doing for him, for mark my words if he does not shake this off I cannot see how he will win a scholarship and my reputation will be shaken. You must be talking to him in English, he must do better. I am not used to this, Miss Jasleen. Please, I am begging you to try again, for all our sakes."

# Three

## *1898 Scholarship*

Jasleen heard Mr Mistry's entreaties in her head constantly. They were written on the ticket stubs, they were printed on the file covers, they were everywhere; but as she worked diligently she could see no solution. Her brother continued to sit in lethargy: light gone from him, his active mind no longer alive. He ate without tasting his food, he thanked her by rote and hugged her without feeling.

She took Mangaldas to the temple and made sure he did his morning *pujah* to the goddess of learning, Saraswati. She bought special garlands and Mangaldas placed them around the goddess's neck. It was to no avail. He remained disengaged from both school and life.

She wondered if she should tell him the truth of his parentage. Would it shock him back into life or would it spiral him further downward? It was a conundrum she could not solve. Would her relationship with him deteriorate, built as it was on a lie; or would he feel closer to her and understand the family's dilemma?

Days passed, weeks passed. Mangaldas grew thin, his face grey, his hair lacklustre.

"Come to Jasleen," she tried, "here; I will rub some coconut oil into your hair. It is looking very sad. Much like you."

Sighing, Mangaldas sat at her feet and Jasleen massaged the oil into his dark hair. The love she felt for him radiated into his scalp. He closed his eyes and leant back into her legs, the rigidity in his body finally relaxing. She crooned and then began singing one of the songs her mother had sung to each of them as babies tied tightly around her person. Mangaldas swayed as her fingers gently pulled his dark curls. The darkness in him lifted. He began to sing. Together they sat in the gloom, their song a harmony reaching into every corner of his soul.

It was as if the old Mangaldas returned. He shook himself and went to fetch some *lassi* sitting in a cold tub of water in the kitchen. He placed it in her hands with a small bow of his head. His hands in prayer, "Thank you," he said. "Our parents have been reincarnated. I feel it in my bones." His gravity belied his age. Words of a priest, from a child.

"I don't know what you have been doing to Mangaldas or what you said to him," said Mr Mistry, the next time Jasleen met him, "but he has renewed his efforts. He is applying himself to every lesson and he is answering every question I ask him. I think there may still be a chance that he will sit for the scholarship and be successful. We will see. At the end of this month I will ask you to go and see the Hindu Education Fund and we will hope for wonderful things. Yes, wonderful things we will hope for," Mr Mistry continued, nodding his head and smiling at the change in Mangaldas.

"You have such a special brother, Miss Jasleen. Please be taking good care of him."

"Don't hold my hand so tightly. I know where I'm going. I can walk by myself. you know."

"You're walking so slowly! Mr Gupta said you had to be there by half past eight and it's almost that now. Come on."

Mangaldas scowled and hurried to keep step with his sister, his feet working twice as fast as hers. It was hot and dusty as they scurried down the alleyways towards the Hindu Education Fund building. His sister had been to see Mr Gupta on the advice of the village school headmaster as he had told her that her brother had an exceptional brain and could do well for himself if he managed to get a decent education. He could teach him no more.

"He is beyond what I am knowing," Mr Mistry said. "Perhaps if you take him to Mr Gupta at the Hindu Education Fund he might have a place for him. There are some wealthy benefactors. But perhaps all the places are taken. I am not knowing this."

Jasleen had rushed after work to the address scribbled on a piece of paper. To make doubly sure of arriving at the correct place she had asked Mr Mistry to draw a map which he promptly scrawled on the back of the paper. She held her sari tightly across her face as the familiar places were left behind her. The white building in front of her was shabby, its paint dusty and faded; and on street level was a shop entrance full of piles of tin pans. Shiny utensils filled every shelf and the shop owner looked up with a quizzical smile from his newspaper as he sat on a stool waiting for customers. Jasleen hesitated before a plaque on the wall of a steep and narrow set of stairs. She held up the piece of paper and double-checked the name of the office. She looked around at strangers' faces curiously glancing at this slight woman as she hovered in the busy street. She plucked up her courage. This was for Mangaldas. She would do anything for him. He was her world and everything beyond it.

The stairs turned onto a landing and in front of her she saw a faded blue door, its paint peeling, with the same plaque attached. The Hindu Education Fund. She knocked hesitantly. An impatient voice called out, "Come in, come in." Mr Gupta sat behind a large wooden desk, its surface covered with a collection of stacked papers that reached higher than Mr Gupta's chest. His round face, spectacles perched on his nose, peered over the top of one such stack. He put down his pen and moved a pile of folders so he could look at his visitor.

"I'm a very busy man, Miss. It is a very lovely day but so short and I have much work to do. Is there something you are wanting, Miss?"

Jasleen stood, twisting the ends of her sari in her hands.

"Mr Gupta, sir, Teacher Mistry from Girgaum district sent me. My son. My brother."

"The teacher is your son?" He looked amazed. "Speak in English, Miss."

"No, no, sir. Not the teacher, no. My brother, I mean, he is very clever. The teacher said I should come and see you, sir."

"Well, did he think to tell you how I might help?"

"Yes, sir. He said that you might be able to find him a place at a good school. He loves his numbers. He writes all day long. Numbers and numbers on any sheet of paper he can find."

"Yes, yes. I will need to see him and assess his capabilities, you understand. We can't just send anyone to those schools, you know, we have our reputation to be thinking of."

Jasleen looked down at her feet, dusted a soft grey. Her nose stud glistened as she held her head up and stared at Mr Gupta.

"I can pay some money," she said softly. "I have a job. I have some savings."

Mr Gupta waved his hand.

"No, no, that is not how it works. If your brother is as good as you and the teacher – Mr Mistry, was it? – say, all his fees will be covered. They will pay for uniform and all his expenses. You understand? But he must be good... And you must keep talking to him in English, you understand, his English speaking must be fluent. Keep talking, Miss Jasleen!"

Mangaldas loved school. He loved how numbers seemed so logical to him and the mathematical puzzles set were completed without thought. Logic. It was all to do with logic. What had not seemed logical to him was the death of his father during the recent plague outbreak. He hated passing the building on the corner of Kaladevi Road where his father's death was recorded amongst so many others;

a small red circle. His father who had saved every rupee to send him to the school run by Mr Mistry in the next *wadi*. His father's job on the railway, like his father's before him, paid him a regular salary which was much more than most people who lived around him could earn. His father had learnt to read Hindi when he was young and he instilled this love of learning into his son. Mangaldas remembered sitting on his father's skinny knee tracing letters in the tatty book that his father kept out of reach on the top shelf above his bed. His tin drinking cup sat next to it and his black leather-covered *Bhagavad Gita* which had been given to him by one of the English colonists in the office. He never knew why. It had certainly remained his most treasured possession up to his death. For Mangaldas, thoughts of both his father and mother arose acutely every time he opened the leather cover and transported himself into the world of Arjuna and Krishna, looking for answers to his life.

"We're nearly there," his sister said. "Just down this alleyway and there, see? There's the building."

Mangaldas had expected to be impressed but this building looked the same as any others in his *wadi*. Badly in need of whitewashing, the surface streaked and dirty.

It was twenty-five minutes to nine as they raced up the stairs to Mr Gupta's office.

"You're late," he said looking at his watch as they tumbled through the door. "This will not be making a good impression. Punctuality is most important. If they are seeing fit to give you a scholarship and you are going to the school you must be present on time at every lesson. Every lesson, you understand. No running in five minutes late."

"It's my fault; don't be cross with Mangaldas, please. He was walking as quickly as he could. The streets are so busy, you know, at this time of the morning."

"Leave us now. I will not be hearing any more excuses. You can come back for him in an hour's time. Good-day, Miss Jasleen.

# Four

Mangaldas shuffled and turned his cheek as his sister bent to kiss him. He beamed as Mr Gupta moved a pile of folders, making space for him on a corner of his desk, and set a paper booklet in front of him.

"Take your time, young man. I am not expecting that you will finish in an hour but we will see how well you are calculating."

Mangaldas looked at the smooth white paper and the sums neatly set out in columns. It was delightful; he had never seen so many numbers. He smiled and sucked his pencil. All the sums made sense, he could see that. None of the numbers jumped around as letters sometimes did. He worked through the first page while periodically Mr Gupta looked over his glasses at the concentrating boy. Mangaldas turned over the page and the sums became more complicated but he finished them quickly enough. Mr Gupta opened the window wider and called out to a chai wallah to bring him some chai, throwing him a few *paises* before turning back into the room. Within a few minutes the chai wallah brought up a clay cup of chai. Mr Gupta heard his *chappals* clattering back down the stairs. He held the cup in both hands and took a deep draught of the sweet liquid, clouding up his spectacles.

Turning over to page three, Mangaldas sent a questioning glance up at Mr Gupta but he was sipping his chai and didn't meet his gaze. He couldn't make sense of these sums. He blinked and looked again. He had failed. He had disappointed his sister. He would go back to school with shame written all over him. He had no idea numbers would not deliver up their mysteries to him.

Shamefaced, he handed the paper to Mr Gupta. He said nothing, scrutinised pages one and two and harrumphed at page three. Mangaldas felt hot; he pulled at his *kurta's* fabric around his neck and then padded from foot to foot as he thought he was going to wet himself.

"You may be going outside to wait for your sister. I will be sending word about your results next week. In the meantime, I am suggesting you do more studying. You can never be learning too much, you know."

He gestured a dismissal and Mangaldas dragged his way down the rickety stairs. He counted the knots in the wood and saw patterns in the nails as he worked his way down. Groups of numbers are just patterns. Why could he not have seen the patterns in the sums upstairs? He sat on the bottom step, hands cupped under his chin, and explored the shapes on the stair wall. Damp had drawn clouds, smoke and steam. Hiding behind were gods and goddesses floating down to earth. If only they could have come down and saved him, given him the answers. He stuck his tongue into a hole in his tooth and worried it as nerve pain shot down his neck. Serves me right, he thought. I deserve it. Tears prickled. His nose ran and he wiped the dribble on his *dhoti*.

His sister found him there ten minutes later, his *dhoti* soaked and his eyes red-rimmed. She crouched in front of him.

"What is the matter? Was he mean to you?"

Mangaldas shook his head and wiped his eyes again.

"Then what is it? Tell me."

"I've failed." His bottom lip was trembling and the tears threatened to pour down his cheeks.

"Did Mr Gupta say so? You are not knowing that. You are clever.

How could you have failed? The astrologer said it was a propitious day; he is always right, you know."

The comforting words were spoken in love but Mangaldas could not be consoled and he dawdled behind, a miserable heap, as they made their way home through the winding streets. He entered the doorway to their somewhat austere rooms at the bottom of the two-storey building. Jasleen had said that they were lucky, as the railway company's paperwork had not yet caught up with the fact that their father was no longer employed and as such no longer entitled to accommodation, bare and sparse as it was. However he was grateful for the coolness, it reflected his mood.

# Five

"We are Brahmins, Mangaldas, we are educated people. You deserve this scholarship. I'm sure you will be fine. Teacher Mistry said so. He is very clever, I think. He got a scholarship too, you know."

Mangaldas scooped up rice with his fingers. The *dahl* he loved so much did not please him tonight; he hardly noticed he was eating it. He wondered how he would get to a good school without the scholarship. Jasleen's job at the railway he knew was a good one. It was not usual for women to be working but as the head of the household with no other form of income she had no option. Her father had used his long tenure to wield a little influence and ensure a position for her a few months before he died. It was as if he had known how important this would be. She had been given a trial in the railway ticket offices of the local station as a filing clerk. She derived pleasure from sorting and organising. The folders and binders were kept in a large store cupboard and her job was to file the copies of the tickets that the clerks wrote daily. It was a busy station, the Victoria terminus, and at the end of the day her feet ached. She liked nothing better than Mangaldas' small hands rubbing butter into her heels and massaging her sore toes. It was a gift he could give her; and now, as sad as he was, he set out the cushions for her and put the ghee into a pot on the floor. He brought in a bowl of water with jasmine petals floating on the surface. Gently, he took her feet into his hands and caressed them before washing them.

"You are doing so much for me," he said, his head bowed.

He dried her feet with a coarse towel and dipped his fingers into the ghee. Methodically, he massaged the oil between each toe, under the instep, around the pads of the toes and lastly into the cracked skin on her heels.

"You'll never be having the feet of a *maharina*," he joked, "if you are standing on your feet all the time. One day I'll be having enough money to keep you. To give you sweetmeats and beautiful saris. Just you wait."

"I'm sure you will," she laughed, "you are my clever boy. Come here and give me a hug."

They sat entwined on the pillows as the soft dusk and the scent of jasmine fell around them.


Mr Mistry stood at the door to the *wadi* school shuffling his feet as Mangaldas walked in the next morning. He rubbed his hands and beamed while Mangaldas avoided his gaze.

"*Namaste*, Teacher Mistry." He held his hands in prayer and nodded as he sidled past.

"Not so fast, not so fast! You must be telling me everything. How was the paper? Did you do well? What did Mr Gupta say?"

Mangaldas swallowed. He felt tears prickle. He was too old to cry. Too old to cry like a baby in front of Mr Mistry.

"I don't know, Mr Mistry. Mr Gupta said nothing and… and…"

"And what? Were you doing something wrong? Tell me!"

"The paper was too hard," he blurted out. "I only did pages one and two. The third was making no sense to me. I'm sorry, I've disappointed you."

"Well, well, never mind. You can be trying again next year, I'm sure. Did Mr Gupta give you any mark?"

"No, sir, he just told me to go outside and wait for my sister."

Mr Mistry issued a curt command to all the children to sit on their benches and copy the sums off the board. He knew that

Mangaldas would complete them before anyone else, even the older children. What was he going to do with him?

The following Tuesday Mr Gupta sent word that he needed to see Mangaldas and his sister. His opening words as they came into his office were: "I am having good news. Good news indeed! The school has never seen such accurate work from a boy your age. Teacher Mistry was right!"

"But I couldn't complete the third page, Mr Gupta!"

"No one has ever been doing the third page, young man. That is for college entrants. One day you will try it again and I'm sure you will be finding it easy."

Jasleen and Mangaldas gripped each other's hands. Jasleen was trembling.

"What happens now, Mr Gupta, sir?"

"Yes, yes, I was getting to that. A lot of details. A lot of details. After the summer Mangaldas will be commencing at St Patrick's. Before school ends this year you must go to the bursar at the school and request uniform. Very smart, it is, very smart. Are you knowing where the school is? Not too far for Mangaldas to go every day, I think. Many felicitations, young man, many indeed. It is not often that a prestigious school like this takes one of my recommendations. Do not let me down, no, not at all. I do not wish to be hearing any negative things about you, you hear? Nothing negative, indeed no, I wish to be hearing only good things, only good things."

Jasleen and Mangaldas nodded vigorously and left with the recommendation paper in hand. Jasleen folded it in half and tucked it under her bodice. Mangaldas hoped it was not too hot before they got home. He did not want her to present a wrinkled, crumpled piece of paper to the school. St Patrick's! He couldn't even speak as they made their way home. Jasleen kept up a stream of words, none of which he heard.

Mangaldas worked hard and did not turn away from his studies, despite being teased about his name by the other boys. Jenkins was the worst.

"Mangaldas: what kind of name is that? Sounds like: my Mum has a mangle! Bet you don't even know what one is, do you?"

Mangaldas shook his head. The word had not entered his vocabulary but Jenkins, who had been at school in England before being sent back home to Bombay, did know and thought it was hilarious. He teased him at every opportunity; and when Jenkins finally left school, Mangaldas determined to give himself an English name. Many Anglo-Indian boys had English names; perhaps he could too. He prided himself on his honesty and after much thought, decided on 'Frank.'

Frank started his last year of school top of the class in everything and so far ahead in Mathematics that the headmaster, Father Francis, called him in to talk about his prowess.

"You have shown yourself to be a very capable young man, Frank. You would be in line for the headmaster's prize but I'm afraid we can't give that to a scholarship boy. I would like you to sit for another scholarship, though: a college scholarship which will take you far."

Having been awarded the scholarship Frank began business college, specialising in accounting and bookkeeping. His sister continued to follow his progress with pride; and one day after reading of another scholarship that might be available to him, she spoke to him of her dreams.

"You are wasted here," she said. "I think it's time you spoke to Mr Gupta again. I read about a scholarship which would fund your training in England. Every year they send one student to Manchester College to study. I know as Brahmins we shouldn't cross the sea; but think of this opportunity! They pay for your boat passage and even give you some money to rent a room while you're there!"

Her enthusiasm was infectious and although Mangaldas thought he would not have any chance of gaining the stipend he dutifully sat the exam at the end of the college year during which he had gained Honours in his basic accounting. He allowed himself to daydream of life in England but his imagination failed him. He thought it impossible.

Jasleen prattled on about how life in England would be.

"You will be articled to a famous English accounting firm. You will become rich and can return to Bombay to start your own business." She marvelled at the plans she had for him. Frank did not wish to disappoint her. The possibility of being the one to win this wonderful accountancy scholarship out of the many hundreds applying for it seemed so remote.

As if in a myth, the poor student won the prize and his life was to change for ever. The next few months before his departure passed by all too quickly. He relished his time with Jasleen and spoke often to her about how he would miss her. It still seemed impossible that he would be living a different life.

Jasleen, as a way of hiding her emotions, became the practical one. She took him to the tailor.

"Please make him an English suit," she said. "My brother is going to study in England." Frank thought that a new pair of glasses was more important as his eyesight, which had never been good, had been troubling him with the amount of calculations he had to complete. He squinted now at the columns and often had difficulty focussing.

But his appearance was important to his sister and she scoffed at the idea that he would need new glasses before he left.

# Six

*1910 Voyage from Bombay to London*

Jasleen was determined to send Mangaldas off in style and she scraped together some rupees to buy him a new pair of leather shoes. While she was at the cobbler's she noticed some beautiful leather cases piled up in the corner of the small, dusty shop. Her fingers ran over the strong cotton stitching at the corners, her breath steaming the bright brass latches. With a curious glance she looked over at the cobbler bent over a shoe on a last. She gasped at the price when told.

"But I can give you special price," the cobbler said, "as you have bought some beautiful shoes for your brother. When you return for the shoes I will give you a discount. A very good discount, yes?"

It was a week before Jasleen returned to talk to the cobbler and pick up the strong leather brogues she was sure he would need for the English weather. She laid out the notes she had been going to give to Mangaldas for his journey and hoped that they would be enough.

"Very good, very good," he said. "For that, I will imprint his initials on his case. He will be very proud to carry my good work with him all the way to England. Very pleased, indeed."

With his tan leather case stamped with the gold initials M.L.T., and sporting his new suit, Mangaldas walked along the dock towards the ship. Jasleen walked beside him, wiping the tears from her face with her sari. Before he reached the gangplank, he turned and knelt. His sister sobbed as he touched her feet in respect, before straightening up and brushing off his trousers at the knee, his own vision blurring.

Mangaldas walked up the gangplank to his new life. As he stepped into the ship he turned to wave to his sister; but he could not make her out on the crowded quay. He thought he saw her standing at the back, her golden sari to her mouth, but then he remembered she was dressed in blue today – a beautiful sari that her new husband had given to her.

Life for once had been kind to her, Mangaldas thought. Jarod, a quiet ticket dispenser in the railway office, had been taken with the clear gaze of Jasleen's dark brown eyes and her ready smile. He made discreet enquiries and learned that she was the head of her little family and as such would be in need of his assistance as a husband. He had been widowed some years before and had not been openly looking for a new wife but the thought of perhaps having children before it was too late spurred him on. The courtship was fast; she had no parents to negotiate a bride price with; his parents had given up finding him another arranged marriage after his first wife died. They welcomed his choice of lady into their household. All this had happened while Mangaldas was finishing business college.

"The timing is perfect," Jarod had said. "You can come and live in my house once your brother has gone to England. He won't be needing your help anymore. You have been caring for him all this time, now you can be taking care of me and my parents."

Jasleen bit her lip and forced herself to smile. She would never divulge the secret of Mangaldas' parentage to Jarod. The thought of transferring her caring duties to Jarod and his parents did not particularly appeal to her but the thought of financial security was too tempting. Besides, her devotion to Mangaldas meant that her friendships with others had never developed and she feared the emptiness which would encircle her once he had left.

II

# Seven

## *1910 Chorlton-cum-Hardy, Manchester*

Maree waited at the tram stop amongst the hustle and bustle of workers returning home. She jiggled from foot to foot. What it was to be fifteen and have all the exciting world in front of you! The escapade she was planning with Ruby was so exciting.

She and Ruby had been bosom pals since they entered school together on their first day. She had seen Ruby standing hesitantly by the side of the road opposite the school, scuffing her newly polished shoes in the gutter.

Maree remembered it so clearly, "Are you going to start today, too?" she asked, confident as she held the hand of her elder sister Flo who was two years ahead of her and well used to going to school on her own.

Ruby nodded and looked down again at her shoes, now poking at a piece of wood. Flo was dragging Maree towards the school gates.

"Wait," Maree said, and without extricating her hand from Flo's grip she extended her other to Ruby who took it gratefully, a shy smile on her grubby face.

So, that was how it started. They stood together in the girls' line as they waited for the teachers to inspect them before they were allowed into the classroom. Miss Gilbert, the teacher for the infants, allowed the corners of her mouth to turn up as she looked at the new intake. The little girl with the shock of red curls wore a neatly patched and darned smock. The blonde girl in front of her beamed up at her with a fresh face and laundered pinafore.

Miss Gilbert held her register and ticked off the names.

"Ruby Parkin?"

"Yes."

"'Yes, Miss Gilbert.'" Thinking she might have frightened the small girl on her first day, she smiled and continued calling out names.

"Maree Crymble?"

"I'm here," Maree responded, taking no heed of Miss Gilbert's request.

"Maree, did you not hear me say you must answer, 'Yes, Miss Gilbert'?"

"I did, Miss, but I thought that was for Ruby, not me."

Miss Gilbert hesitated, threw a glance to Miss Shields, the ancient headmistress who luckily had not heard or seen the exchange, and decided to shelve her doubts as to the intended cheekiness of this remark and said, "Never mind. Just remember next time."

Miss Gilbert told the girls to enter first, followed by the boys.

Holding hands, the two girls made their way through the infants' entrance and into the gloomy corridor. The stone floor felt cold beneath their thin-soled shoes and they shuddered as the door closed behind them. They sat next to each other at the strange wooden desks, shared chalkboards and exchanged answers and confidences from that day onwards.

Ruby and Maree strolled arm in arm from school. Their firm friendship had blossomed and their heads were always together in the playground, one red, one fair, despite the protestations of the headmistress, Miss Shields, who was convinced that they were spreading head lice around the school.

Monday morning was inspection day. The girls stood at one side of the playground and the boys in their grubby shorts and scabbed knees on the other side. Maree elbowed Ruby and the two started giggling. In front of them was Felicity, the tiniest girl in their class. Her hair was white, her face pale as icing sugar with a few hundreds and thousands sprinkled across her nose. From the girls' vantage point, they could see the lice crawling through her blonde hair. A large one jumped onto Felicity's shoulder.

"Yuck!" Maree jumped backwards onto Ruby's foot. Ruby gave out a yell and Miss Booth, inspecting further up the line, came bustling back to see what the fuss was about.

"Ew, Miss! Felicity's got nits. Felicity's got nits! Her hair is disgusting!"

The chant was taken up by the boys across the playground. Miss Shields, formidable in black, tried to keep control, swishing her cane as the boys jumped up and stood on tiptoes to see if they could see the nits. One brave soul, Fred the butcher's son, darted across the ground separating the two lines, so eager was he to see the dastardly creatures in the poor child's hair. He was within a few feet before he was chased back with a timely rap on the back of his calves from Miss Booth's ruler, which she kept handy for such an occasion.

Pleased with the chaos she had caused, Maree grinned at Ruby. The more time spent in the playground, as chilly as it was, the less time inside sitting on those hard wooden benches, copying out this week's words from the blackboard. Maree's script was neat but Ruby, being left-handed, struggled as she was forced to write with her right hand, her left tied behind her back. It was a constant battle for her.

On the way home from school that day, Ruby told Maree that her grandma was ill. She was coughing so badly her mother thought she might have consumption. Maree shivered. She had heard her mother gossiping with Mrs Taylor down the road about this awful disease. Mrs Taylor had told her mother that everyone who worked in the cotton mills was terrified they might catch it; and that was where all the women in Ruby's family worked.

Maree swallowed down her alarm as Ruby continued, "Mam says that's what they get for working in 'Cottonopolis'. I make special hot drinks for Nan but nothing seems to help when she gets one of her coughing fits."

With childish disgust she described how she had seen blood on the handkerchiefs which her grandma had been too late to hide from her. In a hushed voice Ruby confided that she had overheard her mother and father whispering about a place called a 'Santa room'. She was not sure what kind of room it was but it was supposed to make her grandma better.

At the first sound of a cough from her own father, Maree scurried down from the little girls' bedroom where she had been sitting on the floor playing with her rag dolls. With her doll Emma clutched in one hand, she looked up at her father who was taking off his painter's overalls before having a bath in the kitchen.

"Da," she demanded, "you're not going to Santa's room, are you?" Her father tilted his head to one side and with his bushy eyebrows drawn together he looked down at his youngest daughter.

"Santa's room? Whatever do you mean? I've been painting in some pretty cold places I can tell you, and it'll get colder before Christmas and Santa comes. I've got a cold, little one, that's all." He sneezed as if in proof and swept Maree up in his arms as he strode into the kitchen to his wife who was waiting, towel in hand, by the tin bath.

"Whatever's a 'Santa's room'? Something at the North Pole? Who's been telling Maree tales?"

"I think she must mean the sanatorium; is that right, Maree?" Mrs Crymble hung the towel over the edge of a kitchen chair and smoothed her hand over her taut belly. Arthur's look of concern faded as he looked at his wife.

"How's my little boy?" Arthur said as he too cradled her bump lovingly. He bent to kiss her stomach and Maree, who had nodded her assent to the unfamiliar word, flung her arms around his neck, nearly knocking him off his feet.

"Kiss me too," she said, and he laughed in compliance.

Over porridge the next morning, something seemed to catch in Arthur's throat and he couldn't stop coughing. Mrs Crymble patted him on the back and when this didn't work, she took to massaging it in a circular motion. Maree's eyes were wide as she and Flo hovered their spoons over their porridge, not taking their gaze away from his contorted face.

"Finish your breakfast and away with your staring, girls," said Agnes. "Your father told you, he just has a cold and now a tickly cough. Hurry up now and clean your teeth in the sink before you run off to school. Your father will be just fine." Nell and Maud, Maree's elder sisters still at home, raced each other downstairs ready for work but stopped short when they saw the concern on their mother's face. She turned away from her husband, whose wheezing was subsiding.

"What's with Da?" Nell ran and put her arms around her father while Maud urged her mother to sit down.

"The little ones?" Maud queried.

"Gone to school," their mother confirmed.

"Stop fussing," their father said. "I'm fine. I'm off to work now, too. Leave me be."

It was a few weeks later that Flo and Maree returned home from school to an empty house. They opened the back door into the small garden, thinking their mother might have been getting in the washing and not heard them calling. Nothing. No one.

They sat on the front step, feet turned in with their elbows on their knees and chins in cupped hands, waiting. They passed the time telling each other stories but these invariably had gloomy endings;

and tears fell as they held each other. None of the neighbours noticed the two pathetic figures and it was almost dark when their mother returned home. Her face was grey; with an arm around each crying daughter, she waddled to a chair and sat down, exhaling loudly.

"Stop your withering, girls. Da is in hospital." Agnes didn't have the energy to explain any more and she was not sure how much she would even say. Her time was near and she felt exhausted. Nell and Maud came home and got dinner for them all. Nell took control and organised the family for the remainder of the week. Her calm plans went awry when the next evening her mother shouted, "Call the midwife!" and took to her bed. The midwife was duly called but as this was Agnes' sixth birth, she knew more than the young midwife, flapping around with towels and hot water.

"It's a boy, Mam," Nell breathed. Agnes smiled.

"Your Da will be made up," she said. "You know he adores all you girls, but a boy... he's wanted a son for so long, this will make him better, I'm sure of it!"

Alice, the eldest married sister, came across from Sheffield to visit and help with the new baby.

"Go and see Da," she admonished her mother. "I can look after baby Arthur."

Maree sighed. Her gaze and her thoughts returned to her surroundings. She looked up at the clock at the back of the haberdasher's. Another twenty minutes. She knew they would pass so slowly. Mrs Hastings coughed discreetly into her handkerchief and Maree turned away from the window and busied herself rolling ribbon and carefully pinning the end to itself. She loved the colours. She loved the feel of the ribbons. The sheen of the silk, the pelt-like softness of the velvet. She was saving her farthings for a tuppenny piece of sky-blue velvet ribbon to dress her navy hat. More often than not, her mother needed all the money she earned to keep food on the table. Ribbons were luxuries, not necessities, as her mother frequently said to all her girls.

"Just because you're working with all that frippery doesn't mean you have to waste your money on it, my girl!"

Maree sighed and walked back to the fitting table. The hat she was working on looked limp. She had blocked and steamed it as she had been taught but somehow it just didn't look right. She would need to undo her work on Monday. She sighed again. Mrs Hastings looked over her glasses at her and she turned her sigh into a cough. No, she had better not cough again, or Mrs Hastings would think she too had tuberculosis. They had lost one of the assistants, Mary, last month. She had coughed and coughed until her slight body was nothing but a wracking cough. She looked drained, pale and grey and after a particularly bad day she didn't come back to work. Maree found out later that she had not been accepted at the sanatorium; it cost too much for her family and there were so few beds. A few weeks ago Maree had found herself, dressed in black along with others, standing next to the freshly dug grave in the Southern Cemetery, tears in her eyes, grasping a white handkerchief to her dripping nose. The weather was icy and her breath sailed over the heads of the other mourners: Mrs Hastings, her stiff expression staring into the abyss and Mary's parents, distraught, propping each other up as they contemplated the impossible.

"Are you dreaming again, Maree? If you haven't finished your work by six o'clock you'll have to stay behind. You're not paid to daydream, you know. I've told you so many times to concentrate on your felting. No wonder that hat doesn't look well. Mrs Harris is expecting that hat next week for the races. You'd better look smart."

Maree turned back to her work, vainly attempting to coax the felt into shape. She glanced over at Elsie, who was simpering as she added the final piece of tulle to the crown of the hat she was working on. Elsie never got into trouble. One year ahead of Maree in her apprenticeship, she had nimble fingers and a way with reproducing the designs from the fashion plates of the Paris magazines.

Would that clock never tick towards closing time? Maree had plans for this weekend and a Friday night walk with Ruby was just the start of it.

The bell above the door rang noisily and Maree and Elsie both looked up expectantly. If this was a customer, one of them would be kept occupied until closing time. But they were out of luck this time. It was Mr Wilson, the owner, who came in. He tipped his hat to the girls and walked over to Mrs Hastings who was standing behind the counter.

"Well, how much did we take today?" he asked.

"Good afternoon, Mr Wilson," she replied, her frosty tone lowering the temperature inside the shop. "More than yesterday, at any road," she relented. "Elsie actually sold two of those hats the girls made last week to a couple of society ladies up from the country for the opening of the ice palace."

Maree's ears pricked up. The ice palace opening was where she was headed tomorrow. Such an extravaganza! She had been saving the change from her salary in an old jam jar at home after giving her mother the rest towards her board and keep. She and Ruby had conferred over the weeks and kept tally on each other's monetary progress. Not just the entry money but money to hire ice skates! She'd seen photographs in the magazines of women dressed in fur coats with hands tucked in muffs, skating effortlessly along a frozen river, frozen ponds or even an ice rink in London. And now, Manchester was getting its very own ice rink. It was too exciting for words. Maree's heart beat fast as she thought of how she would dress up in her finery and put on her jacket trimmed with the tiny bits of rabbit fur she had filched from work over the last few months. You had to have some perks, she thought.

Ruby had been the first to turn fifteen and she had taken up work in the cotton mill where her mother and older sister worked. She had wanted Maree to come there too. "Ancott's Mill isn't so bad," she said. Maree thought how quickly the scare of consumption left you when you were given steady money. "They give you breaks and there's some lovely girls working there." She regaled Maree with tales that the older girls had told her which really made Maree's hair curl, even without the help of her sister.

Maree had looked forward with excitement to the thought of starting the millinery apprenticeship to Wilson Bothalmey and Co. that her sister Nell and her husband John had arranged for her, being, as they said, persons of influence with many businesses in the area. But in reality it was hard work and she hated the smell of the rabbit pelts cured with acid and mercury that she had to handle, and waking up before it was light, stepping out into the cold and fog before she had even had a brew. Being the most junior she swept the floor, tidied the workshop and was general dogsbody to Elsie and to Mary too, before she died. Mary had been in her fourth year of apprenticeship and ordered both Elsie and Maree around as if she owned the place when out of Mrs Hastings' hearing. Maree thought gleefully that soon they would have to hire another apprentice in Mary's stead, one junior to her; and then, mind, she could do some ordering around as she moved up in the ranks. She grinned as Elsie looked at her quizzically; but as the clock struck six, she jumped up and just smiled as she headed to the cloakroom to find her coat and scarf.

Elsie finished pinning the tulle and stood up as Mrs Hastings nodded her agreement for her to leave. Maree hadn't even waited for the nod and was putting on her coat. She was cinching her belt as Elsie hissed at her: "What was that grin for? You're a little madam, aren't you? You'd better watch yourself or I'll tell Mrs Hastings you're planning something."

Maree was in such high spirits now that the working day was over that even the threat from Elsie didn't dampen her spirit. She wrapped the scarf around her neck, pulled out a strand of blonde hair which had caught under it and smirked at Elsie.

"I don't have to tell you anything," she said. "You just think you're better than me, don't you, but then I suppose you are; perhaps next year I'll be as good as you or probably better? Just wait and see." With a flourish she stepped away from Elsie; and shouting a goodbye to Mrs Hastings, she pulled the door open. The bell jangled, the door shut with a bang behind her and she ran off down the street, laughing as she clutched her wage packet in her hand.

# Eight

Maree looked up as the tram jangled into view. She hopped aboard and wondered if Flo was home. Flo had promised to curl her hair for the gala opening of the ice palace the next day but these days she was more interested in Bert and would more than likely be stepping out with him when she was needed most.

The green of Manley Park came into view through the grubby tram window and Maree got up, making her way past a lady with a red hat clutching the hand of a tiny girl sucking on a lolly, and stood ready to hop out. It was Friday night and many other workers coming out of Manchester stood around her, smelling, frankly, of more sweat than she liked; and she wrinkled her nose and took out her handkerchief. But the tram stopped and she was able to jump out before she felt too nauseated.

She shook off her week and strode past the newsagent on Wilbrahim Street and resisted the temptation to spend some of her hard-earned wages on sweets from the Candy Shop, making do with the thought of the sherbet lemons and liquorice twists she would most surely buy if she had any coins left over after the excursion tomorrow. She turned into Barlow Moor Road and towards home. She wasn't sure what time it was, as she hadn't checked the clock in the high street; but she didn't think she'd be late for tea.

"I'm home!" she shouted; and before she could say anything

else her mother yelled, "Put wood in't hole! That fire'll go straight out t'door."

She shut the door and checked that the fire in the lounge was still lit. Her mother must be expecting visitors; the kitchen was swathed in steam. She stopped to plant a kiss on her mother's red cheek.

"I'm in a bit of a mither," her mother said. "Maud and her young man are coming round for tea and I already burnt the potatoes. Make me a brew, will you? Might calm me down."

Maree put on an apron and put the kettle on the stove. She could certainly do with a cuppa too.

While her mother scurried around, taking more potatoes out of the pantry and cutting up some carrots and swedes, Maree started to tell her mother about her day. Agnes Crymble puffed and hummed but before Maree could finish her account, her mother started on about Maud. "Nothing but a struggle; she's no idea what it's been like, raising all you five girls on my own. Ever since Maud turned sixteen she's scorned every young man I've suggested to her. Forty-one I was when your father died. No idea, any of you. This one had better be good; she'll be on the shelf, mind, if she doesn't look sharp!"

After several prospectives – who she thought of as ne'er-do-wells – Agnes was pleased that a new one had come on the scene. Gangly Maud said he was taller than her, was kind and respectful. Arthur would have approved, she thought, but she would reserve judgement until she'd quizzed the lad over tea.

She and Arthur had been a loving couple who adored all five of their daughters deeply; but Arthur still wanted for nothing more than a son to carry on his name. After ten years of trying for another child they had given up and so the birth of little Arthur Edward while Arthur was in the sanatorium was nothing less than miraculous, they felt. Agnes was sure this would be the cure for Arthur. He so wanted Arthur Edward to become a painter and decorator like himself and had made so many plans, none of which came to fruition. Lying in the narrow metal bed he confided to Agnes that he felt he could die happy as she would be looked after by young Arthur Edward. She scoffed at his pessimism; but he did not return home from the sanatorium.

Her husband's desires went sadly awry as four months after his own death, baby Arthur sickened and died. Agnes toiled even harder and saved for a gravestone which she placed in the Southern Cemetery. Sunday mornings were her time for visiting; and before the little girls grew up, and when Maud and Nell were both still at home, she would march them all there in their best clothes after church and they would stand solemnly whilst their mother spoke to her dead husband and her little boy. If she was feeling particularly maudlin, rivulets of tears ran down her cheeks as she stroked the pink stone and traced the words *In loving Memory* with her finger.

"I'll be here soon," she would tell the girls, who looked at each other aghast, wondering what would become of them when that happened. Maree thought it unlikely her mother would lie down at any time and give in, but the fear was in her; and she clutched her mother's skirts to pull her away and back to the thoughts of Sunday lunch.

# Nine

Maree hated the process: the strips of wet rag tied into her hair until her scalp squealed, the discomfort of sleeping, the tossing and turning on her pillow, hoping she wouldn't undo some of the rags which would leave her hair tightly corkscrewed with stray straight bits. That had happened on more than one occasion; but how else could she get those curls that appeared on the covers of the magazines they had at the haberdashery?

Ruby had astonishing red curls which fell about her shoulders and struggled to stay put when she tied up her hair. Maree wanted curls like that. She kept thinking that she could spy a wave in her own hair as she inspected it every morning in the bedroom mirror. Flo had tired of asking her why she was so vain but acquiesced in the hair-curling routine whenever asked. Ruby just laughed and said that Maree was lucky in other ways, as she had such a button nose whereas she herself had a great conk. Maree thought Ruby's nose was Roman and rather magnificent but was not sure that she would have liked it on her own small face.

Maree grimaced and swivelled on the wooden stool. "Ouch, Flo, you're hurting me. Can't you be more careful?"

Flo pursed her lips and twisted the rag tighter.

"You're the one who wants to have curls," she said. "I can stop now, if you like, and you'll have one side curly and one side straight.

Now wouldn't you look a picture."

Ruby sat on the workbench swinging her legs, enjoying the proceedings and tossing her curls more often than needed, which added to Maree's annoyance. She pulled a strand of her own hair between her fingers and studied it intently.

"I thought we were going out for a stroll to the park, anyway. You can't go with rags in your hair!"

"I can," retorted Maree. "I have a lovely velvet toque hat that I got from work."

Flo gasped. "You didn't steal it, did you? Mother will tan your hide."

Maree shook her head, which had the effect of pulling her hair again.

"Ow! No, of course not. What it is, right, was an old one that one of our customers left for us to try to copy. It got shoved behind one of the shelves in the stock cupboard. I saw it and put it in my bag last week."

"I bet Ma will still say that's stealing; it is, isn't it, Ruby?" Ruby shrugged. She was jealous of the hat. There were no perks at Ancott's. She once tried to stuff an end piece of cotton under her apron but the eagle-eyed, sour-faced supervisor shouted at her, loud even over the clacking of the looms, and she had to pretend that she was putting it in the waste bin.

Flo tore off one more rag strip and began to roll Maree's last remaining strands of hair into it. She stood back with satisfaction and surveyed her handiwork.

Maree jumped up and tried to look at her reflection in the kettle. A huge face loomed out at her with tiny white knots sticking up, making it look as though she'd seen a ghost.

"That'll have to do."

She grabbed Ruby and swung her down from the bench and into the hall, snatched her coat from the hook, threw it over her shoulders and opened the front door.

Ruby gaped.

"Haven't you forgotten something?" she laughed. "An 'at to cover those dreaded rags!"

"I was getting to that." Maree took a crushed, faded purple velvet hat from her pocket and pulled it as far down as she could. As it was sized for a lady, and Maree being a fifteen-year-old with a small head, it covered her ears and eyebrows too.

"See you later, Mother!" she shouted into the sitting room, where her mother was resting after the tea ordeal with Maud and Maud's chosen one, George.

Agnes was considering George. He didn't seem good enough for Maud, she thought. He had a crooked smile, which she thought meant he was up to no good. He was too polite to her, too. That marked him out as having something to hide. She had sniffed at him when they left and poor Maud could only colour with shame at her mother's behaviour. It made her all the more determined to marry him.

# Ten

Ruby and Maree strolled from the tram, arms entwined around each other's waists as they made their way to Derby Street. Maree's curls bounced about her shoulders and she delighted in the feeling. She would let Flo rag her hair again, she decided. She had put on her best hat, another one she had managed to remove from the dusty shelves at the back of the shop, and admired her reflection as they passed a butcher's window with scrubbed shelves empty of meat. Ruby straightened her coat and looked down at her buttoned boots which her Aunty Joan had grown out of. Her best outfit was second-hand, too. Her mother had mended the elbows with patches and let down the hem. She certainly felt better than she did in her pinafore at work, with smudged cheeks and raw hands. The girls smiled at each other.

As they turned the corner, their way was barred by throngs of people. It had been a long tram ride all the way to the north of Manchester and they were devastated to find that it had taken nearly all of their savings. Maree's mother had warned her; she said she was mad to go so far and spend good money on such a long journey. Inwardly, Agnes smiled. She remembered badgering her own mother to take her to the opening of the town hall so many years ago. It was deemed the event of the decade and Agnes did not want to be left out. Her mother, too, had thought it a waste of money. Agnes sighed. She knew how determined Maree could be. Maree had read about the ice rinks in London; she had read about the fine ladies and gentlemen who skated there and now in her very own Manchester a rink of similar calibre was opening. Since the news had broken last year she had regaled both her mother and Ruby with tales of ladies in furs and feathers, ladies so graceful, dancing across the ice without a care in the world. This ice rink would be open to all and she was adamant that she would be there to see it open.

"Just think, Ruby, we could mingle with all the ladies sipping chocolate at the edge of the rink. We don't even have to skate but imagine: those ladies might say, 'You look lovely young girls; why don't you come and join us?'"

Ruby scoffed; but at night she too dreamed of finery and longed to be amongst it all.

Pushing their way through suited men and long-skirted and feather-hatted women, they could see the red-brick building in front of them. Maree noted some of the finer headgear and thought about how she would sketch them later so she could show Mrs Hastings and that stuck-up Elsie how clever she was. She would even think of how she could reproduce them, asking the feather and trimmings salesman for samples.

Stepping on a gentleman's toes, Maree flung her pardons over her shoulder as she marched on, pulling Ruby behind her.

"Come on, keep up. We've got to get near the front or we'll see nothing."

They could hear a band playing, almost drowned out by the buzz of the crowd. Maree spotted a gap and forced her way through to the throng directly in front of the white-marbled facade. On this day and only this day, Ruby and Maree discovered admission tickets were waived and they followed Lords and Ladies, doctors and physicians together with families through the portals.

Once inside, they passed the potted plants in the ante-room altogether like a greenhouse, their feet soft on the carpet. Their necks ached when they craned upwards to see the plastered ceiling decorated with an elaborate painting of the Aurora Borealis.

"Cor, look at that!" Maree elbowed Ruby in the ribs.

The wooden balconies tiered above them were already full of elegant ladies and gentlemen. The walls shimmered in terracotta and pale blue. A portly man leaning on a railing above them surveyed the scene through a lorgnette.

"Oh my dear," he said to the bejewelled lady next to him, his piercing voice loud over the hubbub: "it seems to be filling with all manner of 'looky-loos'. I do hope they won't allow them in to skate. Just look at those two below. Mouths agape. My, my. They *are* allowing all sorts in here."

Ruby looked up and stuck out her tongue. Maree elbowed her in the ribs.

"Stop it. That's not ladylike. Don't let them rile you. We've just as much right to come in and see, even if we can't afford to skate yet. You'll see, we'll get more money and come back. That'll show them." With a toss of her head she moved slowly with exaggerated steps to the ringside.

The two girls huffed and puffed in the cold air and exhaled small clouds as they marvelled at the skaters swishing their way across the ice. Men in tight tan leggings and dark grey tunics took turns twirling ladies along the ice. They released them and travelled to the next with one leg held high behind them before they sank to the surface and pirouetted so fast they became a blur to the girls' eyes.

"Where does all the ice come from?" Ruby asked as she gazed at the sweepers marshalling ice crystals to a gate in the rink where they took them up in giant shovels.

"One of our customers, Mrs Robotham, said that there's a factory across the road which makes the ice and that every night it'll churn it up and send it underground pumped through a pipe. Isn't that fantastic?"

A bell rang and the skaters left the rink to be replaced by another eager set. Ruby chuckled as a pompous-looking woman dressed in a long navy gown sporting a hat with the widest brim she had ever seen stumbled in front of her and, on pulling herself up, blew the feathers out of her mouth as the hat, now very askew, threatened to dismantle her hair and certainly her dignity.

The girls walked around to the other side, smelt the chocolate in the tall cups held in cold hands and wished they too could buy one to share. They turfed the coins they had left from their fares out of their pockets; but alas, there was not enough to pay the sixpence needed.

Maree sighed. Her gaze fell upon the skaters again. They were leaving the rink. Another formation of skaters swooped out onto the ice. Men and women held hands as they formed figures of eight, waltzed and fairly skimmed the surface. Spellbound, Maree's gaze alighted on a lady with a shy smile who locked eyes with one of the instructors as he whizzed her around.

"How romantic," she sighed. The bell sounded and the demonstration team left the ice. Her eyes now roamed the crowds above her and she gasped: there in one of the seats sat a princess. She was sure she was a princess. Her fuchsia-coloured sari glinted with gold embroidery and the jewels around her neck and on her hands sparkled like the ice below.

"Saints preserve me," said Maree. "Look at her, Ruby. She's an Indian princess. Oh to be her!"

Ruby guffawed. "Fat chance," she said. "She's got black hair, anyway. You're far too white to be an Indian princess!"

"I don't care. I've never seen anyone so beautiful. I wonder where she's from and what she's doing here?"

Maree continued to gaze at the beautiful apparition who tinkled as she laughed and turned her eyes towards the Indian gentleman at her side leaning towards her.

Before Maree could think, she was telling Ruby a story. "She has been sent here by her father who is a maharajah. He has lost his fortune and he wants her to marry someone really rich. Her name is Indira. The only precious thing she has left are the jewels around her neck; see how they shine. The necklace is called the Star of India. But of course she has her beauty. At home she was surrounded by servants but here she is on her own, apart from her brother. That's him, leaning over her. Her father has sent him with her to protect her honour but he is dastardly and has plans of his own to help assuage his gambling debts. He will sell her off for the highest dowry. His father doesn't know this, of course, and thinks that he is wonderful, the best of all sons."

"What a load of nonsense you do talk!" Ruby replied, nonetheless taken by Maree's invention.

The two linked arms and strolled around for another hour, the crowds having dispersed somewhat. Deprived of the promised hot chocolate Ruby began thinking of the tea waiting for her at home.

"I'm hungry," she said. "Let's go to the tram stop before it gets so busy with all these people wanting to go home. I hope Ma has left some food for me; I'm starving."

"If she hasn't, you can always eat with us. I'm sure there will be some leftovers as Ma always thinks that either Nell or Maud might come for a feed."

"You're so lucky having older sisters, Maree. I hate being the eldest. I can't do anything without being told I have to look after my brothers. I hate it. They are such nuisances."

Maree thought of her baby brother lying next to – or could he be on top of? – her father in the cemetery. She didn't remember him at all. She was grateful she didn't have to look after him, though. Immediately she felt guilty for her thoughts; she knew how often her mother cried and wiped her eyes on her apron when she thought none of the girls were watching. Five girls and then the longed-for son. Such a shame, everyone said when he died. Poor Agnes. Five girls to look after all on her own. It's a cruel world. First lose your husband, then your baby boy. She'd better hope they marry well. She can't keep feeding and looking after them for long. She'll work herself to the bone. She shouldn't turn down help, though. Maree had heard all this but couldn't understand what help had ever been offered. None that she could see. There seemed to be a smirking, a 'Thank goodness it isn't me' attitude from some of the old ducks in their road.

Ruby fidgeted beside her as she tried to look out of the tram window to see how close they were to home. It had been a long day.

III

# Eleven

## 1910 Oxford Road, Manchester

Frank stood in front of the stone steps leading up to a brown door, its paint peeling, exposing an earlier green paint, and worn around the tarnished handle. He glanced at the piece of paper held tightly in his free hand, the other gripping the leather suitcase handle. Yes, this was number eight. The street was shabby, grimy and deserted. He looked again to make sure he was correct: yes, 8 Oxford Road; and as he lifted his head he saw in the adjoining window a twitch of curtain. He could see the shadowed outline of a head, of shoulders, but nothing else. No movement. No welcoming smile.

He sighed and taking two steps in one stride he knocked firmly on the door. He could hear laughter and coughing, and eventually a gruff voice: "Wait up, I'm coming; keep your hair on."

The door creaked and groaned before flying open to reveal a middle-aged woman, her hair tied up in a wispy bun, a dingy white apron covering her long black dress.

She looked Frank up and down as he stood there uncertain of a welcome, although he had been assured that she would allow coloureds into her boarding house. She coughed, mucus gurgling in her lungs.

"What d'you want? I'm not buying." She looked down at his

suitcase as though it might contain contraband.

"I'm not selling, Mrs... er... Mrs Higginbottom. I'm Frank Tarmaster. The new college student. I'm sorry, I thought Mr Gupta had sent a letter to you from the Education Fund telling you I was arriving today from India to start college here."

Mrs Higginbottom looked him up and down again.

"Hmm, they get younger and darker every year," she stated, turning on her heel; and as the door was left open, he took it as an invitation to follow her along the dark passageway, its red runner scuffed, its walls stained with dark patches he thought could be mildew. It was not an auspicious beginning, he thought.

She shut the door into what he took to be the kitchen and turning back gestured to him to take the stairs which emerged from the gloom.

"Second floor, second door on the right. Ten bob a week and extra if you want some scran..."

"Scran?" Frank reiterated, a frown on his face.

"Yeah, you know, grub, nosh, victuals, whatever you call it. But I don't do curry, mind, none of that fancy smelly stuff here. Oh, and no ladies in your room. There's the kitchen if you want a visitor, but not at mealtimes, okay? Anything else you need to know?"

Frank shook his head. He did have questions but thought this was not the time to be asking them. He would take his suitcase loaded with books upstairs, have a look at his room and assess.

He took the stairs with a heavy tread. An overwhelming desire to lie down and close his eyes came over him. It might stop the tears tickling his nose and eyes. The room was as he expected: no more welcoming than Mrs Higginbottom herself. He put the suitcase down, flexed his fingers in relief and walked over to the mean window looking out over the street. The view was grey. He took a deep breath, turned back to the room and was grateful that, at least, tucked into the corner was a small table which would do as a study desk, although it would mean removing the basin and ewer every day. He would ask for a lamp, as the single light bulb hanging from the ceiling would not cast any light into the dingy corners. He sat on the bed. The linens at least looked clean and the blanket, although old, looked warm enough. He unlaced his shoes and slipping them off he lay back, his hands clasped under his head, his legs crossed, his feet touching the metal bedframe.

On the other side of the room was an old oak wardrobe. It was small but his clothing and possessions were likewise. It would do.

Opening his eyes he was surprised to see that the light was fading, casting shadows around the room. He glanced at his watch and realised that yes, he had been asleep. What would Mrs Higginbottom think? It occurred to him that he did not know where the bathroom was and he really should go and find out at the same time as going downstairs to pay his rent. He was used to sharing water taps with his family but strangers were different. He stepped out onto the landing and saw that the only other door was one like his own. It did not promise a door to a bathroom or a water closet. He retraced his steps down to the first floor landing and saw that there were three doors on this floor, two like his own and one plainer one which he gingerly pulled open. No; this was a narrow cupboard with shelves upon which Mrs Higginbottom's spare linen lay. Towels, thin and threadbare, grey sheets and a few blankets were loosely piled together. A faint musty odour was overlaid with a fragrance it took him some time to place. He was used to camphorwood being used for items in storage but this was different. More floral, not woody. It brought to mind St Patrick's and the steps leading up to the great assembly hall. On either side of the steps were huge clumps of lavender, their flowers buzzing with happy bees. Yes, that was it. Lavender. He shut the door and made his way downstairs. He knocked at the kitchen door and Mrs Higginbottom's growl told him to open the door.

"Good afternoon. I wondered if I may know where the water closet and the bathing room are?"

She guffawed. "Bathing room! Hark at him!" This said to two thickset men who were seated at the kitchen table. They turned to him with curious eyes.

"Out the back door and to the left. First one is the WC and the next is the 'bathing room'." She laughed again which brought on a fit of coughing as one of the men jumped up and thumped her on her back.

Frank mumbled his thanks and made his way out of the kitchen. The WC was clean enough, he thought, and on poking his nose through the adjoining door he saw a tub, rusty brown with stains where the water dripped from the taps.

At least it's running water, he thought; and on passing back through the kitchen he left one ten bob note on the table.

"No food tonight, then?"

Frank shook his head. The aromas coming from the pots on the stove were not appealing to him. He was tired. He wanted to go upstairs, unpack, sleep and go out in the morning to find a café for a good breakfast of eggs and toast, he thought.

Back in his room he slid open the window a crack to let out the stale tobacco smell. He took out his clothes and placed them into the drawers in the wardrobe, hanging two shirts on one hanger as there were only two wooden ones with twisted wires. His jacket hung like an extra person in the room on the back of the door. He washed his hands in the small chipped china basin on the table.

Sitting on his bed he consulted the small black, leather-bound book which opened at his favourite passage.

*Those who eat too much or eat too little, who sleep too much or sleep too little, will not succeed in meditation. But those who are temperate in eating and sleeping, work and recreation, will come to the end of sorrow through meditation.*

He smiled to himself and wondered if he should have had some 'scran' tonight but he decided to meditate on the fact that sleep too was necessary. The *Bhagavad Gita* was always right.

# Twelve

Frank's intention for the day was to find the offices of Arthur E. Piggott. He sorted through his paperwork until he found the letter of introduction. He hoped that the address was not too far away and would be easy to find. He thought about asking Mrs Higginbottom but decided to walk around the district to orientate himself and hopefully come across a post office. In Bombay the post office had been a fount of information and he was certain it would be the same here. He could hear the hum of voices coming from the kitchen interspersed with Mrs Higginbottom's hoarse chuckle. He tiptoed down the passageway and opened the front door gingerly, hoping it would not creak and send his landlady out to inquire where he was going. He stood on the doorstep, tugged his coat collar up and wandered down the road. He could not keep the smile off his face. He breathed deeply and shook his head. He was really here. Here in Manchester.

He had been warned about the cold and the damp by everyone who had visited the 'mother country' but the longer he walked the more it seeped into his very being. As he walked down the street he lifted his hat to a lady pushing a pram. She busied herself looking at the child within and did not meet his gaze. Two young men came next, jostling each other and laughing.

"Good morning," he said. "It's a bit of a cold one, isn't it?"

They stopped laughing and stared at him as they passed by. One, the younger by a few years, turned his head as he passed, his mouth gaping. Frank heard the other say, "Yeah, yeah, these darkies can talk English too!"

Shaking his head, Frank continued walking. A woman, dressed in a navy dress, faded and stained, and holding a small girl's hand, sniffed and crossed the street in front of him. The little girl turned to look at him, mouth agape. The woman tugged crossly on her hand and spat in his direction. The smile faded from his face. He looked around and thought twice about greeting anyone again. Perhaps they had never seen an Indian before? But surely that couldn't be true.

As he rounded the corner he caught sight of a familiar Royal Mail sign on a red postbox. It stood in front of the bay window of a shop, and in the window was a sign that said it was a post office, open from nine a.m. to three p.m. He glanced at his watch. It was nearly twenty past eight. He had time to find a café and order some breakfast.

The shops stretched along both sides of this street; and he saw reflected in the window of a tobacconist's a sign for Rosie's Café. He squinted, trying to make out the calligraphy in mirror image. He congratulated himself as he turned around and realised he had read it correctly. Crossing the road, avoiding the horse-drawn carriages and carts, he pushed open the door. A bell clanged angrily and 'Rosie', an elderly, sour-looking woman, appeared behind a counter. She narrowed her eyes. He ordered some eggs and toast and a pot of tea from the blackboard announcing the menu. Rosie folded her arms.

"You got some money, then?" she queried.

Frank thought better of answering that of course he had money; why would he have ordered otherwise? and instead took out his wallet and let the coins answer for him.

She gestured to a table in the corner and told him to wait for a few minutes.

"Face the counter," she demanded, "just so you don't put off any other customers."

He raised his eyebrows and his jaw dropped open, since there were no other customers at any of the four greasy tables; but she disappeared into the kitchen.

A young girl dressed in black with a white pinny and cap brought out his pot of tea. She gave a little curtsy in surprise when she saw him. She lowered her eyes and scuttled back behind the counter. The eggs when they came were two round, staring eyes melting into two pieces of soft white bread. They stared up at him as the girl curtsied again, put her hand over her mouth and disappeared into the kitchen.

Frank shrugged. He looked at his pocket-watch; he would need to eat quickly to make sure he was first in line at the post office.

No one serving at the post office knew of Duke Street. One of the other customers lining up behind him, a tall, skinny man with a shiny hat, thought it was in 'town proper' and he would need to take the number seventy-five tram into High Street and ask there.

Frank was grateful for the man's politeness. He was beginning to think that perhaps he was not welcome here. He had not spotted another brown face in his morning travels and hoped it was just unfamiliarity that had made for those unfriendly encounters.

The seventy-five tram was easy to find. He paid his fare to the conductor, who smiled at him as he asked whether he could tell him when the tram arrived at the High Street. He took an empty seat by the window so that he could look out at the life of Manchester. Once in the High Street he stopped a gentleman in a suit and asked him if he knew of the law offices of Arthur E. Piggott and Sons in Duke Street. He nodded and with a huge sweep of his hand which nearly knocked Frank over, he gestured down the road.

"Follow this street until you come to Fleet Street. Then turn left onto Fleet Street and about 150 yards down you'll see Duke Street on your right. I'm sure you'll find the offices you're looking for." He beamed at Frank, turned on his heel before Frank could thank him and strode away, having done his good deed for the day.

Frank followed the man's instructions and stared up at a three-storey red-brick building. He squinted at the brass plaques and spotted A.E. Piggott & Son. Inside he made his way two stairs at a time to the second floor, the wooden banisters smooth under his hands. He paused to straighten his coat and tie and turn down his collar before knocking on the glass-windowed door. He held his hat in his hands as a clerk, seated behind a desk, turned a quizzical eye in his direction. Before Frank could introduce himself, a tall, grey-bearded gentleman rushed from an inner office, a hand outstretched, his smile beaming and twinkling through his moustache. His blue eyes crinkled as he pumped Frank's hand up and down.

"Welcome, welcome. My dear boy. How wonderful to see you in the flesh! I have heard so many good things. Come. Come into my office. Sam, will you make us some tea? You'll have some, Mr Tarmaster? Or Frank? May I call you that? Forgive my presumption."

Frank nodded assent as he followed him into a small unimposing room with a large wooden desk taking up the majority of the space. The piles of files and papers reminded him of Mr Gupta's desk in the *wadi*, which seemed so long ago and suddenly so far away. He blinked his eyes, looked down and smoothed the creases in his trousers. When his gaze felt steady he raised his eyes to Mr Piggott who sat leaning forward, his hands clasped together, a concerned look on his face.

"So, how are you finding it on this isle? How was your voyage? Comfortable, I hope. And how are your lodgings? The law offices recommend Mrs Higginbottom. She's used to foreign students. It's a lot to get used to but I'm sure you'll cope. – Now, let's have a look at the terms of your contract."

He clearly didn't expect an answer to any of his queries. He shuffled through a stack of files, each one tied with red ribbon, until he found what he was looking for. Sam, the clerk, came in as he was untying the ribbon and looked around on the desk for space to put the tea tray. Mr Piggott shuffled some folders and placed them on an already precarious looking stack and pointed to some bare wood.

"Thank you, Sam. This is Frank Tarmaster – well, I think we call you that, don't we? Although all your documentation names you as Mangaldas Laxmidas. A bit difficult for us ignorant English, I think."

Frank grimaced as he shook Sam's hand.

"It is my name. I adopted 'Frank' when I went to the senior school in Bombay. Boys there found the other a good name for jokes. 'Your Mum's got a mangle'! Even though I had neither a mother nor any clue what a mangle was."

"Boys can be so cruel. I remember... I think that's for another time. You can leave us now, Sam. Let's have a look. Mmm... Now, the articles state that you will be with me for three years at least. Learning all the tricks of the trade, as it were. You will be allowed Thursdays off for your classes although I know you will be taking evening ones, too; and you will need to come in on Saturday mornings until one p.m. I will be paying you one guinea per day for your work. I trust that all that is satisfactory?"

Frank nodded. He did not know how much one guinea would buy him but it certainly sounded satisfactory to him. He would only need to work half a day to pay his rent. He did some quick calculations in his head as to how much he could save in three years. Of course, there would be other expenses; but it was a fortune to him. With glee he thought of how Jasleen would react when he started sending money back to her. Then he wondered whether Jarod would take kindly to this. Maybe better to save it all so he could start his own accountancy firm when he went back to India. For he was going back. He knew that.

Mr Piggott stood behind his desk, his hand extended once more.

"I'll let you get settled in. You can start here next week, if that's all right with you. When do classes start? Let me show you your desk. I'll sort out some work for you. You can help Sam, I think, for the first few weeks. I really am so glad to have you here. I think you will be a great asset, judging by your results so far. Wonderful,

wonderful."

Beaming all the while, he ushered Frank out into the main office.

"If there is anything at all I can help you with, you must come in and ask. Sam will be able to sort things out, won't you, Sam?"

Sam flicked a lock of hair and looked over the top of his spectacles and grinned.

"Yes, sir. Of course, sir. See you next week, Frank."

Frank walked back to the tram stop, his hand grasping the folder with his signed contract. Three years seemed an interminable time. He would be twenty-three. He knew how proud Jasleen would be when he qualified. That was presuming he passed all his exams. He hoped that by that time he would feel comfortable in this new city, this new world. A world where he was not sure where he stood in the scheme of things. Today had been confusing. He had been shunned, ignored, singled out and also helped, assisted and greatly welcomed. What was he to think?

# Thirteen

Sitting in class on the following Thursday, Frank glanced around at the other students. Thirty or so of them, all seated at small wooden desks crammed into a room befitting junior children. Each desk was shared by several students and the atmosphere was somewhat oppressive. Frank ran a finger around his collar. He nodded across the room at a tall, skinny redhead who at first he thought was Sam; but on seeing his puzzled frown he realised it was not him at all. Many of the students were white, pale-faced and ruddy-cheeked. A red turban three desks up from him reassured him that at least there was a Sikh in the class.

The teacher, a rotund gentleman with a waistcoat popping open at the second button, had introduced himself as Smythe: "Mr Smythe to all you gentlemen." His greasy hair was lank and fell almost to his shoulders. Frank did not think that this was a look for an accountant at all. He hoped that his knowledge outshone his appearance.

It was a basic class but he did learn that the first exam for him, along with three other students, was to be the next step up from Licentiate; and he was to sit the Teacher's Commercial Education Diploma the following May. The remainder of the cohort were to sit the Licentiate, so he would need to read up so as to make sure of passing the Diploma and not disappointing his teachers.

Over the next few weeks, Frank found life lonely. He concentrated hard on his studies but he missed the easy camaraderie he had had with fellow students in Bombay. He spent the evenings at the desk in his room, sometimes availing himself of Mrs Higginbottom's home cooking which – to his surprise – was quite palatable. On other occasions he would eat out at the small Indian restaurant around the corner from his lodging house.

It was when he was packing up his books after an evening class that the Sikh man he had noticed on his first day walked over to him and offered to walk with him to a Bangla restaurant. "Not quite like home; they're a Bengali family, but at least they use spices. Not that namby-pamby English food," he said. And then, "I don't think I've introduced myself properly. I'm Harbir Singh; please call me Harbir. Tell me, Frank, what is your good name?"

Frank gave a short laugh and said, "Mine's a mouthful. Mangaldas Laxmidas Tarmaster. But at school I decided to be known as Frank; it was just so much easier."

They chatted amiably as they walked the cold, wet-slicked streets. As they opened the door to the restaurant, a warm, spice-filled fug hit them. Harbir waved to a few other young Indian men sitting around a table in the corner and talking earnestly.

"Come, Frank, let's join them. I'll introduce you to some fellow students. They're studying in different faculties but it is so comforting to talk to them."

The four students made room for them at the wooden table. One, very thin with a neat shiny moustache, smiled and pulled up two more chairs from the adjacent table so that they could both join them.

"I'm so glad you came, Harbir. We were just talking about forming an Indian Association here in Manchester."

"What do you think? And who is your friend and what does he think?"

Frank attempted to introduce himself but the enthusiasm of the others swamped him, as all were talking at once.

"We could hold events, raise money and just have meetings

where we can talk about all things Indian."

"Politics, culture, religion. It would just be for students at the moment, students like us at the colleges. A good idea, no?"

Frank managed to interject a few questions. Where would they meet? How often? How long would the meetings be? Would they need a constitution?

The others laughed. "We can tell you're studying accounting and business! I think it should be social at first. Only social. So we can have some fun and some intelligent conversation."

Manesh, he of the thin moustache, took the lead in the conversation. Manesh wanted the meetings to be at the college. So at the college they would be. Manesh would request a room for their use.

Frank found out that not all the students were on a scholarship like himself. Manesh and Ravi, a slight man with a round face and perpetual smile, were both from families already living here in Manchester. Harbir was also on a scholarship but this was his second year and he strode around the streets with his head high. Frank wondered whether he should mention the perceived criticism he had felt, the veiled dislike. He thought better of it but vowed to bring it up at one of the association's meetings.

# Fourteen

As Frank's days at his studies and the accountancy office began to blend into the year, the association became his social life – his life in England. As he talked in Hindi to his friends, even in the dusty, gloomy room they had been offered as a meeting space, he felt at home. He pondered what home meant. One autumn evening as the wind blew leaves torn from the trees in the park, he walked back from a meeting, a maroon woollen scarf tied firmly around his neck, his collar turned up, his eartips tingling under his hat and the beginnings of a dewdrop at the end of his nose. Thoughts of his sister brought him to stop outside a bootmaker's. How long was it since he had written to Jasleen? Her dark eyes reproached him; she was his family, all he had left, not these students he now called friends. Tucking his hands deep into his pockets, he looked at his reflection in the window; his black wool coat marked him out as a Mancunian but his face betrayed his foreignness. He bowed his head against the easterly wind and strode on, his shoes ringing out against the wet, rain-slicked pavement.

Days, weeks, months passed. The world around Frank continued without his knowledge or interest. He focused on achieving the best results he could. When he achieved First in Merit for the final exam of the Corporation of Accountants, Mr Piggott clapped his hands in glee and invited him for Sunday lunch.

When Frank knocked on the door of the Piggotts' house, Mr Piggott opened it with such vigour that Frank was nearly swept in with the rush. His extended hand pumped Frank's and he covered it with his other as he pulled him into the narrow hallway.

"Here, take off your coat and hat. I'll hang them up for you. I don't think we'll mistake your coat for mine; yours is so new! Look, my elbows are getting shiny; and as for the cuffs, well, best we don't look!"

Frank followed him into the drawing room where Mr Piggott's two daughters sat on a faded flowery sofa. The one with curly brown hair, the elder he thought, smiled at him, dimples appearing at the corners of her plump mouth.

"I'm Hettie," she said, "and this is Gertie." She dug her younger sister in the ribs as she threatened to guffaw.

"Don't mind my sister; she's just young and stupid," said Hettie.

Gertie moved to the other end of the sofa. "No, I'm not," she said, her clear eyes holding his gaze. "I'm just not used to seeing... er... Oriental gentlemen."

"Now, girls," Mr Piggott tut-tutted. "Enough of that. This is Frank Tarmaster and he will be working with me for at least three years and I do hope you will all become firm friends."

Frank had never thought of girls as friends before and the unlikelihood of this happening turned up both the corners of his mouth and one eyebrow.

"What?" bristled Hettie. "Don't you think we could be friends?"

He did not; but instead hastened to say that assuredly they could. What funny creatures these English were.

He heard soft footsteps and a diminutive woman with tight curls and a tiny waist emphasised by a large bustle scuttled into the room.

"My dear!" Mr Piggott grasped her by her elbow and paraded her in front of Frank. "This is Frank Tarmaster. Be kind to him; he has come all the way from Bombay to shower me with his expertise."

Frank made to remonstrate but Arthur held up his hand. "No, no, I must insist! You are a most exceptional young man." He placed his arm around his wife's waist. "This is my darling wife, Frida. She is foreign too, you know, all the way from Denmark!" He seemed amused by this; Frida chuckled, but the girls looked pained.

"I don't think you have met my son, Halvor? No, of course not. He is away at university studying Mathematics; naturally he will join the firm when he graduates. He has all the makings of a fine businessman, a bit like yourself, Frank."

"He is only seventeen, Arthur," remonstrated Frida; "far too young to be thinking of his future yet. Not like you, Frank; you have travelled so far to pursue a career. I really admire you. It must have been very difficult for you. These English can be peculiar people, you know." She turned to smile at Arthur, who took it in good humour.

"Yes, my dear, you're right, I'm sure. Come, let's go through to dine. Everything's ready, isn't it?" Arthur enquired.

Frank stood up to let Hettie and Gertie pass in front of him, bowing from the waist.

"Such lovely manners," said Frida, as she flashed an approving smile at Frank.

He sat shyly on the edge of his chair at the vast mahogany dinner table, passing plates and smiling at the girls. Their words flew around like a swarm of bees looking for a hive; his head was not their destination. Mrs Piggott's smile comforted him. She did not ask questions but beamed at Mr Piggott as he chattered from the head of the table.

As they ate what – Frank was informed – was a typical English Sunday lunch, conversation turned to the latest excitement. Halley's Comet was due to arrive in a few months' time and there had been great speculation as to what this might entail.

"Well, I've heard that there are people in America who are very afraid of the poisonous gas in its tail," said Gertie.

"I don't think it's going to affect us on earth, though," said

Arthur. "I was reading an article on this in the *Manchester Guardian* last week."

"But, my dear, that doesn't seem to have stopped the gossip about the possible destruction of us all..." Frida was interrupted.

"But, Mama, I saw some anti-comet pills for sale in the chemist's shop window last week!" Gertie's eyes were round with amazement. "Just imagine, we could take those and we'd all be safe!"

The family laughed as Gertie pouted.

"You mustn't believe everything you see, Gertie," Arthur admonished.

"But, Papa, you believe what you read in the *Guardian*. What's the difference?"

It was a lively debate. Frida had to remind the family to eat their meal before the lamb was cold on their plates. Frank found the food bland and unappetising; but home-cooked meals were now a rarity, so he tucked in as best he could. He choked down the lamb coated in thick greasy gravy and chopped up the potatoes into smaller pieces. He was, at least, hungry.

"Frank?" Hettie was trying to get his attention. "I was saying, were you going to look out for the comet in May? Would you like to come with us to see it?"

Frank wiped his mouth with a starched white damask napkin, upon which – he was upset to see – he had left some gravy stains.

"I would like to do that, yes," he responded. "I am very interested in seeing it for myself. Did you know that it is the same comet that is embroidered on the Bayeux tapestry?" He was proud of his knowledge and a frisson of appreciation ran up and down his spine as all eyes turned to him, especially the soft brown eyes of Hettie.

It was Frank's first contribution to the discussion but he was soon pumped for more information. The girls were curious as to how he knew that fact. Mr Piggott beamed at his young protégé.

The young housemaid brought in a pudding, her eyes downcast, her cheeks red.

"Now, don't be shy, Nancy, this is Frank; he is my new articled clerk at the firm."

She raised her chin and smiled shyly at Frank but would not meet his eyes. She left the crumble on the table and retreated back to the kitchen. The girls giggled.

"See," said Gertie, "I'm not the only one unused to seeing someone from India."

Was he so strange? So unusual? Frank frowned and wondered again if he was in the right place. Life was not as easy when you were a different colour. The pallor of those around him made him feel his shade was more overdone than underdone.

He enjoyed the rhubarb crumble, perfectly cooked, the fruit a tartness he was not used to; but as he swirled the contrasting sweet custard around his mouth it reminded him of the *kheer* his sister would make for him as a treat; and the warmth of the family around him fell away as Jasleen's reproachful face swam into view. When had he last written to her?

# Fifteen

Hettie was true to her word and a week later sent an invitation to Frank to be part of her Halley's Comet viewing party. She was arranging for a group of friends to walk up the Tandle Hill View Point, where she had been reliably informed they would have an uninterrupted view. She encouraged her friends to bring a picnic and blankets to lie on to better see the comet in the night sky.

Frank, not used to social engagements with mixed company, thought long and hard about accepting the invitation. He had said yes without a thought at Sunday dinner the previous week but the reality of talking to a group of his peers whom he had never met before caused him some anxiety. However, he shook off any niggling doubts and accepted Hettie's kind invitation.

The weeks leading up to the event flew by as Frank became accustomed to the long days at the office and the catch-up nights at college. He studied long into the night. He removed his glasses and rubbed his eyes, closing them for a few seconds. Feeling that he could easily drift off he snapped them open, looked into the shadowed corners of the room and back to his books several times as the optician recommended. It was enough to enable him to study for another hour before he washed his hands and face in the bowl in his room and folded his trousers and hung his jacket and waistcoat in the small wardrobe. He was lucky. Mrs Higginbottom's establishment might not have been the best but at least it was mostly quiet. The noise from rowdy card games or possibly drinking sessions barely made it up the stairs and his concentration was not affected.

Finally he wrote to Jasleen:

*Dear Jasleen*

*Please do not be thinking ill of me. I have been very remiss in not writing to you but I think you will be proud of me! I passed my final exam for the Corporation of Accountants last week with flying colours. Mr Piggott is so kind. He gives me time off before the exam. He says my success rubs off on him and he is so encouraging in this strange place.*

*I often wander the streets and am not always met with kindness or courtesy. It seems that an Indian person must be a threat or at least an alien in this town. It seems strange though as I have found many immigrants from all parts of the world working in the factories here, but maybe not so many studying at university. That is the difference. Maybe they think I am above my station in life. I don't know. I have been shunned more than once; do you know, some people even cross the road to avoid walking past me? I have been spat at and laughed at but I hold my head high and carry on.*

*Mr Piggott's family, however, couldn't be more welcoming and once the youngest daughter got over her gape-mouthed curiosity she, too, is most friendly.*

*The eldest daughter Hettie is remarkably well-read and clever. I do enjoy her conversations and she must enjoy mine as she has invited me to a Hayley's Comet party. I do not know if you will be seeing this in Bombay but do not worry, I shall be telling you all about it the next time I write!*

*I must get back to my studies. I do it all for you. Thank you for all you did for me. Sending you my love, as always.*

*Yours*

*Mangaldas (usually Frank!)*

Frank knocked at Hettie's door and she gushed onto the steps, picnic basket in hand, grabbed him by his elbow and steered him down the road.

"Quick," she said, "I don't want to walk with Gertie; she is being so annoying. She can walk with her own friends."

Frank looked behind to see if Gertie was indeed following but the pavement was empty.

"Let me." He took the basket out of Hettie's hand and they picked up on the last discussion they had had about life in India almost as if they had never left off. Frank entertained Hettie throughout the walk to Tandle Hill, only stopping when Hettie waved to her group of friends. He hesitated, but Hettie pulled him forward and introduced him.

"This is Frank Tarmaster. He is working at my father's office. He has come all the way from Bombay to study here. Isn't that wonderful?"

A tall, smartly-dressed man doffed his hat in a mildly sarcastic manner but his warm smile and handshake were welcoming.

"I have heard about you from Hettie," he said. "She is quite your champion!"

Two of the girls, holding their wool skirts up out of the mud, came forward and smiled shyly at Frank.

Three other men were talking in a group, smoking and blowing wreaths of smoke into the cold night air. Frank noted their pointed indifference to him but he was soon caught up in conversation with Freddie, the tall gentleman.

"Now, tell me, old chap, what is it really like in India? We hear all kinds of things, you know, but I never believe everything I read, so I want to hear from the horse's mouth, as it were." Frank was happy to talk about Bombay and his life before Manchester but he was guarded about his upbringing and some of the poverty he had both seen and experienced.

As daylight faded, a hush fell over the group as the time for the comet's scheduled appearance drew close. All eyes were skyward, each person hoping to be the first to spot it. As it happened, one of the long-skirted girls (he couldn't recall her name), looking in an entirely different part of the night sky from the others, spotted its trail. At her shout there was a rush to find a blanket to lie on for the best vantage point. The silence was magical then, and they looked in awe and wonder at this once in a lifetime event. It was only after considerable oohings and aahings that they broke open a bottle of champagne to celebrate the comet's arrival. Frank, being a teetotaller, declined a glass; but as he stood in the group's circle he cheered alongside them and felt the fizz of a celebratory event throughout his whole being.

It was a wet and windy June day as Frank stood in between Hettie and Gertie, sheltering under their umbrellas. As they turned to look at the horses and carriages coming down the street the anticipatory murmurings of the crowd turned into clapping, drips of rain cascaded down. He shook his head laughing at the beads of rain on his coat sleeves, wondering why he had agreed to come out in this weather.

"You must come with us, Frank, come and wave a flag at the parade. Who knows if we'll see another coronation in our time!" Hettie had said. Now, she tucked her arm fondly under his and threw him a charming smile. Arthur Piggot and his wife stood on the pavement behind them, craning their necks to see the shiny black horses with their gleaming horse brasses as they passed by. Coaches and carriages followed one after the other filled with waving dignitaries who did not have to worry about the rain. Jewels of rain trickled down the coachmen's jackets. Another carriage from the forestry department sported three fir trees and marching workers alongside. Frank marvelled at the trees, precariously poised, and at the grim expression on the leader's face. This was supposed to be a celebration of the king's coronation, he thought. How different to the multi-coloured, joyous parades he had been used to at the temples in Bombay. Marigolds and white blossoms flashed before his eyes; this was so orderly and so gentle, no loud drumming or chanting. Union Jacks fluttered in the breeze as they marked out each shop along the street.

"I can see you're not really enjoying this," Hettie said. "I think you and I should do some walking; there's some interesting things to see."

Frank's walks with Hettie became weekly events. One day on his way to her house he took a turn down a different street from his usual route. His curiosity had him gazing in the windows of every shop. He paused to look at the display of fabrics in one window. He was taken aback by the contrast to the fabric bazaars back home. There, the brilliant sari colours, the turquoise and aquamarines reflecting the bright skies, the reds for marriage celebrations; but here, the greyness of the land and sky were reflected in the grey and brown homespun wool. He had been in England long enough to know that these were the favoured colours, but oh, how dull. A few shops later a display of bright ribbons made him stop and smile. A young girl with the most beautiful soft skin was arranging a tartan bow on a hat and as he watched she placed it carefully on a stand in the window. His shadow broke her concentration. She looked up. He smiled at her and saw the blush on her cheek before he walked on.

One day Hettie asked him to come especially to meet her brother Halvor who was back from university in London.

"You'll be working with him soon, you know, so you'd better meet him and make friends, although he's not the easiest person to get to know, I'll admit."

The meeting had not gone well as they interrupted an argument Halvor had been having with his father. He nodded curtly at Frank when introduced but was not interested in making small talk with Frank and disappeared upstairs with a loud tread. Hettie shrugged her shoulders.

Subsequent meetings at other family occasions had been little better and Frank was sure that Halvor resented his presence in the family and certainly the fondness in which he was held by his father. He hoped for Arthur's sake that the frostiness between them would melt and that Halvor would accept Frank's position in his father's affections.

On one of their walks, Hettie fished a newspaper out of her bag.

"Look at this," she said enthusiastically. "I know how much you like Tagore's poetry; look, he's coming over to England. Wouldn't it be fantastic to hear him read his poems? Shall we try to go to London?"

Bells of alarm rang in the far reaches of his mind. Would he be expected to stay in a hotel with Hettie in London? To journey there as if they were a couple? Maybe not, perhaps this was just a friendly gesture, indicating that she was taking an interest in what he had talked about. He demurred, saying that he had some upcoming exams which would certainly not allow him to go gallivanting off to London. Besides which, he thought, he certainly couldn't afford the money to do so.

The notes which Frank began to receive from Hettie contained small endearments which only confirmed his alarm. He was certainly very fond of her but he began to worry that she might be taking their friendship to another level. Would that be so bad, he wondered? He enjoyed their sparring, appreciating her quick mind; and her liveliness was a good foil for his own solemnity. The thought of finding a wife in England had not really entered his mind but now he wondered whether that should be an objective of his. Conversations in the office had led him to believe that men with a stable family life were more likely to be considered for partnership; and although he was a good few years away from that, it might be a good idea to start looking for a suitable matrimonial partner.

As he thought of Hettie, with her rather round face and soft brown eyes, he knew she did not appeal to him in 'that way.' He considered that as a man he should love and desire his future companion in life. His thoughts wandered to the bright young thing he had spotted in the haberdashery window so many months ago. He had deliberately walked that way on several occasions to see if he could spot her again. A few times, he had been successful. She had not yet smiled at him but it was her face, not Hettie's, that he saw as he floated into dreams on his single bed at night.

He ignored the next invitation from Hettie and to the next one he pleaded absence due to a heavy workload. He felt rather a cad but as he said to himself, he didn't want to give someone a false impression, and he was not confident enough to explain his feelings to her. After all, she was just a friend; and he knew she had a wide circle of acquaintances to keep her busy.

He started avoiding Arthur at work as he turned down yet another family function. It was starting to become really embarrassing for him. Should he knock on Arthur's office door and explain himself? But what would he explain? How could he say that he was unsure of his feelings towards his daughter, his daughter who had so kindly taken him under her wing and introduced him to Manchester and included him in so many family events? He felt enmeshed, tangled in emotions and politeness and knew that this meant Hettie was not for him.

# Sixteen

## 1914 Manchester

Maree turned from the navy hat she was trimming. She was now a senior apprentice and as such she took delight in ordering the most junior one, Maisie, around.

"Maisie," she said, "don't just sit there. Mrs Hastings will be back soon and I do so want this hat finished. Can you go into the stockroom and look for some ostrich feathers? It's just what's needed. I think there are a few there on the second shelf. Hurry up!"

It was increasingly difficult to reproduce the hats seen in the magazines; shortages in the trimmings made the girls even more inventive.

Maisie scurried away in obedience to Maree's wishes and within a few minutes brought back two beautiful ostrich feathers, their downy fronds so soft and white in her hands. Maree smiled at her then and, checking the feathers against the brim of the hat she was working on, she began sewing.

"It's right beautiful," breathed Maisie. "I wish I could make one so lovely."

"You will, one day, if you do as I tell you. Now go and tidy up all those ribbons and the laces. You don't want Mrs Hastings thinking you've been idle all day, mind."

Maree picked up the bonnet with its sweep of feathers and netting and took it to the window, the better to see how her creation appeared in the sunlight. It was a surprisingly sunny day and shafts of sun were slanting through at a late afternoon angle.

She held the hat this way and that and pursed her lips. She took a fold of the netting and tucked it further back. Pleased with this, she looked out of the window. It was knocking-off time and many of the shop assistants were leaving and walking briskly down the street to their trams. She spotted clothes she liked and hats she thought she might be able to copy before realising that someone was staring at her.

He had round glasses, a neat suit and tie and a faint smile on his well-formed lips. But, oh my, he was an Oriental gentleman. Surely he wasn't looking at her? She glanced over her shoulder to see if by any chance someone else in the shop had caught his gaze. Highly unlikely, she knew, as the last customer had been served and left five minutes ago. What should she do? She decided the best action would be no action, so she studied the hat again, narrowed her eyes and walked back to the workroom.

The next day, Maree was measuring out some ribbon, the perfect blue velvet that she had yearned for so many years ago, when she spotted her observer again sauntering past, a faint smile on his lips and his dark eyes solely on her. This would not do. She stammered a goodbye to her customer after thrusting the ribbon into a brown paper bag and quickly turned her head.

It happened every day for a week. Never having seen this gentleman before, she now suspected that he was passing her shop with perhaps the very purpose of seeing her. She longed to tell Ruby. When the following Monday he did not come past, she felt a small surge of disappointment.

"Oh, Ruby," she said, "do you think he is really looking at me? I don't know. And why would he?"

"Nothing too shabby about you, you know. Maybe he'll turn you into that Indian princess you always wanted to be!" Ruby laughed.

"Well, he would be an improvement on Thomas Jeffries. I know there's not much choice these days with the war on, but really!" The last young man her mother had tried to set her up with, the son of an acquaintance, had been an unctuous disaster. Fawning over her and licking his lips before every utterance, he had made her skin crawl. She shuddered at the recollection.

"What could he be doing here, in Manchester?" she asked Ruby, who shrugged and said, "Well, he's not coming by any more, is he, so I wouldn't worry about it."

But she did. She could not get him out of her head. She mentioned him to Agnes, who gave her short shrift.

"What d'you mean? An Indian man? Whatever next! Screw your head on, girl, and don't you go looking at him again. What would the neighbours say?"

Two more days passed before he wandered past again, this time stopping to look in the window, perusing the notions on display, his forehead creased in concentration. He glanced up as if as an afterthought and caught her eye. This time the smile was definite. A slight nod of the head and he was gone. Maree caught her breath. She had been holding it all the time he stood there. What was wrong with her? His smooth dark skin had shone. His teeth dazzled as he smiled.

The next day he stopped again to look and Maree found herself returning his smile with a shy one of her own. She placed an anxious hand to her hair and bobbed the back of it. She looked around. No one else in the shop was looking, Maisie tidying the storeroom and Mrs Hastings taking an order from Lady Muck (as they called her): a customer who took an enormous amount of time and effort in describing a creation she had seen at the races and how she wanted one of the girls to sketch the same and make one just like it! She was never satisfied with whatever they made and Mrs Hastings often ended up selling the hat at a discount to someone else as a special order not picked up.

The gentleman on the pavement smiled and nodded once more

before moving off. Maree had been holding her breath again. What a to-do over nothing, she thought.

After a few more days of making sure she was towards the front of the shop at the time the gentleman usually passed, but to no avail, Maree was in the stockroom when she heard the ring of the doorbell. Mrs Hastings being busy with accounts in the office, she put down the material she was wrapping and walked onto the shopfloor.

Her cheeks, which had been a delicate pink, now darkened as she saw the Indian gentleman smiling and nodding at her.

"How do you do?" he said with such formality in his voice. Maree straightened her collar and smoothed her damp hands on the sides of her skirt.

"How d'you do?" she responded in a like manner. "How can I help you?"

"I've taken rather a fancy to that lace in the window," he said.

"For your wife, sir? How much do you need?"

He just smiled. "Two yards, please."

Maree held the lace in her hands and admired the intricate pattern. Who was the lucky lady who would receive this? She played the lace through her hands and against the bronze measuring tape embedded in the wooden measuring table. She revelled in the nearness of this exotic man. He watched her hands intently. She could feel his gaze on her and she felt a prickle of embarrassment at the thought of how her workworn hands with the jagged nails would appear to him.

"Have you worked here long, Miss...?" His question took her by surprise and she returned his gaze, her cheeks tingling pink.

"Crymble, Miss Crymble." She replied curtly, as out of the corner of her eye she could see Mrs Hastings watching her through the office window. Fraternising with the customers was frowned upon even for the most senior apprentices. She followed her reply with an apology of a smile and raised eyebrows and was rewarded by a grin as he looked towards the office to show he understood her caution and embarrassment.

She folded the lace into a paper bag which she tore from a string tied below the bench, pleated the top and handed it to him.

"Thank you, Miss Crymble. How much would that be?" Again, that formal tone.

"Tuppence halfpenny, sir." She watched his long slender fingers with perfectly manicured nails count out the change. She was ashamed to extend her palm to collect the money.

He flashed another brilliant smile, turned on his heel and left the shop. Maree let out an audible sigh. Mrs Hastings was next to her in no time.

"And what did he want? I'm not so sure we should be serving the likes of him," she hissed.

Maree creased her brow. What did she mean? He was so well-dressed and polite!

"These Indians coming to our city, they'll be taking our men's jobs next. They'll take advantage of our men being away fighting for God and country, you mark my words." Mrs Hastings crossed her arms tightly under her substantial bosom and huffed.

"He was beautifully spoken, Mrs Hastings. Educated, you could tell."

"Even more chance he could take someone else's job, then," she threw over her shoulder as she went back to the other workbench where another customer was choosing between two hat designs.

Maree sighed and looked around to see if Maisie had heard the interchange. Would she think the same? Would Ruby? Maree's only encounter with a person of Indian heritage was that beautiful princess she had seen at the opening to the ice palace all those years ago. She still dreamed of her and her family even after finding out that she was a famous suffragette, Maharani Sophie, who had no desire to be finding herself a husband or of being manipulated by her father. Anyway, she had no illusions that this gentleman was a Maharajah. Maharajahs would never enter the shop where she worked. They would have sent a servant to do their purchasing.

# Seventeen

Maree and Ruby sat, heads together, huddled over cups of tea. Mrs Crymble peeled potatoes at the sink while fragments of their conversation floated by her. She knew what they were talking about. Maree had mentioned that Indian gentleman again. It had been a long time since someone had caught her eye. Mrs Crymble had despaired of her finding a husband. It was not easy, she kept telling Maree, with the war on and all the eligible young men off fighting. If this man wasn't fighting, then who was he? Should he have been given a white feather? It seemed as if the flower of Manchester youth were being mown down in the trenches. It was a horrendous situation. Only last week she had been speaking to Mrs Brown, her next door neighbour, who told her, tears flowing down her cheeks, that both her brother and her nephew had been killed in the same battle over there in France. It was frightful. At this rate there certainly wouldn't be choices for Florence and Maree. A few years ago Nell had married John, a local shopkeeper, and thankfully he wouldn't be called up. He told her so with great satisfaction as he puffed on his cigarette.

"I'm essential to the war effort," he boasted, "supplying all with food; well, the food I can get, at least. Nell won't go short and neither will you, Mother."

It certainly was a relief. Agnes's housekeeping work had been cut short as her only employer Mrs Robotham rattled around in the big draughty house with her two boys off to the war.

"I won't need you all day, Mrs Crymble. Just come in the morning and give the house a quick clean and perhaps prepare some dinner for me. That will do."

So it was certainly lean times; and making ends meet for the girls remaining at home was difficult. She thought she might have to take in lodgers. Agnes stared out of the small kitchen window, her attention caught by a tiny spider, industrious in the corner, fixing a small hole in its creation.

"It's easy for you," she grumbled. "You make a trap and the food comes to you."

Maree looked up and asked her mother what she had said. She didn't respond, just shrugged her shoulders.

"You were talking out loud, Mam, you'd better be careful." She laughed.

"It's all very well, but you'd better look sharpish and catch yourself an eligible man. I can't be looking after you all your life, you know. Nearly twenty and not even stepping out with someone. What do you think, Ruby? Your Tim is a nice boy. It's a shame he has flat feet but at least that meant he is still here for you. Does he have a brother?"

She knew the answer to that question as she asked it every time she saw Ruby. She had been going to ask Mrs Brown about her nephew until she had told her the fearful news. In fact, she looked everywhere for eligible men for her daughters; but every day the pool was drying up further.

Ruby had met Tim at the mill. He worked on the machines and as he raced around she couldn't see any sign of flat feet but she was glad of it as his time came to be called up. He had failed the medical and remained working, more valuable as so many men had left the factory short. They were making canvas for tents now, not fine cotton. Tim raced around to fill the jobs of thirty men. Men lost in the mud of war, some never coming back. Mr Fothergill, the supervisor, read out a list every week, calling all the mill workers to stand by their machines while he read in a sombre tone the names of the missing men. It was hard to bear. Sometimes, a woman would clutch her apron to her face and moan as a name was read out. Ruby felt invulnerable. Her fella wouldn't be one of those names. How grateful she felt as she smiled across the shop floor at him, his cap in hand as he bowed his head. She watched the light slant across and set his hair on fire. A joyous beacon amidst the prevailing sadness.

# Eighteen

A week passed. Maree had not seen her gentleman friend, as she now thought of him. She had peered out of the shop window at every opportunity but she had not spied his tall, immaculately dressed figure walking along the pavement. Of course, just when she had begun to think he might never appear again and she had stopped looking up every time the bell rang, he was there in front of her at the counter.

"Good morning, Miss Crymble," he said. "I need some assistance with choosing some ribbon. Can you help me?"

She felt her cheeks glow hot and admonished herself for it. This man must have a wife, a family; he was older than her, she could tell. Mature, she told herself; why was he not fighting in the war? She didn't know and most probably never would.

Ribbons? Must be for his little girl. She showed him the array of silks, satins, velvets and their varying colours. Which would he prefer? Might he tell her what it would be used for?

For a special person, he replied; and her heart sank. Of course he had a special person. What had she been thinking? He was just someone who had merely smiled at her and sent her glances, into which she had read so much more. What a fool she had been to even think that she could ever be that special person. She measured out the requisite two yards of the chosen delicate pink silk ribbon and handed it to him in the brown paper bag. His fingers touched hers – could she imagine that they lingered? – and he smiled that beautiful smile at her, his eyes glinting behind his glasses. She gasped involuntarily. No, she *was* right. He was sending her messages.

"Thank you very much, Miss Crymble. You are too kind. I will let you know if she likes the ribbon." He turned and left the shop, Maree's hopes a-swirl around her feet. She blinked and shook her head. How foolish she was being.

Mrs Hastings swooped up to her. "And what did he want this time? I hope you're not encouraging him," she said. "Why is he even here and not away fighting like the rest of the young men?"

"Well, I don't know why you would expect me to know," Maree retorted, stung.

It was with a dragging heart that Maree gathered her belongings that evening, tied her scarf around her neck, pulled her hat down around her ears, threw the leather strap of her bag over her shoulder and shouted a curt goodbye to Mrs Hastings and Maisie.

She clipped down the stone steps and walked towards the corner; and there he was, leaning against the bank building, a knowing smile on his face.

"Good evening, Miss Crymble. May I accompany you?"

"I… I don't know. I'm just going to the tram stop up the road."

"Miss Crymble, my name is Frank Tarmaster. I'm so pleased to meet you." He offered her his hand. "I have been wanting to speak to you, privately, for quite a while now. I have never seen an English woman with such a soft face. You are very beautiful."

A severe blush spread from her throat and up to her cheeks. Despite the cold she felt she would have to take the end of her scarf and dab her upper lip and her forehead, but how unladylike would that be? Glancing down at her shuffling feet, she considered his offer.

"I need to know something about you. I'm not sure my mother would approve."

"Dear Miss Crymble. Please do not be worrying about me. I

am studying at Manchester College. I am nearly finished with my accountancy exams and I will soon be working full time for Piggott and Co., the chartered accountants. You must have heard of them."

She hadn't and didn't wish to display any more ignorance by asking him what a chartered accountant was. She thought that it sounded sufficiently posh that perhaps she should allow him to walk her to the tram.

She could see the tram in the distance and increased her pace to make sure that she would not miss it.

"May I see you tomorrow?" he asked.

She nodded vigorously and hopped on behind the last man in the queue. The conductor in his long double-breasted coat looked at her curiously as she said goodbye.

She found a seat next to a buxom lady who sniffed her disapproval at her when she sat down but she did not dare look out of the window in case he was still watching her. What was she going to do?

Ruby was excited. So exotic, she said. "Go on, you must see him again. Find out where he's from, and all that."

Her mother decided to swallow her doubts about an 'Indian man' and was equally approving. "A professional man. Mmm, Maree; you really should encourage him. He could be the one we have been waiting for." Maree scowled at the 'we' but slept fitfully amongst dreams of golden saris, horses and jewels bestowed upon her as she rode out on the exotic plains of India.

He must be lonely, she thought; but what had happened to that special person he had talked about? She needed to find out much more about his history if she was going to consider walking out with him, no matter what Ruby and her mother said. She had felt keenly the dearth of young men and had pondered on her future many a sleepless night. The war was continuing. More and more men were being conscripted and if not conscripted were lining up in droves at the recruiting stations to have a chance of fighting the Hun. The last queue she had come across astounded her. The men standing there, joking with each other, were adolescent boys, young brothers of girls she knew in her neighbourhood, the fluff of manhood barely apparent on their cheeks. At this rate, she thought, there would only be girls and women left on her street. No one she knew was studying at a university; most had barely been able to finish school. The sheer achievement of it shook her. And if he were so clever, why would he be interested in her? A lowly shopgirl, even if she were at the finishing end of her apprenticeship. Her future was staying in the haberdashery, serving customers, making and trimming hats and finding herself under Mrs Hastings' thumb.

Every night after work that week he was outside waiting for her. He told her about his scholarship, about his sister so far away in Bombay and his wish to start his own business. She was relieved there was no mention of a wife or children either here with him or back in India. With a little more prompting he told her about the medals he had won for his exams. He told her of his successes without pride, just as a matter of fact, which she liked. He listed the exams he had passed: Commercial Knowledge, Bookkeeping, Commercial Law, Economics – none of which made sense to her; and she thought he must think her very silly as she had left schooling so early, but it did not seem to faze him. On Friday he said he wanted to give her something and he held out the brown paper bag in which she had placed the pink silk ribbon. Tucked inside were both the ribbon and the previously purchased lace.

"I told you I was buying it for a special person," he grinned. It was all too much for Maree. She needed time to think. She ran to the tram, leaving him standing on the pavement still holding out the bag, a quizzical expression on his face.

"Mother, can I accept a present from him? I hardly know him!" she burst out as soon as she entered her house.

"Of course you can, you daft thing. This isn't Victorian times, you know. And what with the war on, you need to take all the pleasure you can get. Although I think it's high time you invited him here before you start stepping out with him, my girl."

The next week followed the same pattern, with Frank waiting outside the shop for her and walking her to the tram stop. On the third day he tucked the brown paper bag containing the lace and ribbon into her coat pocket. She gave him an almost imperceptible nod. Each day they walked on further to arrive at the next tram stop. There was so much to say and so much to learn about each other. She asked him if he would come to her house on Saturday for tea; her mother wished to meet him.

Maree baked scones and a gingerbread parkin using up all the flour her mother had for the week's rations. This was a special occasion, after all. It was not every day that a fine Indian gentleman came a-calling. At three-thirty on the dot there was a knock at the door. Maree raced along the hallway, skidding on the hall runner before bursting open the door. He stood on the steps holding a small bunch of pale yellow primroses, a posy of early spring sunshine radiating and filling the whole smoke-filled street.

As she led him through to the sitting room where a coal fire burnt in the grate casting orange light over the sombre furniture, Mrs Crymble, still in the kitchen, whipped off her apron, ran a comb through her greying hair and pinned up the curls falling onto her shoulders. She strode down the hallway, stopped at the sitting room door, peeked in and announced herself with a short cough.

Maree jumped up as Frank also got to his feet and stepped towards her with his hand outstretched. Maree admired his confidence. Her mother seemed daunting to her but Frank took her in his stride and was smoothly enquiring about her health and telling her about the sharp cold outside.

"Please, come and sit with us," he said, as if it was his sitting room and he were entertaining. Frank was never at a conversational loss. His aplomb was astonishing to Maree. She had never dreamt of being courted by such a worldly conversationalist. Maree left her mother and Frank laughing together as she fetched the tea and cakes.

Frank was extremely complimentary about Maree's cooking and she blushed with a feeling of accomplishment. Frank talked about his lodgings and how he was delighted to taste some good Lancashire cooking although of course he missed the Indian cuisine. He kept smiling over at Maree but continued talking to Mrs Crymble, who found herself warming to him despite her reservations; and when he talked about wanting to start his own accounting company once he had finished his articles, he rose further in her estimation. The visit was a success and although Maree did not have a chance to speak to Frank privately, he left her in no doubt as to how he felt about her. It was all in the glances framed by the dark lashes, the twinkle behind his glasses.

"Where will you be walking out with Maree?" her mother asked him and he looked perplexed.

"Walking out?" he queried. "What does that mean?" Maree jumped in.

"I always enjoy Boggart Hole. Let's go there tomorrow. What do you think, Frank?"

"I do not know of this Boggart Hole. It doesn't sound so appealing. I had thought perhaps some gardens."

Both Maree and her mother laughed.

"It *is* a park with beautiful gardens, even in winter; you'll enjoy it."

The bleak sunshine of the day had dulled with storm clouds heavy over the roofs by the time Frank left. It threatened snow but he said he would return the next day for their outing to Boggart Hole, no matter what the weather.

# Nineteen

The next morning when Maree drew open the curtains in the bedroom she shared with Flo and looked out of the window, she gasped with delight.

"Oh look, Flo. It's beautiful." The fields past the village spread out like a soft sparkling blanket, the houses on the street capped with a fluffy layer. It was the first heavy snow that had fallen that winter and it lay unsullied at this early hour.

The elation soon turned to disappointment as she was convinced that Frank would not keep his promise. It would be hard to travel from the city to her house and then on to the park. She was still eating her porridge, scraping out small spoonfuls at a time, a gloomy expression on her face, when there was a rapid rat-a-tat-tat on the door.

Maree looked at her sister sitting before her, with surprise on her face. Could it really be him?

"Well, I wouldn't be getting all excited," said her mother. "I don't think he'll be coming today!"

Maree began to rise but Flo, having finished her porridge, pushed back her chair with a squeak and dabbed her mouth with her napkin.

"I'll get it. It's probably Ruby." Maree sank back into her chair. What was she going to do all day? She supposed she could tell Ruby all about yesterday, but what then?

From the hall she heard a man's voice, a cultured voice with an exotic accent – and she realised that Frank had made the journey. He had braved the snow and the slow trams and kept his word to pick her up for their day out.

"I was not sure if the park would be open and I had to wait for a train as the trams were snowed in. But, Maree, I am a man of my word and I would not disappoint you."

With luck, the tram to Boggart Hole was one of the few still running. The entrance gate pillars were still capped with snow when they arrived and the magic of the snow glistening in the sun which pushed through the hanging clouds lent a magical air to the park. Maree found it enchanting. She skipped along the tree-lined avenue, her hands in her pockets to keep them warm, as she showed Frank the boating pond, a frozen disc now. She told him how in the warmer weather you could hire rowing boats and sit on the edge with your feet dangling in the cool water. The usual crowds of people out enjoying a Sunday perambulation were thinned today and only the hardy had ventured out, scarves wrapped tightly and hats pulled low. She spotted a woman with a fur hat which she pointed out as having come from her establishment. With pride she showed him the bandstands and the stone fountain, quiet today with frozen icicles draped over the scalloped edges.

The sculptural trees, bare in all their majesty, spread around the park, dazzling bundles of snow creating thudding sounds as they dropped to the ground.

"It looks like a giant has been icing cakes," Maree said. Frank laughed and they continued on, too cold to stay in one place. They came across a newly completed thatched shelter, its wooden spire spearing the sky.

"I'm surprised they finished this," she said. "There was a lot of talk about it not being essential and that men had better things to do in this time of war."

"It is a beautiful place. It gives people pleasure. I believe they need this. When the times are dire we must take pleasure in the smallest of things." He touched her sleeve affectionately and Maree wondered about the pleasure they could take from each other. Her mother was now keen for this slight acquaintance to be a serious relationship but she was not sure. The future was so difficult to think about. No one had expected this war to continue for so long. No one had realised that death and devastation would be a daily occurrence for what was now nearly two years.

She had thought that by now she might be like Nell, married and expecting a child; but this darned war had delayed everything. She became silent as they walked back to the tram stop, thinking about the person beside her. She needed to know more about him. He had told her next to nothing about his family in Bombay. He was a mystery man. She did not know about his friends, and the only dream she was aware of was his wish to start his own business. She knew that this was an uphill struggle and in these difficult times she did not see how it could be achieved. Maybe he had some money. She did not know but she had heard that banks certainly were not lending any money to anyone. She had overheard Mr Wilson complaining to Mrs Hastings how he might have to sell one of the small cottages he rented out so that they could keep the haberdashery afloat. Customers were scarce, as was the money to keep them ordering outrageous and extravagant hats. She had wondered whether she would lose her job but it was more likely that Maisie might go as Maree was the only one with sufficient hat-making skills if custom did pick up.

He too sat silent next to her, deep in his own thoughts, vaguely wondering if he had said or done something to offend her. He bowed slightly when he left her at her door and set off without mentioning if and when he would see her again. As she watched his back recede down the road Maree felt a panic rise; her heart beat fast and tears prickled.

"Where is Frank?" her mother asked, as on stockinged feet Maree tried to creep down the hall and upstairs to her bedroom. She was mid-step as her mother's face appeared from the kitchen door.

"He had to go," she said. "It looked as if it might snow again." And indeed it did. He had probably been thinking that. He must have been in a hurry and forgotten to discuss their next meeting. She consoled herself with this thought. She sat at the dressing table in her room and brushed her hair through. She put on a blue woollen cardigan her mother had knitted her, wrapping it tightly around her frame. The tips of her fingers were white. She went downstairs in search of warmth.

Pouring herself a cup of tea from the pot, she pulled up a stool next to the stove and sat teacup in hand trying to thaw out. She had not realised how cold she actually was. It must have been the silent ride home. No animation or movement to set the blood flowing.

"Pour me a cup, love," her mother said. "It's right parky in here."

They sat together drinking the steaming tea, mugs under their noses until Flo came in.

"I can't believe how cold it is in here," she said. "Bert said we shall have a fire in every room in our house when we get married."

"Well, let's hope he has money to get enough coal!" her mother said tartly. "That Bert thinks he's real fancy."

"Talking about fancy, where's that fancy man of yours, Maree?" her sister deflected. "I thought he might be here out of the cold. Did you actually go to Boggart?"

Maree shook her head, stood up, hurried down the hall, grabbed her coat off the peg and headed out of the door, shouting behind her, "I'm off to see Ruby!"

Her half-drunk mug of tea lay steaming between Flo and her mother, who looked quizzically at each other.

"Well, she did go to Boggart, I think," said Agnes. "I don't know what all that's about. She's a queer'un sometimes."

# Twenty

Maree made her way carefully down the street, her boots slipping on the icy pavements which had been cleared of snow earlier in the day but which were now threatening to spill every passerby. Her nose dribbled and her eyes were watering. In her rush she hadn't taken hat, scarf or gloves and she was glad how close Ruby's house was.

Ruby answered the door to her and ushered her in, a cold, shivering, pink-faced bundle.

"Ooh, Maree. You don't half look cold! Come in the kitchen by the stove. The others are sat by the fire in the sitting room." Maree's distraught face told her of the need to be private.

Ruby shut the wooden door, which squeaked on its old hinges, and stood with her back pushed against it, her face questioning as she turned to face Maree who had crouched down by the stove, her head on her knees.

"For goodness' sake, Maree," she whispered, "whatever's come over you? You look right awful!"

"I think I've lost him before we've even become a couple," she managed to get out. "We were having a lovely time. You know, I showed him all the places in Boggart that we like and then he made a comment which got me thinking and I went all quiet, you know like I do, and then so did he and we never spoke another word until we got back to my house and he just said goodbye and nothing else." She groaned.

"That doesn't mean owt," Maree said. "You'll see: he'll be back outside the shop waiting for you tomorrow, mind."

Maree shook her head. "I wish I could be so sure."

It was the longest day in the shop on the Monday. The foul weather continued and few people were out on the streets. Even Main Street was deserted after the workers had hurried into the shops out of the cold. It was hardly a day for shopping.

Mrs Hastings kept walking to the shop window, wringing her hands as if she could magic some customers into it. She barked at Maisie who as usual stood around without direction. She found fault with the order Maree was working on and made numerous cups of tea to keep her own hands busy.

Maree tried hard not to glance out of the window and a few minutes before closing time she asked Mrs Hastings if she could leave early as the sky was so dark and snow was coming. This was partly the reason; but it was also so that she would not actually know if Frank had come for her or not, as she would have left the shop.

The weather remained bleak all week and the snow lay in dirty heaps by the sides of the road with treacherous icy black patches on both the pavement and the road. She concentrated hard each day on arriving at the tram stop without a fall on the ice. Her boots slipped and more than once she grabbed onto the sleeve of another pedestrian, murmuring her apologies as she did so. She wished it was Frank's sleeve she clasped; but he made no appearance.

It was a miserable weekend. Her mother rolled old clothes under each door but still the bitter wind found its way around their ankles. Nell did not visit and Flo and Maree contented themselves with crocheting doilies as they sat around the fire, jumping up when a piece of coal threatened to fall or if the fire needed banking up.

On Sunday morning after church Ruby braved the ice and came to visit. She had news. She positively glowed and it wasn't from the cold, as Maree soon found out.

"You'll never guess!" she gushed. "Tim… Tim came round yesterday evening and wanted to see Dad. I stood outside in the hallway and listened. I even put my ear to the keyhole as he hadn't said anything to me… I couldn't make out many words from their murmurings so then I glued my eye to the hole and then Dad got out of his seat, pulled down his jumper, stuck his hand out to Tim and said 'Congratulations'."

Maree's curiosity only went so far and she couldn't wait for Ruby to get to the point.

"Congratulations? What for? Did they want him to do a different job at Ancoat's?" They had discussed this possibility before as the male workforce dwindled.

"No, you silly," Ruby blurted out. "He's asked me to marry him! We know we can't find a house or anything until the war's over but isn't that exciting? Next week we're going up town to find a ring. Oh, I can't wait!"

Maree forced a smile.

"Aren't you pleased for me, Maree? I thought you'd want to help me plan a wedding. We haven't got much money put aside and there aren't many things to buy anyway but we'll make do and manage."

At the sound of Ruby's excited voice, Mrs Crymble came in, wiping her hands on her pinny; she asked what all the fuss was about.

"I'm getting married, Mrs C! Isn't it exciting? We'll have to wait until next year, maybe, or even longer; but I'm so made up!"

Mrs Crymble's long arms embraced the girl and she planted a kiss on her pink cheek.

"Look at you," she said, "as pretty as a peach. Why've you got a sour face, miss?" as she addressed Maree. "Just because you let your young man get away."

"He wasn't my young man and I didn't let him get away, he just stopped coming by. I don't know why." And she burst into tears, the hot flushing of a week's emotion coursing down her face.

Ruby wriggled out of Mrs Crymble's embrace and threw her

arms around her friend.

"Don't you worry," she said. "He'll be back; I feel it in me waters."

Maree stopped snivelling long enough to laugh at this and her sobs subsided into hiccups.

"Well," Mrs Crymble said, "I think we all need a brew. I'll go and put t' kettle on."

# Twenty-One

As it happened, Ruby's predictive waters turned out to be accurate; and the following week as Maree stepped out of the shop, she saw Frank hurrying around the corner towards her.

"I'm so sorry," he began, "there was an exam that I had to take. I was studying every night and I did not tell you when I last saw you. That was why I was so silent. I had been thinking of nothing but the examination. It was a Diploma in Banking and Economics. I need a good result for this one!"

Maree's smiling face gave him courage to continue.

"It is so important for me to pass that exam; without it I will not be able to start working on my own. I would have nothing to offer you. Please be kind to me."

In answer Maree tucked her arm in his and they walked the familiar route to the tram. Frank didn't stop talking all the way. It was such a relief that she didn't really listen to what he was saying; she just enjoyed the sound of his voice, his kind brown eyes on her, his hand clasping hers and his breath so close.

She held her head high, even higher when she noticed a disapproving glance from an elderly lady they passed. The woman lifted her hand to her nose and continued watching the young couple, her neck twisted so far round that she tripped on a paving stone which would have delighted Maree if she had seen it; but she was too busy looking to see if Frank's face had registered the rudeness.

Spring seemed to be nearer every day now, even though the ground was still hard and the snowdrops in the park had barely shown their white and green heads. Maree felt light and full of energy. She acquiesced to Mrs Hastings' every request, beamed at Maisie and hummed as she worked. Mr Wilson, when he dropped by, came up to her and demanded to know what was making her so happy with all the horrifying things going on in France. These events were a world away to Maree. A different world of which she was no part. She saw the horses and carts on the road but was indifferent to their passage. More than once a bobby had to motion to her to step back on the pavement as she was about to step out in front of one. She came to, as out of a dream, and just smiled at the harassed coachman who was about to shout at her. She stopped and looked into Bostock's and wondered if she could afford a new pair of boots for spring. Her old ones were looking rather shabby, she thought; but eight shillings and sixpence was a huge amount of money to her and she knew her Mam depended on her wages to get by.

Counting out some spare coins she had in her pocket she went into the local toy shop to buy her mother a block of her favourite Fry's chocolate. Maree looked at all the toys displayed in the window. She should be thinking of what she could buy her sister Nell's little baby when it was born. Her wages would be better spent on wool for a baby blanket. She didn't want to think of the chocolate as a bribe but she had used it before when she needed to get her own way. It was amazing how amenable her mother became after tucking into Fry's peppermint chocolate. Maybe there might be some change and Maree would be able to persuade her mother then to allow her the expense of the new boots. She felt rough around the edges when she walked out with Frank. The shiny patches on the sleeves of her wool coat and the thin cotton of her blouse made her feel embarrassed and she wanted to be as well dressed as he was; but she was not sure that she could do so on her wages. Material was getting scarcer and her mother said her poor hands were getting too rheumaticky to be doing any hand sewing.

Frank hopped down off the tram. The conductor, in his smart double-breasted coat, tipped his hat to him. Frank turned the corner past the Chorlton pavilion and whistled as he made his way up Barlow Moor Road. The evening was quiet and the street unusually deserted. He spotted a group of four or five young soldiers in their military green at the top of the road. They swaggered down the pavement, full of themselves and, Frank thought, probably full of Dutch courage.

As he increased his pace, he watched as one threw the cap of another into the middle of the street. The young man staggered to pick it up and as he did so, he spotted Frank.

"Oy, what have we here then?" he enquired. The others followed his gaze.

"Hey, you, wog, where are you going? Where's your uniform?"

It was too late for Frank to turn back and they quickly surrounded him. Frank was not sure if he should say he was at university or whether that would inflame them further. His heart pounding he attempted a genial smile.

"Cor, think you're better than us, do ya?"

"You tell him, mate!"

They started shoving him between them and then it was impossible to get away. The first soldier pushed him onto his knees; he felt the gravel through his thin trousers. His first thought was that he would need a new pair after this was over but he didn't have time to follow this thought. A sharp kick was aimed at his back which sent him sprawling. His glasses flew off and the next five minutes was a blur of pain.

"Go... home... you... bloody... wog..." Each word was accompanied by a kick from heavy boots. Frank gasped: his back, his kidneys, his legs. He tried to protect his face and his chest by curling inwards and thinking of his wonderful numbers which had soothed him before; but this time they did not help.

Soon the soldiers tired of their sport and, dusting down their jackets, they spat on him as they left, their guffaws echoing in his roaring ears. His left hand scrabbled to find his glasses. The frames were broken and looking through one lens was like looking through a snowflake. He got to his knees and groaned as he pulled himself straight. Still no one on the street. He was sure he saw the twitch of a net curtain, but no one brave or compassionate enough to come out to help him.

He hobbled towards Beech Road, stopping at Brooke Road Bridge to catch his breath.

He leaned against Maree's door, his face stinging.

"Blimey!" Mrs Crymble said as she opened the door. "You've been in the wars. What happened? Come on in and I'll get you a wet flannel to wipe the blood off your cheek. Best do that before Maree sees you."

Maree clattered down the stairs and stood on the bottom step looking over the banister into the living room.

"Frank!" she shouted. "Your face, your clothes! Just look at your knees! What on earth went on?"

Frank shook his head, unable to speak. He wanted to weep. He wanted Jasleen. He swallowed and tried to stand up straight but the pain wracked his body and showed on his face.

# Twenty-Two

Frank kept accruing high honours and medals with every examination he sat. In May he arrived at Maree's house with a silver medal in First Class Company Law. He waved both his certificate and the medal in the air with great glee.

"I feel my goal is getting nearer," he said. "I need to start thinking of what I will do when I finish my articles."

Arthur Piggott had taken a shine to Frank and encouraged him the most of his young articled accountants.

"Numbers come so easily to you, Frank. Our clients all ask for you; they reckon you are magical with figures. If I don't watch it I will have no clients myself!"

Working with Piggott and Co. had helped Frank's pockets and he was now able to afford for himself his own rooms in a boarding house in Sale, which was a shorter journey for him to visit Maree. He could walk down the main street and arrive there after dinner to spend the spring evenings with Maree. Invariably, they would wander the streets of Chorlton and as the cricket season started he delighted in stopping to watch them practise in the nets of the cricket pitch and would applaud wildly at the fine shots.

"When I was a very young boy, I used to wander over to the

*maidan* sometimes after school before Jasleen came home," he recounted. "It wasn't far from the *wadi* I lived in and I would sit with my sums and watch both adults and children playing. Hearing the thwack of the ball and the shouts makes me feel nostalgic, although I myself didn't play." Maree tucked her arm under his and looked up at him fondly.

"I would sit on the sidelines offering encouragement and occasionally I just sat reading, as it was a peaceful place away from the hustle and bustle of the *wadi*," he continued.

Here in Chorlton he again admired the cricket whites. The team was made up of young men, too young to be called up, and older men, too old to be fighting. Young Tim, Ruby's beau and soon to be husband, encouraged him to join in.

"I'm really not a sporting man; well, not in that sense," he chortled, "and just because I'm Indian does not mean I'm a great cricketer."

He was happy to watch and support the local team. Maree prepared and poured tea at the Sunday games but only so that she could spend more time with Frank, who was content to sit on the bleacher seats and not think about figures or business.

At home, Frank sat at his desk perusing the papers for business opportunities. He was aware of Mr Piggott's favouritism and felt that this might assist him with a glowing reference.

He circled possible jobs and sent off letters to as far away as London, but so far he had been unsuccessful.

His correspondence with Mr Gupta from the Hindu Education Fund kept him abreast of possibilities in Bombay; but he was a long way from persuading Maree that their future might lie there.

Mrs Crymble had been dropping less than subtle hints about making an honest woman of Maree; but Frank was convinced that he had to be more secure in his work before he would offer marriage to her. He was not sure how they would be accepted as a couple here in Manchester, nor how it might be in India.

Towards the end of the year, he sat for Fellowship of the Chartered Institute of Secretaries and Maree complained bitterly that she never saw him. He was focussed on his studies rather than her; and once again she doubted his intentions. She sighed and shrugged when questioned by Ruby, whose trajectory was so firmly entrenched. She did not, however, want what Ruby had. She and Tim were going to have to live with her parents until they could afford their own place. As lovely as Tim was, he had not been promoted at work and another even younger man had been promoted above him. Ruby didn't really mind. She would rather have a kind, generous young man than a miserable, bossy one. Tim felt slighted but the joy of seeing Ruby every single day at work soon overshadowed this and he continued being the general dogsbody around the factory with his usual good humour and ready smile.

The hours that Frank spent huddled over his books paid off and he was accepted as a Fellow and also was noted as a medallist of the Royal Society of Arts in London, which together with his now five years of service articled to Piggott and Co. proved his membership of the Institute of Chartered Accountants. He had explained to Maree how important this was for him but she pouted and her congratulations were rather perfunctory, as she felt she had been in second place for too long. Mrs Crymble, however, lost no opportunity in regaling Mrs Brown and any other neighbour who would listen with the achievements of her prospective son-in-law.

"Well, I'm not sure it makes up for him being Indian and all that," Mrs Brown said, her arms crossed over her chest, "but I'm impressed all the same. You have to hand it to him..."

Mrs Crymble made up stories about Maree and Frank, how they were going to live in a fine house in London, or how they were going to live in Singapore – why there, she didn't know, but the very place name sounded exotic to her. She was not sure that she would enjoy Maree living so far away but she would be out of her care and responsibility, which was definitely something she looked forward to. Flo had left last year after a small wedding to Bert who, being so much older than her, had managed to avoid being called up. Agnes counted up her grandchildren, using the fingers of only one hand. Mrs Brown boasted of her six grandchildren with one more on the way. It was a lot to keep up with, thought Mrs Crymble.

In early December one of Frank's applications turned up trumps. An offer came to him to work for Meugens, Peat and Co. from Birmingham in their Calcutta office. Calcutta was not familiar to him but the company name and prestige were hard to turn down. He negotiated a first class passage on the first boat out of Southampton in the new year with a war insurance in case the boat was bombed. A deal was struck with a handsome salary of three hundred and sixty pounds per annum with an annual increase of forty pounds.

Frank was jubilant; but he had to tell Maree. It would mean leaving her in the deprivations of war. He could not think of taking her with him until he was settled; and would she even consider it? He had kept his foreign applications out of their conversations and she, he knew, was envisaging a post in either Birmingham or Manchester, or at the greatest distance of London. Maree had not been too far afield; an outing to Blackpool with her sister Nell and her husband John a few years ago had been the furthest she had ventured.

He would write to her from Calcutta every day telling her of the wonders of India and the plans for settling her into a beautiful home. He was not sure how well the post was functioning and possibly many of his letters would not arrive or would arrive out of sequence, but no matter.

Having decided on this course of action he determined to tell Maree that evening. It was another cold night, one which reminded him of the time he had taken her to Boggart Hole. It had become one of their favourite places and he had seen all its seasons: yellow with daffodils, pink with roses and russet with leaves. He would miss it.

Ruby and Tim were at the house as were Nell and John, visiting from Altrincham. The conversation was lively as they sat sipping cups of tea around the fire. Frank fidgeted in his chair as he could see that his chance of finding a few quiet minutes with Maree was very remote. Mrs Crymble, her ankles made thicker by her wrinkled woollen stockings, sat in an armchair, knitting and listening to the conversation. She interrupted a few times but seemed content to revel in the nearness of family and friends. How was she going to feel when the last of her brood had left? It was not a scenario that she wanted to envisage, so the present would be enough for her at this time. No thoughts of the future would disturb her contentment.

IV

# Twenty-Three

## *1918 Voyage to India*

It was on a brisk morning that Frank walked up the gangplank onto the P&O ship *Nellore*. It was the second time Frank had sailed such a distance but this time he was going first class. He was returning to Bombay in style. The February winds whipped his scarf into his face with such force that he thought his glasses would fall into the murky harbour water.

He was ushered into his first class cabin where his luggage awaited him; no lugging suitcases himself this time. He smiled with pleasure at the sitting room with its round desk that he could work at, seated on a comfy chair. Space to pace and a porthole with a view, he allowed himself to chuckle. He lay down his treasured magenta and gold Onoto fountain pen, a parting gift from Arthur Piggott. Arthur had smiled as he handed him the pen nestling in its box.

"I have every confidence this pen will serve you well, Frank. I read that Florence Nightingale used one very like this one. I have it on good authority that it will work in any condition, be it very hot or cold. Just the ticket for you, my boy."

Frank placed a business textbook and some papers he wished to peruse next to the pen on the mahogany table.

It was time to go on deck to wave goodbye to his old life and set off for the new. Leaving Maree behind had been a wrench; and the last glimpse he had of her was as she stood on the Manchester Central platform waving a damp handkerchief as the train left the station for London. Despite all his explanations and entreaties, he was not convinced she would join him after the end of the war, which by all accounts had been dragging on for far too long.          M r s Crymble had not taken the news of his appointment very well. It was too far away and she was outraged that he was leaving without a ring on Maree's finger. Frank's explanations fell on her deaf ears.

Frank had said he was not afraid of being attacked. The journey might take longer due to delays from troop ships, he had been informed, but his optimism about a safe passage remained high.

Frank suspected that he would not be the only Indian in first class but he wanted to make sure that he upheld the position he had been put in. He dressed carefully for dinner that night in his new dinner suit and sauntered to the dining room, saying good evening to the couple he saw emerging from the room next to him. Well, he thought, they don't seem to have made much effort, as they were still in day clothes. On entering the dining room, he froze. Well, he would certainly make an impression: he was the only one 'dressed' for dinner. How had he got it so wrong? Arthur had said that first class passengers always dressed to eat on the ship. He turned back along the corridor and upon finding his Goan steward he asked him why no one else was dressed. The steward sniffed.

"Sir, *everyone* knows you don't dress on the first night of the voyage," he said, with a slight curl of a contemptuous lip.

Clearly, I am not everyone, Frank thought, and hastily changed out of his dress suit into his lounge jacket and hurried back to the dining room.

As they made their way across the Bay of Biscay, its legendary swell sent dishes scooting along tables and many a genteel lady exited the dining room, napkin to mouth. It did not bother Frank; he had the stomach of a camel, he would say. He acknowledged two other Indian gentlemen sitting at a table on the other side of the room. Perhaps he should make his way over to them and engage them in conversation; they might be good contacts, he thought. After he had finished his meal, he pressed the snow-white linen to his lips, pushed back his chair and wandered over to make their acquaintance.

The ship had to forgo docking at Marseilles where three travellers were waiting to embark. German ships had been seen in the area and it was safer to keep sailing on. They did, however, make a very brief stop in Gibraltar where from the railing Frank saw a large hessian mail sack being tossed down onto the dock. It fell with such a clatter that it surprised him and he suspected someone's precious package might no longer be intact.

As *Nellore* sailed into the Mediterranean, the sea immediately became calmer and the grey gills of many passengers were restored to their customary pink. The two other Indian gentlemen that Frank had spoken to the previous night came on deck, deep in conversation. Frank wondered whether he would join them but thought that as they were otherwise engaged it might be better for them to seek him out after they had completed their talk. After a few turns around the deck, the couple stopped to talk to him.

"Mr Tarmaster," the shorter one said, "how are you this morning? I'm sorry, we were needing to talk business. We were not ignoring you. Why don't we go to the smoking room for some conversation and tea; or do you drink coffee?"

Frank learned that Mr Patel and Mr Chakrabarti had been in London and Manchester on business, negotiating a trade deal for Indian cotton to be shipped into the country since the mills were not able to produce enough capacity due to the reduced workforce during wartime. They had been successful. It was an exciting time for their company and they were pleased to extend their bonhomie to Frank, inviting him to join them for dinner that night.

"You can tell us all about living in Manchester, Mr Tarmaster. You must be quite the expert."

Frank was pleased; he would be able to tell them of his plans, his desire for his own company, his appointment to the prestigious firm of Meugens, Peat and Co. He did not like to think of himself as a trumpet blower but he was going to have to feel more comfortable about it if he were to attract powerful clients.

Making headway through the Mediterranean, the ship kept as far from the African coast as it could, skirting Crete before turning towards the Suez Canal. Although German ships were spotted, they did not approach the passenger ship; and the guests heaved sighs of relief as they docked safely at Port Said.

Frank watched as two officers parted to allow an Arabian man up the gangplank. His long robes fell off a skinny frame; his nose was beaked with a slight twist to the right, which gave him a mildly sinister air. He had come on board to entertain the children, who watched in awe as he produced chicks from beneath his voluminous robes. The parents and other interested spectators were not so enthralled. His smile showed broken and missing teeth which heightened their feelings of unease; and when he stooped down and breathed into the faces of their children, they drew them back sharply and waved him off.

# Twenty-Four

The wait for the convoy was interminable. The usual excursion to the pyramids and Cairo was naturally not on offer. The hot air was thick and pungent with the smell of oil and spices. Frank saw how the two ladies who usually strolled the first class deck had collapsed into deckchairs and were fanning themselves in a frenzy, dabbing themselves with their hankies, feverish spots on their cheeks. Frank knew that the heat would become more intense as they left the port and progressed through the Red Sea. He noted with glee that his cabin was on the portside of the ship which would alleviate a little of that direct heat through both the Red Sea and the Indian Ocean. He breathed in the air and revelled in the thought of returning to his beloved India. He was used to the heat but years of living in England had made him soft, he decided. He would need to acclimatise, too.

Eventually the convoy was formed. As they sailed through the Suez Canal, the deserts glimmered pale and unearthly in the moonlight; soft, dark shapes of camels plodded in trains. Frank thought of the wind-blown Bedouins and the stories they would have to tell. He thought back to the tales of the Arabian nights and Scheherazade's spellbinding words which his father had once read to him so many years ago.

Frank tossed and turned in his bunk. He had thrown off the sheet and lay trying to sleep; but the oppressive heat that night, even from his favourably positioned cabin, drove him on deck. He saw that some passengers from the second and third class cabins were sleeping out on their decks, only moving when the *lascars* hosed down the wooden planks in the morning. The huge cowled ventilators which caught any breeze and sent it down below were not effective in this stifling heat and even the scoops on the portholes did not stand a chance of cooling the cabins.

Frank had never eaten so much food. It seemed as though hardly had his plate been cleared away when another buffet was being prepared at the long tables in the dining room. After the morning wake-up of orange juice, coffee and biscuits at seven, a full breakfast was served at eight-thirty. Once, he had entered the dining saloon early and seen the nannies with their charges, of whom there were many: the nannies wiping faces, keeping the peace between quarrelling siblings, and cutting bacon into small bite-sized pieces. He could see that the Anglo-Indian children had *ayahs* in saris while the British on their way to the colonies had brought their own English nannies with them. He stood to one side as one particularly buxom one with her hair swept severely from her face shepherded out a crying child. Nanny looked harassed, and child looked distraught. Where were the parents, he queried? In their cabins, dressing leisurely for their breakfast.

Frank sometimes worked through coffee time at ten but was then in search of lunch before the twelve-thirty offering. Cakes and pastries were on offer at four o'clock with dinner served at seven. Once, he worked through dinner, but was pleased to see that sandwiches and sweets were placed out at ten before bed. The food he thought was mostly anglo but there were Indian offerings. He tucked into *jalabis* when they were offered at teatime; and one dinner featured a scrumptious *palak paneer*. It was certainly a blended cuisine, he mused.

"How many first class passengers are there?" Frank asked a young steward who was passing by as he sat out on the deck. "I'm thinking there must be about three hundred, and possibly the same number in second class?"

"Yes, sir, you are absolutely right!" Ha, he thought to himself: always good with numbers. Yet it was surprising how many people were travelling in wartime. He allowed himself this sitting time on deck to give his brain a break from swirling numbers. He smiled at the young Indian boys dreamily polishing brasswork in their snow-white suits and scarlet turbans, their faces as shiny as the brass with the effort.

Frank was on deck again when the hostile red cliffs of Aden hove into view. Their steep sides reflected the scorching heat and on the boat in the tiny channel it felt to him as though he were baking in a tandoori oven. The two ladies Frank had often said *Good day* to had removed some of their outer layers of clothing and replaced them with cotton lawn garments: none too soon, he reflected. He mused that the stouter one of them might have fainted dead away in the heat and he might have been called upon to carry her to her room. No, of course he wouldn't, there were stewards everywhere from four o'clock in the morning to ten at night at the passengers' beck and call.

For much of the voyage he felt an outsider. As evening fell and the sky grew darker he watched the frivolity of the young participants playing quoits on deck. All passengers on board regarded the once weekly fire drill as entertainment and Frank too stood and watched as the *lascars* in all their finery of bright red hats and white uniforms directed the procedure, blowing on shiny whistles dangling off silver chains. The imaginary fire they had been called to put out inevitably saw a member of the audience wet from an 'accidental' mishap with the water bucket. A guffaw went up from the crowd.

Frank stopped to look at the blackboard as he entered the dining saloon. A group of chattering passengers were gathered around the notice.

*'The one and only famous Arabian Nights party will be held once we leave Aden. No war will stop us! Fancy dress mandatory!'*

Frank was contemplating what this might mean when Mr Patel and Mr Chakrabarti came up behind him.

"Don't you worry," Mr Patel said. "Follow us into the bazaar and we will be finding the most suitable attire!"

The market stalls were full of costumes which the Bedouins laughingly displayed. At one point Frank felt his sleeve being pulled and instinctively he felt for his wallet. A grinning salesman held out some snow-white robes for him to see. Mr Patel proved himself a superb negotiator and Frank was full of admiration as after some severe bargaining they managed to buy three costumes for the price of two. As they were leaving, a stallholder thrust a packet of food into Mr Chakrabarti's hands.

"Come, come, eat this. It is wonderful, sir."

The other two shook their heads as he tried to stuff more packets into their hands.

"Come on you two, it's delicious!" Mr Chakrabarti said; but a stall of silver jewellery caught Frank's attention and he wandered over to try out his own skills in obtaining a particularly fine bracelet for Maree. He also thought of Jasleen – so many years since he had seen her – and he turned back to purchase a finely wrought silver chain which he could give her.

That evening, Frank ventured out in his robes. He felt conspicuous. It was an odd feeling as a Hindu to be costumed as a Bedouin, his small face framed with the red and white checked *shemagh* which the seller told him was a sign of his male status. He had tried to imitate the tying of the *agal* rope but had to resort to calling for a steward to help him tie it correctly. His shiny glasses and clean-shaven chin looked back at him from the mirror. It would have to do, he thought.

He joined Mr Patel in the smoking room where they waited some minutes for Mr Chakrabarti. Mr Patel looked at his watch.

"We will wait five more minutes and then I will be calling the steward to go and see if he is wanting something."

The steward was summarily sent and returned in a few minutes.

"Mr Chakrabarti will not be joining in the party tonight. He is feeling rather unwell in the stomach. He said," reported the steward, "that it must have been the *mansaf* that he had been persuaded to try in the bazaar."

Frank and Mr Patel were relieved that they had both declined the offer. Mr Chakrabarti was paying for his weak will, they laughed.

At the end of the third week, Frank noticed a restlessness on board. There was no enthusiasm to play quoits. The deckchairs were more often than not empty. Passengers paced the decks, shielding their eyes as they scanned the Arabian Sea looking for a sign of land. Children ran screaming past him, nannies and *ayahs* showing no inclination to hush them. Huddles of men stood on deck, smoking. Conversation had dried up but companionship was apparent in the small groups as they stood or sat around.

Sitting next to Mr Patel and Mr Chakrabarti, Frank exchanged contact addresses with his two new friends, who vowed to come and visit him when they were next in Calcutta.

"We will send a letter of introduction to Mr Agarwal at Jamall & Sons. I am sure they will be looking for a new accounting firm as they expand due to this new contract we have secured. We will be recommending you highly."

Frank stayed out on deck, abandoning his paperwork and missing a few days' letters to Maree. He had promised to write every day but of course the letters were piling up as it had been a while since he had managed to send some for posting in Aden.

His patience was rewarded and he was one of the first to spot the moist swampy lands of Gujarat coming into view. His heart thudded in his chest. He took off his glasses and wiped them with his chequered handkerchief before tucking it back into his breast pocket.

He had not heard back from Jasleen before he left England so was not sure if she knew the exact date of his arrival. He had informed her of the name of the ship so she should have been able to go to the P&O office and enquire as to the exact time and date. But he was not certain that she would have done that. It was with a sinking heart that he realised that he might have to make his own way to her home. He was sure of a welcome from her but felt unsure of how he might be received by her husband, Jarod, who had been only too glad of his departure more than six years ago. Jasleen had sounded happy in her letters to him but of course one could never tell from words. One look at her face would tell him, without a doubt.

Excited chatter brought his attention back to the faces around him. Full of laughter and the longed-for release from the restriction of shipboard life, passengers milled around the decks. He strode over to where Mr Chakrabarti, who had completely recovered from his bout of sickness, was leaning on a rail; and they shook hands as the ship made its way into the dock.

# Twenty-Five

Jasleen's beaming face told him all. She was plumper now, even matronly, he thought, the slimness of poverty long gone. He was glad she was happy. During his Manchester days, when he had allowed his thoughts to return to Jasleen and Bombay, he had felt guilty at leaving her in Jarod's care. He suspected that she would become a slave to Jarod's parents but this had not been the case. Jarod's promotion had allowed an increase of servants who took great care of his, by now, very elderly parents. Jasleen was at pains to describe her days, now filled with ritual and prayer, as very satisfying for her.

Jasleen could not stop touching Frank.

"Mangal, my darling brother," – she still did not wish to reveal herself as his mother – "you must tell me all about yourself and your life in England. You have been away so long."

Frank laughed. "I have told you most of my news in my letters, Jasleen."

"Yes, but I want to hear it from you. Are you ready to settle down now? A wife, maybe?"

Frank swallowed. He had not told her about Maree. He wanted to tell her in person; somehow he knew the presence of an English woman in his life might not be appreciated.

She continued, "I have consulted an astrologer and he has said

123

that it is a very auspicious time for you to marry, Mangal."

Frank swallowed again but before he could find the words she said, "I have been speaking to a matchmaker, Mangal. There are some very good girls from good Brahmin families I have been looking at."

She was so eager. Frank did not wish to disappoint. Perhaps he should let her continue with her investigations. He was unclear in his mind. Prevaricate.

"Jasleen, you are so caring. But let me rest and re-acclimatise to life here. As you said, I have been away for some time and my ways are somewhat English, you know."

"That is no mind, Mangal. I have been looking at educated girls for you. Ones who will be appreciating your intellect and your sojourn in the 'motherland'."

"Please, Jasleen. No more talk of marriages at the moment. I am tired. And besides, I want to hear about you and your life."

Jasleen knew enough to let the subject slide; she recognised the signs of Frank's stubbornness and realised she would need to pick her time to talk to him again. She would not rest, however, until she had shown him the candidates she had chosen.

It was a few days before Jasleen felt she could broach the subject again.

"Come, Mangal, sit down beside me." She patted the red sofa cushion next to her. Frank sighed. Why did he still feel like a small boy in her company? He tried hard to formulate the words he needed to explain his love for Maree, his plans for her to join him once the war ended, and his need for his sister to desist from her matchmaking. Words were never as easy as numbers. One thing he knew. He was loyal to Maree. She was all he needed.

Jasleen drew out some papers she had stashed next to the sofa.

"I really am needing to get back to these families, Mangal. Tell me, what do you think." She handed the biographies of the prospective brides to Frank with a flourish.

Frank gave them a cursory glance, shuffling them together after the perusal. He looked over his glasses at Jasleen's anxious face.

"Well, which one do you think, Mangal?" She leant over to look at the one on top of the pile. "I think she would suit you really well; her parents are assuring me she has been educated in the best schools money can buy. She has a kind face, no?"

Frank sighed. He placed the papers face down in his lap.

"Jasleen," he began slowly, "however kind her face is, she is not the one for me. I am sorry. You will not like this, I know, but I met a lovely young lady in Manchester." Jasleen's face brightened. "But no, she is not a Brahmin, nor is she Indian of any caste." He saw the brutality of his words register on her face as Jasleen's eyes registered hurt and incredulity.

"But, Mangal," she said curtly, "you must marry a Brahmin, it is our responsibility to keep our caste pure."

Frank reached out for her hand but she snatched it away.

"When I sent you away, I didn't think you would find an *Angrezi* woman." She spat out the word. "So where is she, this wonderful woman? Why is she not here with you? Maybe she will never come?" Frank could tell she would cling to this thought.

She stood up. "I have to go out. I have some chores to do for Jarod. I will see you later." She swept out of the room, tears glistening but not spilling.

Frank wanted to visit some of his old haunts. In an effort to ameliorate the tension at dinner he asked Jasleen to accompany him the next day to Chowpatty on Back Bay.

"Do you remember, Jasleen? I was so young, but you took me to see that air flight along the sands. I remember you holding my hand so tightly. I think we were both frightened and were sure it would crash into us!"

Jasleen smiled and softened as she remembered the feel of his hot little hand in hers. She felt again the trust he had had in her, the obedience he showed after their parents died. Perhaps, she thought, he might trust her judgement again and relinquish his plans for an *Angrezi* bride and bow to her lead, as any son should. But he was not aware of his parentage and it was something she had vowed she would never tell him. She sighed. He was an adult; he had lived for many years in a foreign country; he had experienced life like she never had. Her sphere was small; his had expanded to include another culture. She wished Jarod were home to discuss this with, but he had gone to a great-aunt's funeral in Unai a hundred or so miles away north and would be away with his parents until after Frank had left for Calcutta.

She shrugged her shoulders. She must spend as much time now with Mangal as she could. She did not know when she would be able to travel to Calcutta. It was a long train journey indeed, across the whole continent of India, for which she would need much courage and fortitude.

They strolled along the beach, bare feet in the sand. Mangal looked out across the Arabian sea. It was a long way back to England and a long way for Maree to travel on her own. Doubts began to niggle. He must write to her tonight. Jasleen pointed to an old man shuffling down towards the waves breaking on the sand. He held a painted wooden idol in his hand. Frank knew this would be dipped into the water in honour of Ganesh's birth. As he watched, others came to join the old man. They were all clutching idols. Pottery idols, ceramic idols, and other crudely carved ones. Three *sadhus* sat on the sand, their eyes closed, their faces covered in sandalwood paste, a red mark of Shiva on their foreheads. This was part of his birth culture, an intrinsic part of his life before England; but he stood at a distance, mentally and physically. He viewed it as a moving picture in shades of black and white.

Jasleen touched his elbow and spoke; gradually the colour returned.

"I'm sorry, Jasleen," Frank said. "I am feeling rather dislocated. I feel like I am floating. Let me sit down for a few minutes and then let's go to Babulnath Mandir. Do you remember we used to go to pray after Ma and Baba died? I always felt like Shiva listened to us, didn't you?"

Jasleen smiled. "What a wonderful idea. I'm glad you haven't lost your religion at least. I can make it up the hillock; I'm not that old," she laughed.

They slipped off their shoes and strolled clockwise around the temple, Frank giving thanks for his safe arrival in his birth land and Jasleen fervently hoping that Frank would think again about an *Angrezi* bride.

# Twenty-Six

*1919 Maree's voyage to Calcutta*

Maree stood on the dock looking at the ship, the *City of Karachi*, towering above her. She had never seen anything so huge. She closed her mouth as she realised gawping would not do. She gripped the handle of her suitcase in her gloved hand as she waited for the customs formalities to be completed.

Her train trip from Manchester to Liverpool had caused as much excitement in her family as the voyage to India itself and all her sisters and her mother had come to wave her off. The grandiose stone building of the Manchester Victoria station loomed through the morning fog, the clock face barely visible. Both confused and sound advice bombarded her from all sides.

"Which door should we go through?" "Have you got your ticket?" "Don't forget to put your passport away safely in the inside pocket of your coat." "Where are your sandwiches?" All the words fell around Maree's ears as her eyes looked from right to left and then back again. She wondered whether there would be other passengers heading for the docks when she arrived in Liverpool. However would she find her way? Frank's letters of advice became jumbled in her mind as her heart beat frantically. She clutched her mother so tightly that she thought she would burst with the effort and her mother had quite the breath squeezed out of her. Her sisters, she saw, stood, quite oddly, in height order to say goodbye. Maud, tall and gangly; Alice the eldest a head shorter; Florence lean and angular, almost the same height; and short and stout Nell, all waiting their turn.

Maree's eyes were swimming with tears; she could hardly see her sisters' faces. What was she doing, leaving them all to post war deprivations and heading off across the seas to an unknown fate, and heaven knows when she would see them and their families again? She was unused to her high-waisted skirt; and the wool of it, scratchy and new, she thought would be of little use once she was in warmer climes. She had packed few clothes in her suitcase, preferring to wait and see what she could have made in Calcutta. Frank had said that the tailor around the corner from their flat in the law offices would be able to make up anything she wanted so she had tucked in a few women's magazines for the dress patterns to copy.

Now that she was thinking of something other than leaving, her tears began to dry and she could ensure that she hugged each of her sisters in turn with a gentle comment that of course she would see them soon. The journey only took three weeks. She was sure she could come back any time because Frank said he was earning enough to send her back whenever she wished.

Her sisters were sad that they were to be deprived of a wedding.

"Write back and tell us all about the ceremony and whether you get married in a church or a temple or even a registrar's office!" Nell said.

"Ooh, I hope there'll be Indian music and dancing. Frank would look so handsome in his Hindu wedding robes!" Flo chimed in.

Maree's face remained impassive. She dared not look at her mother. It had been a huge contention between them when Frank left the country without having married her and now he expected her to sail away on a promise of a ceremony in a different country.

"You know the marriage probably won't be legal; and then

where will you be? Don't you have any bastards; I couldn't stand the shame of it!" her mother had shouted. "You make sure you're well and truly married in English law. Promise me you'll go to the Viceroy's office in Calcutta and talk to the officials there. They'll know what to do."

"You don't have to worry, Ma, Frank intends to marry me as soon as I arrive in the country."

She had no doubt he would whisk her off the ship and to the registrar's office so that there might be no gossip of impropriety. She did wonder, however, how practical that was and whether in the joy of their reunion a few days or even a few weeks might pass before this happened.

With a last hug to her mother, she jumped into the carriage before the conductor blew his whistle; she could see him drawing it out of his pocket. She found her seat quickly so that she could pull down the window and wave goodbye. She placed her suitcase on her seat.

Her gloved hand and shining face disappeared as the train slid along the platform and the family of sisters and mother huddled together, feeling a strange mixture of grief for her departure and elation at her bravery.

"Well, it's no use moping here, girls. Let's find the Lyons teashop. I reckon we could have a celebration to see Maree off right and proper."

The sisters, each with her own thoughts about their youngest sister, agreed. Alice and Maud each tucked an arm under their mother's elbows, kissed her on her cheek and walked out of the station as they had come in, in a huddle.

# Twenty-Seven

Maree felt curiously deflated. The emotion of leaving had departed with the last wave of her hand and she sat down with a thump on top of her case which she had forgotten to put on the luggage rack. Without thinking, oblivious to the weight of it, she hoisted the case up and then sat down again. Her mind was blank with fear. After twenty minutes or so had passed, she looked across at the woman seated opposite who had been staring at her. Her young boy was playing with a small toy train, running it over his knees and down the maroon fabric seat, "choo-chooing" all the time. Maree smiled at the two of them, shook her head to clear it and realised she hadn't even taken off her hat. She stood up and placed it neatly on top of her suitcase in the luggage rack, its net bulging with the weight of packages and parcels belonging to the other occupants of the carriage.

Next to the woman and child sat a moustachioed gentleman almost hidden behind his *Manchester Guardian* with its startling headline, "The Fanatic's Rage at the Ballot Box". Maree's grasp of politics was minimal and she realised with gratitude that she would have no need of any of this election nonsense to deal with in Calcutta. The general election of a few months ago, held just before Christmas, had passed her by without exciting much of her attention; but she had been quizzed on it by Frank who was certainly more interested than she. She had found out for him that it had been called the "coupon election" but was unsure what that really meant. She was far too busy arranging her upcoming departure. Ruby, who was heavily pregnant, she knew would be unable to come to bid her farewell and so she spent as much time as possible with her and her first child, the little boy Timmy, who was now two years old and into much mischief, causing poor Ruby to race around. Yesterday, they had sat with arms wrapped around each other, weeping copiously into each other's shoulders while Timmy pulled on his mother's skirt, tried to clamber onto her lap and asked over and over again if Ma was all right.

Now, in the train, Maree felt a slight panic set upon her as, patting her coat, she could no longer feel the folded cardboard cover of her passport. With her stomach churning and her heart threatening to leap out of her throat, she put her hand inside the coat and touched the paper passport and her ticket for passage in the pocket where she had put them. She had laughed at the description of herself on the folded piece of paper. Forehead: large. Nose: large. Eyes: small. Well, she thought that could be many other people indeed. She was indignant about the large nose description; Ruby had described it as a button nose – but then any nose would be small compared to Ruby's; maybe it was large for her small face; and she certainly felt that her eyes were not her best feature, being quite well set. So what was it, she thought, that Frank saw in her? His suave behaviour, his intelligence and his knowledge all threatened to dwarf her, but he was so tender and loving and wished for nothing more than to take care of her and provide for her and their hoped-for family. She drew out his last letter, its creases already beginning to tear, and read again the loving endearments sailing across the oceans to her. She took courage from his plans and his conviction that they would carve out a wonderful life for themselves in a city unfamiliar to them both.

Her eyes must have closed because the second hour of the journey had almost passed when she sensed the slowing down of the train which signalled its entry into the city of Liverpool. Hurriedly, she replaced Frank's letter in her pocket next to her passport.

The gentleman in the corner reached up and brought down Maree's suitcase; she rewarded him with a broad smile. Should she tell him she was travelling to India? Would he even be interested? She decided against it and after thanking him she put on a confident air as he stood back to let her pass. On the platform she stood hesitant until she saw a conductor and hurried up to him to ask the best way to get to the P&O shipping dock. He was most helpful; he had just answered the same question a few minutes ago, he said, and smiled a buck-toothed smile as he gestured towards a young couple heading up the stairs in front of her.

"I suggest you catch up with them, ducks, they're going to India too. Likely be on the same ship."

And they were. A young couple from Manchester, too, who had recently been married. They had returned from India for the wedding and were setting off back to India to start their new life together. Maree felt jealous; she would have loved to have a husband by her side as she set out on such an adventure. Mrs Stephen Phillips, for that was her name now, the lady told her, was only too glad to have the prospect of Maree as a friend for the long journey and chatted continuously as they made their way to the *City of Karachi* moored at the dock.

Waiting for immigration, she lost her new friend in the crowds but soon spotted her rounded figure already on board as she herself made her way up the gangplank. Maree was lucky that Sadie, as she was soon to confide, was travelling in second class too, along with her husband Stephen, a very junior consul being deployed to the Viceroy's office.

Mr Stephen Phillips stood tall and silent to one side, as he was to do for most of the voyage, twisting his moustaches while looking down his nose in an attempt, Maree thought, to appear superior to those around him. She hardly wasted a word on him. Following Sadie, she arrived at her cabin down the corridor from theirs, a cabin with bunk beds, shared with three other young ladies. She unpacked her clothes into the drawers and sat down on her bed, her hands in her lap, stroking one with the other.

The rhythm of the days became a routine. Sadie would knock on the cabin door in the morning. The three other girls in her cabin were usually still asleep but Maree was happy to escape from the fug of a shared cabin and be out in the fresher air on deck. She and Sadie stood on deck all through the passage through the Suez, marvelling at the lonely, hot, shimmering desert. They felt as though the waves of heat were knocking them back from the railings, so intense was it. As they arrived in Aden, they could not believe that the temperature had risen even more; and abandoning their long-sleeved blouses, they changed into short-sleeved ones and even shorter skirts. Maree was not used to showing her ankles so readily and kept trying to pull the skirt down as she caught men's eyes straying to them. Not that she was proud of them. Far too thick, like her mother's, she thought.

Now that the war was over, outings from the ship had been resumed; and Sadie and Stephen made the excursion to the pyramids.

"Oh, please come with us, Maree. I shall be so bored without you. Stephen won't talk to me. It'll be such fun," Sadie begged.

Maree's finances did not stretch to taking excursions so on their return she had to make do with Sadie's enthusiastic account of the camels, the monuments and the Bedouin Arabs. Sadie fanned herself as she sat on the red-striped deckchair and related her story to her captive audience. One day, Maree said to herself, I will do that. I will ride on a camel and visit the Egyptian tombs.

At each port, Maree sent a letter to Frank. She told him about the three other girls sharing her cabin who did not have much to say to her, being quite a few years younger. They were on their way back to India after being at boarding school for the duration of the war and had been unable to return until now. They clearly thought that they should have travelled in a first-class cabin; and after the initial enquiries into Maree and her family they showed little interest in her. She was hurt but did not show it; only at night when they were giggling together at a private joke did she allow herself to feel sad and lonely, burying her face into her pillow.

She told Frank about all the food they were given to eat and although it was not up to the standard of the first class meals he had described, it was far more than Maree had seen for many a year. Food supplies were severely rationed in England and had in truth been scarce for most of her life. This abundance seemed both outrageous and exotic. She related the fun she had playing deck games with the other single passengers and that she was really rather good at quoits, a game she had never heard of until the voyage. Sadie often joined in although she huffed and puffed and complained that she didn't have the energy to throw anything heavier than a feather. Stephen looked on.

The ship sailed south around the tip of India into the port of Colombo. Maree was sure she could smell spices and her skin shivered with the strangeness of it. Her eyes filled with tears; she felt so far from home. She wished for her mother's strong arm around her and again the feeling of the unknown rushed from her feet to the crown of her head, infusing her with a weakness which caused her knees to buckle.

"Hold my arm, Maree," said Sadie. "Whatever is the matter? You nearly collapsed. Come and sit down. You aren't... with child, are you?" she whispered.

Maree turned a shocked face to her.

"No, no. I... I ... I think I just feel faint, it is all so strange to me."

"There, there," said Sadie. "I felt the same the first time I came over. It is a different world, indeed. Come, listen to the singing from the women on the dock. They are welcoming us to Ceylon."

Maree stood up, her knees still feeling weak. She held Sadie's plump hand between both of hers and followed her to the railing where many of the passengers were hanging over, watching as the *lascars* made the ship ready for docking. The crew members threw heavy ropes down to dockhands who tied them around massive posts. The drawbridge was wheeled up and the first passengers leaving the ship here were saying their farewells to the ship's captain and the crew.

"One more leg to go," Sadie sighed. "We'll be there soon and your young man will be waiting for you at the end of the gangplank, I'm sure."

Maree had been quite coy about telling Sadie about Frank. From a comment Stephen had made about "bloody lazy Indians" and the stories Sadie had told about the Indian servants, she judged that they might perhaps think differently of her if they knew that Frank was Indian. For perhaps the first time, the reality of being married to an Indian began to sink in.

# Twenty-Eight

The anticipation of the remaining passengers built as the coast of India could be seen far off in the distance. The breeze from the ship did little to carve through the oppressive heat. It lay thick and muggy on the passengers like a wet carpet. Maree felt she could hardly take a breath. The air felt hot and damp as it coursed through her nose and into her lungs. Three weeks of heat had not prepared her for this.

She had packed her suitcase the night before with its meagre selection of clothes, the wool skirt never worn on the voyage at the bottom of the suitcase. The visit to the tailor was definitely the first thing she would need to do after she arrived at her new abode.

As the now familiar shouts, clanking, and throwing of ropes signalled their arrival at port, Maree sat on a deckchair. She could not drag herself to the railing where Sadie and Stephen stood together with the boarding school girls and other passengers she had had a nodding acquaintance with for the duration of the voyage. She closed her eyes. It was all too much. What had she been thinking? Her mother's small house and lowering grey skies seemed so so far away. Perhaps she should just stay for a few weeks and then return. She could get her job back at the haberdashers. Mr Wilson and Mrs Hastings had been displeased that she was leaving and they both knew they had lost a good worker. Nellie had long since gone to a rival establishment and Maisie still needed to be told what to do. With the end of the war they had anticipated an influx of business; but money was scarce and the frivolity of buying expensive hats still seemed far away. Maree sighed as she recalled the shocked face of Mrs Hastings when she told her she was leaving and marrying the Indian gentleman who used to call by the shop. They could manage quite well without her, they had said quite emphatically.

Dragging herself out of the deckchair, Maree staggered to the railing where Sadie made room for her.

"Come and see. Look at everyone waving! Can you see your young man? Oh, look, Stephen, there's Vishnu from the embassy. They've sent a car for us, I'm sure."

The closeness of another body caused Maree to reach for her fan and as she fanned vigorously her eyes skimmed the dusty crowd. Colours blurred; the unfamiliar fetid smell arose from piles of rotting vegetation that she could see scraped together in some semblance of street cleaning. Flies swarmed above the crowd, people swatting at them and waving fans or covering their faces with brightly coloured saris. There were no princesses that Maree could see. But there amongst the many dark faces she thought she spotted Frank. She lifted a small, limp hand in greeting.

"Have you seen him, then? Where is he? Point him out!" Sadie demanded.

Maree pointed, the sleeve of her blouse damp and clinging to her arm, to where she had last seen him; but she couldn't now make him out. Perhaps it hadn't even been him. Perhaps he wasn't coming. Perhaps she would have to find her own way. Perhaps she would be whisked away and sold into slavery. Perhaps...

"Come on, Maree. They're letting us off the ship. Look, the first class passengers have already disembarked. We're next."

Maree let herself be swept up. She looked around for her suitcase but it had been lifted onto the turbaned head of a bearer, many of whom had swarmed on deck to carry the luggage. She couldn't summon the energy to worry about it. It was so, so hot.

She observed her feet as if they belonged to someone else as they trod into this new country, down the gangplank and onto Indian soil. Officials in uniforms tried to keep back the crowds as they surged forward and surrounded the new arrivals. She looked around at the strange faces, smiling, frowning, shouting and most of all sweating. It was so, so hot.

She lost sight of her suitcase for a moment and wondered whether she would ever see it again. Her mother would not be pleased at its loss, she thought … But then everything faded away, there was a faint buzzing in her ears, and she was crying as if her life had ended. And then she felt Frank's arms around her.

"You're here, you're really here," he said. "I didn't know what I would do with myself if you didn't come. It has been a long wait, Maree. A long year indeed. Come, let's get you to the car."

Maree let herself be half led, half carried to the waiting car where miraculously she saw her suitcase being loaded into the boot. Tears were still running down her face as she tried to blink and take in all the sights and smells of this place. The strangeness of getting into a car, having a driver open the door and usher her into her seat, Frank beside her – all this left her speechless. She looked around to wave goodbye to Sadie, but she had gone, lost in the seething crowd.

But Frank was there; he was sitting next to her, he was talking to her, pointing out the landmarks… and suddenly there, directly in front of the car, was an elephant. Her eyes widened and she twisted her head in astonishment as they made their way past it. Dusty grey skin, folds and folds of it on the thick legs, on the sagging belly, the ears almost translucent in the sun flapping to keep cool, its bright carapace glowing. And the *mahout* sat on the *howdah* cross-legged, brandishing a small stick.

"It's a real elephant," she managed to blurt out, "on the road!" It wasn't the only strange thing they saw as the car made its slow way into town. People walking, people on bicycles, cows, carts full of people, carts full of vegetables, all spilled into sight. And so many dark faces. She looked down at her white skin. Where were all

139

the white people? Wasn't Calcutta a colonial capital or something? That's what Frank had said; but she saw little to no evidence of it.

Without warning, the crowded streets fell away and the road widened. On her left she could see a great expanse of parkland, its green grass somewhat yellowed but giving home to numerous cricket matches. She could hear the familiar thwack of the ball, claps and shouts. The teams consisted mostly of Indians as far as she could tell, but a few were mixed: white faces looking very out of place as they raced in as they bowled, with their faces reddened and pink arms.

"That's the *maidan*," Frank explained. "We're not far now. We can walk there and sit under the trees and have picnics, just like in England."

Maree wondered whether anything would be 'just like in England' but she smiled wanly at him all the same, hoping it might be true. A huge white marble edifice rose from the trees, massive steps guarded by marble lions. "The Victoria Memorial," Frank informed her.

"It does look like England," she said, twisting in her seat as they passed. "I'm sure I've seen photos of those same lions – oh, where are they? Ah, I remember: in London, in Trafalgar Square!"

Frank, pleased to see some animation in his wan fiancée, smiled at her fondly. He took her hand in his and patted it gently.

"Next up, the law courts," he said.

On the right she could see large stone buildings looking altogether like the centre of Manchester, she thought. So this was the city. The other bit must be the outskirts, areas she would never dare to go to, she thought. The car stopped.

"This is home. For now," he said as he escorted her by the elbow into the dark cavernous hallway. She heard the clicking of typewriters. There were numerous offices, all glassed in, their louvre windows open, fans whirring overhead. Electrical cords hung from the ceiling. Brown wooden pigeonholes were fixed in rows to the right of her, each one with a brass plaque, the names on which she didn't have time to read. But they were so shiny.

The doorman had welcomed Frank and *salaamed* Maree who, confused, followed Frank's lead in greeting him with a stuttering "*Namaste.*" Frank grinned.

"You see, you'll get used to it!"

He had written that they had a large, spacious flat on the top floor of an office building; this, however, was not what she had envisioned. A wide staircase appeared out of the gloom and a doorman hurried in front of them and opened the metal cage doors of a lift which she had not even spotted. He ushered them both in, bowing and nodding his head in a way she found disconcerting. Was he pleased to see them or not? His words and expression said one thing but his head belied it. She looked back and could see the car boot open through the open double doors with the driver standing back, letting one of the bearers take out her suitcase. She lost sight of him as the lift ascended and four storeys of balconies and rooms flicked past her eyes in bands of dark and light.

"Don't worry. He will bring up your case," Frank said, reading the question in her eyes.

As the door opened on the top floor a young girl dressed in a pale green sari – cotton, not silk, Maree noted – stood to greet them, her hands in prayer at her chest, her head bowed.

"This is Rani," Frank said. "She will look after you and see you to your room."

Maree followed dumbly. She was so tired and so hot. This strange place, this strange house: now, her home. Following Rani into a large shuttered room she collapsed onto a chaise longue in front of her. Her head ached. Her mind whirred.

A girl to help her. She, whose mother had been the servant in someone else's home, now had her own servant. What a strange thought. She closed her eyes and felt the faint breeze fanning her as it wafted through the wooden shutters closed against the midday sun. She would just sleep for a few minutes and then find out where the washroom was. She would wash the dust off and the sleep out of her eyes soon, really soon.

It was cooler when she woke and much darker. She sat up in fright, her heart pounding, and then remembered where she was. The dark shiny furniture glowered. She gasped when she saw Frank sitting still in a chair, watching over her.

"You must have been so tired," he smiled. "I had hoped to go to the registrar's office to get married today but it will have to wait until tomorrow, now. I hope you don't mind. Do you feel hungry? Daruk has made some special food for you. Come."

She held out her hand, still feeling dazed. "Wait. I must wash first and put on some clean clothes. Do you mind waiting?"

"I will send Rani in with some water. Your clothes are on the bed, ready for you."

A soft flowing, pale lemon skirt and a crisp linen blouse were laid out. She felt cooler just looking at them. Rani entered her room on soft padding feet. Maree gave her a nervous smile. Should she speak to her? Did she understand English? This was a new world for her. She would have to find a way of coping, of talking to servants. It was too much to contemplate in the heat. She sighed.

# Twenty-Nine

Maree looked up as Rani walked into her room, a cream silk dress draped over her arms.

"Here, Memsahib, the dress is ironed," she smiled as she laid the fine garment down on the bed.

Maree stopped brushing her hair and stood up to gaze in wonder at the fine embroidery. Frank had explained that white was not an auspicious colour for a wedding dress and that it should be red according to Hindu custom. But Maree could not countenance the idea of sending a photo of herself dressed in red as she got married. Her mother would definitely think she was living in sin and would be unable to show off the photo of her daughter in her finery so far away. White was virginal, white was traditional as far as Maree was concerned and in this she remained stubborn, although she allowed that cream would certainly be acceptable.

It was Frank who came up with a compromise. An official wedding ceremony presided over by an official at the British Consulate? Maree could wear cream, Frank a linen suit and then afterwards a blessing by Frank's priest at the Hindu temple. Maree could change into the red sari he had chosen for her before she arrived and he would also wear his traditional white *dhoti* and jacket.

The discussion had been going on for weeks as Maree realised they were not going to just rush off to the local government offices as Frank had intimated on the day of her arrival. Maree had thought that she might enlist the help of Sadie and therefore Stephen, who worked as a lowly clerk at the registry office, but her notes sent to Sadie remained unanswered.

Maree was not used to having the housework done for her and the first few weeks here in the top floor flat were difficult. Her initial surprise at the amount of leisure time she had quickly turned to boredom. She wandered around each room of the flat, arranging trinkets or moving small tables. This became a game for her, as by the next day everything had been returned to its original position. The initial inability she felt to do anything because of the heat dissipated and one evening as they sat down to dinner she asked Frank if she could go to the market with Rani for something to do.

"Of course you can," said Frank, "but I think Rashid should go with you as well. I don't want you wandering around and getting into trouble."

"Trouble? What do you mean? Is it dangerous? Should I wait and go with you? I just want to get out of the house."

"Maybe you should just get Rani to take you to the *maidan*; you might meet some other ladies there. Maybe Sadie?"

When she arrived there in the cool of the morning, many ladies were perambulating under the shade trees, parasols held high. She looked around eagerly but was unable to spot Sadie; she was sure she would have known her padded figure. She nodded politely at others strolling around keeping as much as possible to the shade. They glanced at her impassively and turned back to their conversations. She envied them their ease with each other, their chatting and their laughter. She was a long way from home and Ruby. She swallowed and blinked rapidly. She turned to Rani.

"I think that's enough for today, don't you?"

Rani nodded in agreement and followed Maree back along the crowded side streets until they saw the familiar towers of the law courts.

"Home sweet home," Maree said brightly.

"Yes, memsahib," agreed Rani.

Maree walked over to the window and looked out over the rooftops. Frank had promised to be home soon. He had to attend to some urgent business at the office. Should she put on her dress, put on the little make-up she had, or should she wait? It really wasn't much good asking Rani; she would agree to whatever the memsahib said. Rani's dark eyes glittered as she waited with hands together for Maree to decide. If she put on her dress and sat waiting, would it look like a reprimand for Frank? If she wasn't ready when he came back, would it mean that she really didn't care and the ceremony could wait for another day? Since arriving in India she had found it hard to make decisions and even though the heat was not as debilitating as she had first found it, it certainly decreased her mental acuity. Sighing, she sat back down at her dressing table and stared at her reflection. How she wished Ruby were by her side, chattering and making her laugh; how she wished her mother were laying out her clothes, and Flo were curling her hair. She shook her head and jumped up as she heard the front door to the flat open.

Frank's smiling face peeped around the door. He beamed at her. "You look beautiful, as always," he said.

Maree laughed. "I'm not even ready," she said. "All I've done is brush my hair!"

They walked up the wide stone steps each flanked with neatly trimmed camellias in large marble urns looking like stern sentries. Maree offered up a nervous smile as the guard challenged their entry to the grand building which housed the registry office.

"What is your business here?"

Frank pulled down his jacket sleeves. "I think you'll find we have an appointment in the registry office," he said. "Tarmaster."

The guard looked them up and down, Frank resplendent in his linen suit and Maree radiant in cream silk, before consulting his list of appointments for the day.

"Down the corridor, turn first left and then first right. The office door on your left will have a brass plaque. Knock before you go in!"

Maree's heart beat fast and she held onto Frank's arm, his confidence giving her strength. She smiled shyly up at him as their footsteps tapped along the long, gleaming corridor. Her chest felt hot and her hairline began to prickle. She hoped that she would not start sweating. Frank rapped on the door, and they entered a sparsely furnished room, ceiling fans whirling madly, the off-balance blade of one clanking regularly as Maree looked around. A gentleman behind the counter glanced up at them with a quizzical look, cleared his throat and asked if they had an appointment. His adam's apple quivered as he did so as the collar of his shirt was far too tight, Maree thought.

"Of course," Frank answered looking over the top of his glasses: "Tarmaster."

He smiled down at Maree and said, "We're here to get married. Tarmaster and Crymble." Maree blushed.

The clerk sniffed, cleared his throat again and asked for their paperwork.

"I will need birth certificates, passports, proof of residency, entry permits and anything else you might have which will allow this marriage to take place."

Maree looked up in alarm, but Frank passed over the file folder to him with a smile.

"I'm sure you'll find it all in order," he said.

The clerk rifled through the papers, peering closely at the details. He held two papers up together and compared the information.

"All seems to be in order, Sir, Madam. Take a seat; I will get Mr Robinson, the registrar."

By the time Mr Robinson appeared, Maree was starting to become alarmed. Frank held her hand and patted it.

They stood up as a tall man appeared out of a connecting room, wiping his forehead with a handkerchief. He held out his hand and ushered them into a room that was small and plain with a shiny mahogany desk in the corner.

Later, Maree could not recall what vows she and Frank made to each other or who were the witnesses. She stood in a daze. Mr Robinson coughed, "I now pronounce you man and wife."

Frank felt two inches taller than when they arrived. He grinned at Maree, squeezed her hand and then brought it to his lips while his brown eyes held hers with such love and devotion that Maree began again to blush.

"We will register the marriage, Mr Tarmaster, and you can send someone to collect the certificate next week," Mr Robinson explained.

Maree felt light as they skipped out of the office, back down the corridor and down the glistening steps. She was married. She was no longer living in sin, as she thought. Frank took her around the corner to the photographer to capture their image in sepia to send to her mother.

Once they were in possession of the certificate, the temple priest agreed to bless them. Feeling awkward but looking magnificent in a red and gold sari, Maree followed Frank. Their wrists were bound and they processed around a small fire as the priest intoned his blessing. It was all a dream, thought Maree. How could this be happening to that young girl from Chorlton? She glanced up at the images of Ganesh and Shiva in all their bright colours. The smell of incense made her dizzy and as she could understand nothing of what was being said she retreated into herself and blindly followed directions, trusting Frank, trusting him as she always had. A smile illuminated her face as he looked down at her, his love, his delight. Bound to each other in this world and the next.

# Thirty

## 1920 Calcutta

Maree sat on the chaise longue, her feet tucked underneath her, the fringe of the upholstery tickling her ankles. She twisted a scarf over and over through her fingers, wrapping it tight until her finger pulsed; and then she jumped up and raced into the hallway.

"Rani," she shouted, "is the bedroom prepared? Did you put out clean towels and fill the basin?"

"Yes, memsahib," Rani replied, bowing her head, "I have done all you asked me to. I will be checking again before they arrive."

"What about the kitchen? Wait, no, I'll go and check," and then: "Rashid, Rashid, where are you? What are you doing now? Did you see to the fan in the bedroom? I'm sure it's not working well. What will sahib's sister think if she's too hot?"

Rashid came out of the bedroom on soft, bare feet.

"I am here, memsahib. The fan will be working, you will see."

Maree nodded and went to check the kitchen. She found it hard to manage all the tasks someone else was responsible for. It was a different life and she was beginning to find out that work was not always done in the timely manner she expected. Giving instruction to others was not easy, especially as she was not sure of how much she needed to explain or even what needed doing. Her brain felt foggy. She was hot all the time. She sat on a stool in the hallway as Rashid returned to his work, adjusting the fan. A few moments, that's all she needed. She leaned her head against the wall behind her and looked up at the brass tray that hung on the wall. The coloured dancing figures around its rim were whirling before her eyes, turning to laugh at her, she was sure. The splendid tray was a wedding present from Jasleen, sent over from Bombay with the promise of a visit in a few months' time. At the time of the wedding she had been quite ill with an undisclosed sickness.

Maree closed her eyes and took in a deep breath of the muggy air. Just a few minutes. Now, what did she need to do?

The kitchen preparations were in full swing. Poor Daruk was not used to catering for so many and he flitted from one job to another as he ordered the kitchen boy around. He jerked his head up as Maree entered his domain. Nodding and smiling, he assured her all was in hand.

Daruk had sent Rani to the market just after daybreak to get the best choice of vegetables. She had disturbed an old onion seller, who was napping after arriving early to get the best selling spot. She picked over the cabbages, pumpkins and cucumbers. Weighing the aubergines in her hand, she had chosen the firmest and shiniest. She paused before the pulse sellers, registering the beautiful colours of the lentils, the greens and golds piled in neat cones. She went through the list in her head, mentally ticking off the items Daruk had asked her to purchase. She checked twice; it was easy to come back without a vital ingredient and she did not wish to start her day with an upbraiding from Daruk, let alone the memsahib, who for the past week had been so irritable. She returned, her baskets laden, and waited for her next instruction.

Frank and Maree stood together at the entrance to their apartment as Jasleen and her retinue arrived.

"Who are all those people?" Maree whispered to Frank. "And where are they all going to stay?"

"Welcome, welcome!" Frank addressed his sister, who stood in a cloud of patchouli as her bearer carried a large trunk up the stairs behind her. "You are looking well, I'm so glad to see; we were quite worried about you."

Jasleen caught her breath. "Why is your lift not working, Mangal?" she queried. "I cannot be climbing those stairs every day. I am not completely well, you know. Now let me see you." She raised her glasses which hung from a string around her neck. "Hmm, you are looking thin."

Her eyes had so far avoided meeting those of Maree; but eventually she turned to her, running her eyes up and down as Maree stood in an anguish of embarrassment at the scrutiny.

"Jasleen, this is my darling Maree." Frank placed his hand protectively around Maree's waist. "I'm sure you will love her as much as I do."

Jasleen harrumphed. "Where am I sleeping?" And then to the bearer, who was sitting cross-legged outside the door: "Ranjit, bring my trunk this way."

"I will inspect the kitchens after I have had a rest," she continued. "Mangal, it really is so good to see you." She caressed his cheek with an uplifted hand, her bangles tinkling as they fell down towards her elbow. Without so much as another glance at Maree she snapped her fingers at her maidservant and disappeared into the bedroom prepared for her. Maree held her breath, half expecting Jasleen to sail out with a criticism.

Maree fell to twisting the scarf in her fingers. "I don't think she approves of me," she said.

"Give her time, Maree. She is not used to a white person in her home."

"But it's not her home," Maree protested, as Frank led her into the sitting room, saying, "Come, we will wait for her here."

"I... I think I need to lie down. I am feeling rather faint," Maree said as she stood up, with the scarf still twisting in her hands.

"Yes, my dear. That's a good idea. Rest now and you should be fine by dinnertime. You can get to know Jasleen then."

Dinner was delayed. When Jasleen woke up from her rest, she sailed into the kitchen and started inspecting the food Daruk was preparing.

"It really won't do," she told him. "I need my staff to prepare my food. This is a white person's kitchen!"

Daruk protested that he was a good Hindu but she would not listen.

"But you are not Brahmin," she bristled. "I need a Brahmin cook. My food will not be clean otherwise. You are dismissed." Summoning her bearer, she told him to bring in her cook who was waiting patiently outside. Daruk shrugged his shoulders and sat in the corner of the kitchen. His carefully prepared food was thrown into a bin and Jasleen's cook began again. Jasleen sailed out to inform Frank of the change.

"I cannot be eating the food prepared in your kitchen, Mangal, it is not pure. My cook will prepare food for us while I am here."

Maree sat without uttering a word, her eyes darting between Frank and Jasleen. She felt the slight. Her kitchen was not clean. That was because of her, she was sure. Jasleen was not making it easy for her. She understood well enough that Jasleen did not approve of Frank's marriage to an English woman and she was making that perfectly plain.

While Frank was at work, Jasleen took charge of the household. She uttered commands and orders to her own staff and to Frank and Maree's. She swept around the apartment, sniffing at the pile of fashion magazines which Maree had brought with her. She tut-tutted at any dust she found, moved ornaments around and generally made the space hers. She placed a shrine in the hallway which was garlanded with fresh flowers daily. She prayed in front of it and several times Maree was prevented from passing as she did not wish to disturb her ritual. Maree shrank into herself and retired to her bedroom, where she sobbed silent tears into her pillow. What had she expected? For Jasleen to love and accept her like Frank did? Between them, there were no barriers. He was Brahmin, certainly, but he had never allowed his caste credos or his religion to come between them. She was very glad that Jasleen lived in Bombay. How long would this visit last? Daruk and Rani had both spoken to her: if they were not required they would return to their villages.

At night she cried to Frank, "I feel anxious every day. Jasleen does not speak to me at all. She treats our flat as hers. She takes charge of everything. She makes me feel more useless than I already feel. When is she going home?"

"Shh, my dear. I will talk to her. She means well. She wants to make sure I am happy."

"Well, she's going a funny way about it," Maree retorted, "and she's certainly not thinking about me and whether I'm happy!"

It was a long week for Maree before Jasleen decided she would return to Bombay. Jasleen was satisfied that Frank was doing well for himself in business and the efforts and sacrifice she had made to send him to England had paid off; even if clearly she did not approve of his marriage. After she swept out with her staff, still complaining about the non-functional lift, the flat held its breath. Frank accompanied her to the railway station, leaving a wan Maree to sink once again onto her familiar chaise longue, her body finding the indentations she had made over the weeks after her arrival. Rani, Rashid and Daruk crept back into their familiar roles and a general sigh of relief seemed to rise from the very floorboards.

# Thirty-One

## *1921 Calcutta*

Maree lay on the chaise longue. Dressed in nothing but her chemise and covered with a fringed silk Spanish shawl, she didn't care if she shocked the servants. It was just so damned hot. Rani, however, was used to her and no longer hid her face when she came upon Maree dressed, or rather undressed, like this. Her mistress's peculiar ways were something the three servants had long finished gossiping about. The concern was for the baby, and for the new one on the way.

Ernest had been born in January, thankfully the coolest month of the year. As Maree told anyone who listened, if she were to have a child due in the middle of the year she didn't know what she would do. Ernest was a small baby, with thin long legs and a thicket of black curls plastered to his head. He never cried but stared up at everyone and everything with wonder, his eyes bright and knowing. The *ayah* who had been brought in to look after him held him and crooned to him while Maree lay exhausted.

She was constantly exhausted. The pregnancy depleted her. Her days were spent mostly sleeping and she only awoke and dressed when Frank returned up the stairs (as the lift was broken again) and entered the apartment, Rashid scurrying around to take his briefcase and place it in his study. Frank's first question was always about Ernest as he snatched him up from the *ayah* and perused his solemn little face. He had wanted to call him Govinde, his father's name, but had to be thankful that this name was even second on the birth certificate. Maree had been adamant that an English name was to be first. His name certainly suited him.

Now, he gazed up at his father, his brown eyes pools of ancient knowledge. Six months on and his frame was still long and lanky. He did not seem to be putting on any weight. Frank frowned as he looked at him. Ernest held his gaze and the glimmers of a smile appeared at the corners of his tiny mouth; and Frank broke into a grin.

"He smiled at me!" he shouted. "Come and look, Maree; he smiled!"

Indeed, from that day on he smiled regularly at his *ayah*, at Maree when she held him after his bath, and at his father when he came home; but his legs remained skinny and he often fretted when asleep. Any small whimper caused the *ayah* to rush to his mahogany crib and rock it gently. He would settle but then again, as if disturbed by ancient thoughts, he would let out small sobs which echoed in the quiet of the night.

Frank's workload increased and although his office was very close by, in fact just across the road, he found it increasingly hard to spend time with his fretful child and wife. The business world, he had heard, was becoming concerned with the intimations of self-rule and the unrest this was beginning to cause. It was a problem he would not concern Maree with, but he spent many an hour in discussion with his colleagues. Vishnu Patel, a solicitor friend, had an acquaintance in the police force who kept him informed about the goings-on of 'activists' who were following Gandhi's proposition for self-rule. Recently, a certain prominent activist had been caught, supposedly masterminding a plot of insurrection. Frank found this rather extraordinary, as he understood any follower of Gandhi to support passive, non-violent action.

After many months feeling very much alone in Calcutta and seeing less and less of Frank as his business demanded more of his time, Maree made a friend of Nataline, a Portuguese Goan who was married to Vishnu. She stepped out with her several times a week to walk around the *maidan*, which she managed as exercise during her blossoming pregnancy; and she visited her in her house on Park Street where they sat in the garden and drank tea and gossiped about the life they led.

It was after one of these outings that Maree arrived at her top floor flat (out of breath, for the lift was yet again not working) to find Rani hovering at the front door, her hands wringing out what she could not say.

Without stopping to question her, Maree rushed to where Ernest lay, small and feverish in his crib. He had lately taken to pulling himself up, holding tightly to the bars, but not today; listless and glistening he lay, his eyes unfocused.

"Have you sent for the doctor?" Maree managed to ask.

"No, memsahib, I am waiting for you. Shall I send Rashid for the doctor sahib now?"

"Yes, Rani, quickly, go."

Maree cradled Ernest and wiped the sweat off his brow with a cotton napkin. What was the matter with him? She positioned him on her lap, smaller now with the protrusion of her belly. She took off his nightshirt which was sticking to his back and wiped him again with some cool water. Her tears dripped down her nose and onto his face. He blinked.

"Oh, hurry up, Dr Chandra," she muttered to herself. "Why are you taking so long?"

As Ernest's skin grew hot again, she put the napkin back into the bowl of water and squeezed it out with her free hand, its coolness dripping onto his stomach. At last she heard voices in the hallway and shouted out, "I'm in here, Dr Chandra. I don't know what's wrong with him."

While Dr Chandra was examining Ernest, Maree stepped outside the room.

"Rani," she shouted, "tell Rashid to go and tell the sahib. I don't care how busy he is. No excuses. He must come now, at once."

Dr Chandra busied himself with his stethoscope, making soft humming noises as he moved it around the boy's chest and, after gently turning the child over onto his front, listened some more.

"He is having a fever, Mrs Tarmaster," he said.

"Even I can see that," she snapped, "but why, what from?"

"I am not knowing that yet. He may have an infection. I will be giving him some medicine and you will see how he is tonight. If he is still having a fever I will come back."

Frank came racing up the stairs with Rashid behind him and breathlessly had a conversation with Dr Chandra just as he was leaving. Maree could see Dr Chandra nodding as he talked. That head-waggling disconcerted her. She could never tell if it was positive or negative. Frank might not tell her what the doctor said; but she would make him. She felt sure it was more than the doctor wished to divulge to her.

Frank came inside and, placing his arm around Maree's shoulder, he led her to the sofa. She shuffled, dread falling into her stomach and down to her feet, making her legs wobble as he settled her gently down. Her fear was much alleviated as he explained that Dr Chandra felt that it was not serious and that she should not be worrying too much; but he would look in again tomorrow, if not later that night. Feeling calmer then, they both got up and looked over the crib at Ernest, now sleeping soundly with little breath puffs, calm and regular.

"Now, I don't want you standing here all afternoon worrying, Maree. Let's leave the *ayah* in here with him and you can go and rest. I don't want you sick again, too. I have to go back to the office; I can't leave Mr Basu on his own for too long, but I'll come home earlier than usual. Send for me if he gets worse." Frank planted a kiss on her forehead and nodded at the *ayah* who was sitting on a chair in the corner of the room.

Maree hesitated and stared at Ernest before she acquiesced; she did feel exhausted and needed to rest. So there she was on the chaise longue, drifting in and out of dreams and of nightmares of losing Ernest, his disembodied dark eyes floating in front of her, fading as she ran closer and reappearing further along the street; bullock carts moved out of her way as her legs felt heavier and heavier the further she ran, until his eyes disappeared totally.

She woke up, her heart pounding, and leapt up to see how he was. His *ayah* was sitting nearby. She smiled at Maree.

"He is sleeping soundly, memsahib." Maree was not sure if this was good or bad but on feeling his forehead, now dry, she thought that he didn't feel so febrile. She opened the shutters wider and then closed them again after a few minutes. She was leaving the room when she changed her mind, walked back to the window and opened the shutters once again. A soft breeze, bringing the smells of Calcutta, drifted in and she thought that, on the whole, even though germs might come in, the coolness might help Ernest.

She woke as the shawl slipped to the ground and the cool evening breathed over her bare shoulder. Her muddled thoughts cleared; and placing her bare feet on the floorboards, she padded in to look at Ernest. She looked around in panic as he was not in his crib but then she heard the *ayah* crooning to him as she sat in a dark corner of the room with him in her arms.

"Ba... ba... ba," he smiled, drowsy-looking but awake enough to wave his little hands at Maree.

"My baby," she sobbed, scooping him up in her arms and kissing his soft cheeks. His hair still felt damp; but half an hour later, when Frank came home, Maree was sitting peaceably with the baby on her lap, singing him an old Lancashire lullaby that her grandmother used to sing to her. Ernest was reaching up to her chin, tickling her and twisting a lock of her hair in his fingers. He glanced around as his father came into the room and smiled up at him. Frank's relief showed as his shoulders dropped and his frown of worry was replaced by a grin which lit up his face and his whole being. He fell to his knees and took Ernest's free hand and covered it with butterfly kisses. His solemn child giggled, which took both their breath away.

"I'll call Dr Chandra. I'll tell him the medicine worked," said Frank. He stroked Maree's belly. "You'll see," he said, "everything will be fine. You mustn't worry so much. You have another little one to think about, too."

# Thirty-Two

## *1921 Decisions*

Max was born in early August, the time Maree had dreaded, hot and humid. But luckily the birth was easy and Max was a sturdy boy with a perpetual smile on his tiny face. Ernest had had a few months of good health and both Frank and Maree began to breathe more easily and did not race to his cot every time they heard the slightest sound. At the beginning of September, however, the rains had begun to ease but Ernest was again wracked with a high fever. His damp clothes were first blamed on the humidity but soon it was apparent to his *ayah* that he was hot to the touch, and pink spots glowed on his golden cheeks. A gentle wheeze escaped him and Maree's concerned face was enough to cause the *ayah* to start crying. Dr Chandra having been summoned, he examined Ernest in his thoughtful way and spent many minutes with the stethoscope on the young child's chest. He did not hum. Pulling the stethoscope out of his ears, he told Maree that she was not to worry but that he would like to come again in the morning.

"If the boy is starting coughing, will you please send for me again."

Maree assured him she would. During the night she awoke to the sound of a cough. She sat up in bed and sure enough, there was another one.

"Wake up, Frank, wake up! We must send for Dr Chandra at once." Maree nudged him awake. Bleary-eyed, Frank tied on his dressing gown and rang for Rashid. He told him, "Run to fetch Dr Chandra; never mind the time."

Maree sat frozen by Ernest's bed, dreading the return of a cough. She knew what it meant. Ruby's grandmother had had a cough. And so had her father. Frank had reported office clerks coughing and leaving work never to return. Fear made her hands tremble; for once the heat made her feel cold, her toes tingling.

Dr Chandra confirmed their worst suspicions. Ernest most certainly had tuberculosis and the doctor did not have the latest treatments that were needed. He advised them most sincerely to think of travelling to England if they had any hope of saving him. The local newspapers declared in bold headlines that tuberculosis was now rampant in Calcutta, more so than in either Glasgow or Birmingham. Many of the deaths of infants, it was reported, were due to a tainted milk supply.

"But Ernest has only had breast milk; he should be fine," they both thought. Only five hundred tuberculosis beds available in the whole of India, a headline screamed. Fear again grabbed Maree by the gut and she spent the next few weeks in a stupor, alternatively crying or sleeping, the latter aided by draughts Dr Chandra prescribed.

Frank looked up from his desk.

"Maree," he said, " I took the liberty of writing to Dr Lingard in Birmingham. Do you remember Dr Chandra told us he is considered the authority on tuberculosis? I didn't want to raise your hopes but I have heard back from him. He said that if we get Ernest there soon, we'll have a chance of him living a longer life. But we must make up our minds quickly."

Maree assented without any thought as to what it might cost Frank in work. In her heart she felt excited to be going back to the cool greyness of the North but then felt guilty as she remembered the reason for the return. Her firstborn must be saved at all costs. Even if Frank lost his job, she reasoned, he could find one again in Manchester, surely.

It was a fraught voyage that took far too long for all of them. Frank had no alternative but to accompany Maree with the two baby boys. He managed to obtain leave until the end of the year. They considered taking their *ayah* with them but decided against it. Where on earth would they all stay when they got to England? Maree sent letters to both her mother and Flo advising them of their imminent arrival. They would first be travelling to Birmingham and then to Manchester to stay with Flo who at least had a spare room that they could use while Ernest was undergoing treatment. After that, they were not sure.


It was a blustery late autumn day, the day of their arrival. Maree felt the cold wind on her face with grateful thanks. She felt sharper, more awake, not so listless. Her stomach clenched and gurgled with the anticipation of seeing her mother and her sisters. What a joyful reunion it should be! Her heart pounded with the worry of Ernest, miserable with coughing, his tiny chest convulsing and his body wracked with the effort of spitting out phlegm. It was horrific to see. Frank had kept by his side while Maree took Max upstairs for air and out of the cabin. She could not bear to think that he might catch it as well. It was a heart-stopping consideration.


Dr Lingard proved to be a smartly-dressed physician whose matter-of-fact statements inspired confidence in his knowledge and expertise. His face was thoughtful as he examined Ernest. Baby Max had been left in the surgery waiting room with a nurse who was only too happy to "ooh" and "aah" over this beautiful little boy with his smiling golden face and his dimpled cheeks. The doctor prescribed new medications and prepared the forms for Ernest to be admitted to a specialist child sanatorium where he could be properly looked after. He had taken one look at the drawn faces of the parents and felt they would not be able to comply with the necessary regime which would give this poor emaciated child a chance at continued life.

Maree's shoulders dropped in relief and her emotional goodbye to Ernest was tempered by the knowledge that he was in the best of places if there was to be any chance of recovery. Frank's money had made sure of that. But Ernest's little face looking at them through the cot bars quite tore her heart in two.

Frank made a booking for them all to return to India towards the end of the year but as their weekly visits to the sanatorium showed, Ernest seemed unlikely to return with them. So Frank extended their date of passage to the New Year which would give Maree a longer visit with her family and more time to recoup some of her strength after the quick succession of births. Each visit saw his hope for a recovery for Ernest diminish. The boy was pleased to see them, certainly, but his little body had not filled out and his coughing had not lessened one iota. Frank questioned the doctor as to the efficacy of the cure but he replied that sometimes the bacterium was very stubborn and would take longer than expected. After extending their return date yet again it seemed incontrovertible that Ernest would need to be left in England. Maree's sisters would visit him and report back to them in regular letters. It seemed the only thing to do. If Frank did not return to his position with Meugens Peat he might lose his job and all the contacts he had worked so hard to acquire. Maree was torn. Should she stay in England? How would she survive without Frank to look after her and provide income?

"Your place is by the side of your husband," Agnes said, her heart wrung out as she recalled the death of her own little boy so many years ago. How cruel life was, and how family history seemed to repeat itself. Maree's life was with Frank in Calcutta, however hard she found it to leave Ernest.

Frank secured a passage for the three of them to Bombay which gave him the opportunity of planning a visit to his sister, Jasleen. The planning and the anticipation kept him busy as the desolation of leaving Ernest hit Maree hard. As much as Maree turned her attention to Max, now an inquisitive, bonny six-month-old, she could not stop seeing Ernest's face, solemn as ever, staring at her through the cot bars. Cheerful and babbling, Max kept her occupied in her body but not her mind. She had never been to Bombay and after last year's disastrous visit from Jasleen, she was wary of the welcome she might receive at her home. They had certainly not got off to a good start. Frank, however, was using his glee at the prospect of seeing his sister again to douse his distress at leaving Ernest. He didn't discuss his sense of dread with Maree. He wished to pass on his optimism to her, to scour out the despair: he wanted to transmit a tangible feeling of delight to surround her and lift her gloomy mood.

# Thirty-Three

Aware of Maree's feeling of loss at having left her eldest boy behind, Jasleen tried her best to enfold Maree into her own family; but Jasleen's love was for Frank, and he – as her golden boy – received the majority of her attention, which also disgruntled Jarod. A thin veil of jealousy on Maree's part overshadowed her relationship with Jasleen as she felt lost with her lack of understanding of the language and the nuances of the Hindu culture. She and Frank had amalgamated their cultures into their own small world but here at Jasleen's she was at a loss, a ship adrift. She stayed in her room, feigning exhaustion and sickness while Jasleen's *ayah* looked after Max. Frank's cocoon around her was partially torn as he spent time talking to Jasleen, leaving Maree resting. He ignored Jarod as much as was possible. Jarod had never been friendly to him as he resented the time and focus that Jasleen gave Frank. But in all the time Frank spent with Jasleen, he never forgot to jump up every hour or so to check on Maree and to order the servants to take her drink and food.

"I know you don't feel well, darling, but Jasleen is trying, and it would be lovely, and would show gratitude and respect to her, if you came down for dinner tomorrow evening. Jasleen has made a special effort for this: our final meal with them," he attempted to persuade her.

She wrinkled her nose. "I... I don't really like their food, Frank; it is too spicy for me."

"At least come and sit with the family while we eat, even if you don't feel like eating the food they've prepared. You know, it seems as though you're acting just like Jasleen did when she came to visit us. Refusing to eat food not prepared the way you're used to," he chastised.

She sighed. "All right, I will. For your sake, Frank, not for Jasleen. I know she really doesn't like me."

Maree felt oppressed by the heat and the dust, the noise and the smell. She longed for the familiar winter of the north of England. She longed for her other baby to be by her side and she questioned their decision to leave him alone to recover, in spite of her family's good intentions to take care of him. On the morning of their final day in Bombay, she received a letter from Nell who wrote to say that they had been to see Ernest and he was looking better, beginning to fill out; and although he remained the same solemn child, his coughing had diminished. This was enough to rouse Maree; and with a forced jollity she was able to join in the final family dinner before they left for their long journey across the country by train. She even felt optimistic enough to offer hospitality to Jasleen and her family despite the previous debacle, forgetting that their flat would not be able to host more than two people and certainly not the retinue which Jasleen would like to bring with her.

The journey across the continent was tedious but uneventful. Maree and Frank took it in turns holding Max who was entranced by the constant moving pictures out of the window. The dry dust gave way to tropical green rice fields, and dark muddy rivers in flood rushed beneath the railway bridges. Maree watched women washing clothes in streams and laying clothes and bedding on the stones to dry. Men made bread dough on large flat stones by the water, crouched over, intent on their work. Elephants and bullocks paraded the lanes and byways, causing chaos and confusion as they ambled along. At one point, the train slowed as cows crossed the tracks, oblivious. Frank put his head out of the window, as did many others, curious to see what was happening. The shout of *'cows on line'* passed down the carriages as Maree sat fanning herself in the stifling heat, Max now grizzling as his entertainment had stopped. The train driver and engineer dismounted and encouraged the trundling beasts to move to where a conductor stood holding out straw for them. Finally, the train moved off with a gentle tug and Max stopped whimpering and was once again content with the fleeting views.

As they pulled into Howrah station, the familiar red stone building with its Mughul tiles stood against the dawn sky, pink streaks staining the Hooghly river behind. It was early, but Calcutta was never quiet. Traffic outside the station was being directed by a policeman in his white belted jacket and white pantaloons. A bullock cart passed, the red-turbaned driver sitting cross-legged, the large wooden wheels creaking as he went past.

Meugens Peat had sent a car for them and it was with relief that Maree tumbled into the back seat as the driver held the door open for her. There were a few residents parading down the wide street for their early morning constitutional before the angry heat of the day, protected by black umbrellas held high. But Maree did not see them; she had shut her eyes and leant back on the leather seat, her face pale and set. Frank placed Max on the seat between them and spoke softly to the child who was waking from his sleep. Bearers who had run in front of them out of the station, suitcases on top of their turbaned heads, placed them now in the boot of the car.

"Welcome back, sahib, memsahib," the doorman greeted them. He snapped his fingers and a bearer came running to fetch the suitcases from the boot of the car. Maree managed a small smile at him in greeting, and clutching Max to her heart, she headed for the lift.

"I'm sorry, memsahib," the doorman said, "the lift is not working."

As tired as they were, Frank and Maree turned to each other and laughed.

"We're certainly home," Frank said. "Let's go upstairs. We can go slowly, there's no rush."

Frank supported Maree under her arm. He looked at her with concern. He was not sure how she would face entering Ernest's room, viewing his cot, empty now. The *ayah* came to greet them, beaming all over as she saw Max in Maree's arms. She looked at Frank's empty arms but thought better of asking about Ernest.

"Oh, my darling little one," she cooed, "I am missing him so much, memsahib. Let me take him while you sit and rest." She whisked Max away. Reluctant to let Max go, Maree turned a distraught face to Frank.

"It's all right, my dear," Frank said. "She will look after him, you know she will. Max will need a little time to get used to her again. It's best she does it immediately. It will give you time to acclimatise."

Maree wandered into the sitting room and flopped down onto the couch. Rashid, bowing with hands clasped in greeting, smiled with pleasure at the two of them.

"I will get cook to bring some refreshments, sahib," he said. "He has been cooking all day for your arrival. We are all so happy to see you... and the baby." Clearly he too was embarrassed to ask about Ernest but knew it was not his place to ask. The sahibs would tell him if and when they were ready.

Maree tiptoed into the babies' room. The two cots were there, garlanded with marigold flowers, the linen fresh and clean. One empty; in the other, Max lay on his back, staring up at the wooden ceiling. The *ayah* looked up guiltily as Maree swept up the blooms from the empty cot and inhaled their pungent smell.

"It's okay, Devi," she whispered. "You weren't to know..." Tears spilled and rolled down their cheeks.

"We are still hoping, Devi, that he will return to us. We must have hope."

# Thirty-Four

Frank sorted through the pile of letters on his desk, discarding those he thought he could afford to open later when he was not so tired. One he turned over in his hands, intrigued by the postmark. On opening it he was elated to find that he had been offered a Professorship of Accounting at Mysore University. He had been actively seeking a post in academia but was not sure that he would actually accept one. He was not convinced that was the direction in which he wanted to take his career. Especially since the Maharajah of Mysore expected him to start in June of this same year. He paced the room. Would Maree wish to move to Mysore? He was not sure. Did this fit in with his business plans? He was not sure of this either. Before he left for England he had approached Meugens for an increase in salary due to the number of new clients he had brought into the firm, mostly through his involvement with the Masons. Joining them had brought about the success he had anticipated. What a perfect way to meet and gain influential business clients who needed a trustworthy accountant! One of his earliest clients in Calcutta had extended the invitation for him to be taken into the Masons and he discovered that he enjoyed the rituals and mythologies abounding in the society. The added bonus of finding clients who recognised the handshake was something he had not firstly considered. His 'Indianness' was not an issue with this fraternity. It was something deeper, a connection of minds, a culture to which he could belong wholeheartedly. He longed for a group where colour was no barrier. In the Masons he found it.

As Frank suspected, Maree was not in favour of moving to Mysore. He had undertaken some research before telling her about the offer. Its location in the south of the country and its reputation as a cultural centre might endear itself to her, he thought. The weather was also milder than Calcutta, he said; to no avail. Reluctantly, he declined the offer and concentrated his efforts on building a solid base of clients. Frank had plans to open his own accounting business, even to commence a school of business; and with this focus in mind he wrote an article which was published in the *Calcutta Commercial Gazette* promoting the idea of a school which offered after hours classes to the highest level. Providing only daytime classes precluded clerks who were already in employment from availing themselves of further tuition, he argued. It was important to upskill the local workforce; not everyone was as lucky as he had been to be granted a scholarship to study overseas; and he wished to give back to his local community.

Mr Doherty called him into his office.

"I see you're making a name for yourself..." he shook the paper in front of him; "and I presume this means you will be seeking that raise in salary? I am beginning to have a suspicion that your ambitions lie outside this office, Frank."

Frank's protestations did not assuage Mr Doherty. He sent Frank a testy memorandum stating that he would not be increasing his salary and the current agreement would stand as it was. Frank continued with his article writing and put into place the necessary scaffolding to be able to start out on his own. He negotiated a contract with the Law Courts to be in charge of requisitioned property and businesses which had failed, to act as the liquidator. He knew that although the government of the day enjoyed the prestige of allying themselves to a well-known international accounting firm, eventually they, as Home Rule loomed ever closer, would be looking at the extra profit they could make by employing a local firm who of course would undercut the rates charged by Meugens Peat.

Frank was bursting with ideas. He really did not know which opportunity would give him the best progression to his career. He wanted to discuss the options with Maree but by the time he came home, although Max had been put to bed, Maree was once again lying on the chaise longue.

"Maree," he said, "I have some exciting things to talk over with you." She waved a small hand at him and with her eyes closed murmured, "I have a headache, Frank. You must decide things. My head hurts; I can't think clearly."

Her vague malaise became even more acute when in the New Year a letter arrived from Alice closely followed by one from her mother and one from Nell. Rani opened the door to Maree's room, smiling broadly. She knew delivering letters from Maree's family in England caused her much delight. Maree tore at the envelopes. At first she hoped they were missives sending seasonal greetings; but the first one from Alice announced that Ernest had a cold and was not doing so well. Her mother's could not begin to prepare her for the worst news. A bout of pneumonia had swept through the sanatorium; and by the time she opened Nell's, with a band of black around the envelope, she was struggling for breath. Tears rolled soundlessly down her cheeks and she sank into the chair, while Rani wrung her hands, her bangles tinkling as she swayed from side to side wondering whether she should fetch memsahib some water or whether she should send Rashid to the sahib's office.

A high-pitched wail from Maree brought Rashid running in. Taking one look at the memsahib he ran down the stairs, leaping two at a time, and across the road to Frank's office. Frank jumped out of his seat as he saw the stricken face of Rashid; and like him, he raced up the stairs two at a time. The lift was working but he could not bear to stand waiting for it. He found Maree on the floor of their bedroom with her arms wrapped around herself, sobbing loudly and rocking back and forth, with Rani still hovering ineffectually in the background. He picked the letter up from the floor where Maree had dropped it, cream against the mahogany floorboards, and hurriedly read it. All the breath rushed out of him. He dropped to his knees and taking her arms from around herself, wrapped them around his own shaking shoulders. With his forehead on her shoulder, his cries echoed around the flat. Rashid stood at the door; Daruk, the cook, joined him and they exchanged frightened glances with Rani. As the wailing showed no sign of abating, Rashid gestured to Rani to leave the room with him and Daruk as they crouched in the kitchen, silent in their shared grief for their sahibs. Devi joined them with Max in her arms and they waited for a break in the sounds that seemed to tear the walls apart. Was it memsahib's mother? Or sahib's sister? They did not know.

"I need to go and see him," wept Maree. "I can't bear to think of his little body lying there without his mother."

"Shh, shh, dearest." Frank tried to comfort her. "Think of it. They cannot keep him until you get there; remember, it's a three week journey… your mother and sisters will take care of him and make arrangements."

"I should never have left him. It was selfish and wrong of us. Why did we do it, Frank, why did we?"

Frank whispered to her in soft tones and reminded her how sick Ernest had been and that he would have died earlier if he had stayed in Calcutta.

"Yes, yes, I remember, but at least his mother would have been holding him. I just can't bear it."

"We must be strong, my love, we have Max to think of. He needs you too."

Maree's face was ghostly white and her eyes red-rimmed like those of a ghoul. It was time to send for Dr Chandra. Her breath was fast and shallow, her dizziness increasing as he led her to the bed. She needed a sedative. Through his grief, Frank tapped into

171

his organisational strengths and leaving Maree in the good doctor's hands he sent a telegram through to England, to let them know that they were in receipt of the shocking news and to ask them what arrangements had been made for a funeral and burial. He knew how quickly tuberculosis patients were interred. It was mandatory, in order to prevent any excess spread of the disease. It was hard for him to think of his solemn firstborn son lying in unfriendly soil, heaven knows where. He needed to know for Maree's sake as well as his own.

He sent another telegram to tell his sister the tragic news, knowing that she would want to come to visit and take charge of the household. Did he want this? Could he share his grief? He solved this by adding that he did not want her to come all across the country as they might be in England, even though he knew this was not a possibility.

For Maree, the tragedy was everything that she had feared after hearing the first little cough searing through Ernest's tiny chest. She remembered the dread she had felt when she first heard her father's cough, too. How could she be sure that Max would not fall ill or that she or Frank might succumb? She felt the cut as of a knife's edge. The abyss in front of her offered sweet oblivion whilst behind her everything was dark and swirling.

# Thirty-Five

*Maree's dark days* was how they referred to them later. More months than days. More years than months. The death of her firstborn left her nervous and timid. She hovered in indecision. Frank arranged everything. Frank cosseted her and brought her food and tea. He bought her a diamond necklace, the star of India he called it, after the necklace she had described so long ago: small diamonds arranged in a star-shaped white gold setting. He knew she liked pretty things and he had the necklace made up by the jeweller whose accounts he had been handling, at a very special discount of course. He was bursting with pride when he presented it to her but had to swallow his disappointment as she just smiled and said thank you and put it down on the sofa next to her; it did not crack her gloom. He searched the sari shops for the brightest sari he could find. The stalls in the bazaar were packed tightly together. The swirl and busyness of it washed over him. As he stood in indecision he was beckoned up a step into one, with a cup of cha held out for him. He sat cross-legged as sari after sari was laid out in front of him. None seemed to be the exact colour he was looking for. The hustle buzzed in his ears as the layers and layers of colours reminded him of the ribbons in Maree's haberdashery all those years ago. He could see her face, so unlined and fresh, her beautiful skin, smiling her shy smile as she noticed him standing on the pavement. His eyes watered and he shook his head. No, that was not the one. Nor that one either. The stallholder clapped his hands and his young assistant brought yet another pile of saris from a shelf at the back for him to view. There, among this pile, was the colour he was looking for. Brilliant fuchsia edged with exquisite gold embroidery. How vividly Maree had described the sari on the maharini at the ice palace all those years ago. The assistant draped it over his arms. Frank felt the fine silk and nodded his head. This was the one.

He opened the shutters in the living room where Maree lay on the chaise.

"Look, my darling, I have something very special for you." He gently unfolded the tissue paper. She let him wrap the sari around her, holding her close as he placed the beautiful edging around her shoulder. She lay her head on his shoulder and sighed. But it was not a sigh of contentment or delight. He wished he could have his delightful Maree back. His beautiful princess.

"Come, my dear, let's get you ready," Frank said, a week later. "I think a supper out would do us nicely tonight," he continued as Maree looked up at him without any interest in her eyes. He pressed on, "I've heard there's a new restaurant opened on Park Street. The Red Fort, I think it's called. Let's go there."

Maree arose and allowed Rani to choose her outfit and lay it out on the bed. She washed her face and hands, brushed her hair listlessly and waited for Frank to raise her up from where she sat on the end of the bed. Frank grasped her elbow and led her downstairs. He watched her as she seemed to float as they descended in the lift together.

His face was all concern as he flagged down a rickshaw and helped her up. He hoped the change in routine might force some conversation from her but although she had a faint smile on her lips she spoke not at all. He felt a bit like a babbling idiot as his monologue continued, telling her about his day at work and the new clients who were clamouring for his expertise.

The rickshaw-wallah set them down outside the restaurant and stood with his hand outheld before the doorman waved him away. He opened the door to Frank and Maree with a curt nod of the head. It was early and there were few people dining. The maître-d' bustled towards them, a tall, skinny frame with a haughty face above a starched collar.

"Do you have a reservation?" he asked, his finger now on an opened book of reservations.

"I'm afraid not," Frank said. "I heard this was a good place to eat."

"There are no tables available," came the reply.

Frank raised his eyebrows. "There seem to be many," he retorted.

"They are all booked." He would not meet Frank's eye but looked past Frank's shoulder to the timid woman standing behind him. "You may find another table at another restaurant," he sniffed.

Frank turned on his heel, shepherding Maree out. He was gratified that at least she had not recognised the snub. A hundred years ago, he thought, mixed marriages, albeit usually between an Englishman and an Indian woman, were considered quite normal and a recognition of the amity between the two countries. But now, especially now when tensions were rising with the spectre of Home Rule, there was no easy relationship between the two.

He organised a trip to Mangalore; he thought it might lighten her mood, give a fillip to her. But she remained in a daze, a fog, smiling vacantly as Frank pointed out the sights. Frank was not sure if the draughts which Dr Chandra prescribed were helping. Was it better to have her emotionally raw or in this vague unemotional state?

A narrow flight of whitewashed stairs led up to the roof of their spacious flat in a two-storeyed arched building. Frank took Maree by the arm every evening and led her onto the roof. He ordered a small table and two chairs to be set out, the table covered with a tablecloth, with a drink for each of them; and he held her hand as the sun sent carmine and purple ribbons into the horizon. Frank looked at Maree and thought ruefully that she could have been anywhere; her eyes remained glazed. She smiled at him when he smiled but never initiated one herself.

Wandering along the shore, they stopped to watch a snake charmer. Mesmerised by the snake, Frank watched as it wound itself around the neck of the charmer who sat perfectly still in the grass, his creased brown hands lying loosely against his crushed, dusty white *dhoti* pants. His turban flopped as the snake encircled him tightly, crushing the breath out of his skinny body. The watching bystanders gasped; but in response to a hand command from the charmer, the snake loosened its grip and fell into its master's lap, its head swaying, its tongue flicking in and out as though singing a song. Frank turned to Maree but she was looking beyond the man into the distance of what would never be. Frank had begun to worry about Max and how his mother's indifference to all was affecting him. He would soon be ready to go to school, which Frank was not sure would aid in Maree's cure. With more time on her hands, she could retreat further into her inner world.

On their return to Calcutta he sent a message to Nataline, who had been away visiting her mother in Goa, to please come and visit Maree. Nataline arrived, bringing a breath of Goa into the flat. Maree, who had been sleeping on the sofa, looked up; and for the first time, she smiled voluntarily.

"You poor darling," Nataline said as she took Maree into her arms. Maree cried.

"Cry, my dear friend; cry your heart out and then perhaps you will return to feeling better. I cannot imagine how this is."

An hour later, still wrapped in Nataline's comfortable embrace, Maree began to tell her how she was.

"I have no feelings left," she said. "I am a hollow woman. I let my child down. I failed him. I failed Frank. I failed Max. I am a miserable mother..."

"No, no, dear. Don't say that. Frank certainly doesn't think that and you have a beautiful son who needs you. No one can imagine how you are feeling and you mustn't listen to those who tell you to shake it off. Everyone's grief is their own. I know." She sighed as she thought of the seven miscarriages she had endured: each hope and anticipation dashed. How easy to have felt herself a failure as a woman, a wife, a mother. After the first, she had thought it was normal for a young woman to lose her first baby. She hardly gave it a thought, it having been so early in the pregnancy, before she even knew she was carrying. So easily she conceived the next and so easily it, too, was lost: a blob only, seen in the toilet pan like an afterthought. Ah well, third time lucky, she said to Vishnu. But it wasn't lucky. This time she carried for longer and was sure she was out of danger until one day after a walk on the *maidan*, the cramping pains in her belly could no longer be ignored; and after lying on the bed, dozing off through the agony, she woke to both a spreading redness and the realisation that once again she had lost a child. A bonny baby boy. Her next pregnancy she approached with fear and trepidation and the tenderness with which she carried her rounding belly was shattered when after four months she again miscarried.

She almost lost count. But one miscarriage for every day of the week was how she remembered it. Vishnu's sad face for weeks after each one was a reminder of her ineptitude. Doctors had told her – she had seen more than one – that she should never try for a baby again. The toll was too great on her body. Her sense of dereliction of duty became part of her; and as such, she could so well empathise with Maree after the loss of her own child. A real child; a child with a face, unlike Nataline's own who lived only in her imagination. She had named each lost child, its imaginary features branded on her mind, each one smiling and jolly, unlike the solemn Ernest, so aptly named.

In telling her story to Maree, Nataline felt lighter. It was the first time she had told anyone. Only her husband knew of the hidden sorrow of her psyche. Maree was shaken by these revelations. She found herself comforting her friend, her arm now around Nataline's shoulder as she cried out the grief and stoniness in her own heart. What was her loss compared to these repeated losses? She had a living child and could, most probably, have another; whereas her dear friend had no hope of altering her childless situation. Her self-pity slid off her and lay around her ankles, swirling until it disappeared through the cracks in the floorboards. She had a mission. To keep her friend happy. To support her.

Nataline and Maree did indeed prop each other up. Nataline kept up her accustomed cheerful facade while Maree endeavoured to enjoy all the outings and walks that they did regularly together. Maree blossomed under Nataline's watchful eye and with Maree's encouragement, Nataline came to accept her lot. Maree and Nataline were like two peas in a pod, their husbands said, although physically they bore no resemblance to each other. Their circumstances of having married Indians gave them another common thread. They did not fit into Anglo-Indian society.

In fact, they had both been snubbed. Maree's embryonic friendship on the ship with Sadie had been smothered by layers of racism and snobbery. Sadie had spied Frank upon arrival at the dock; and when after a few weeks Maree attempted to make contact, she had ignored the message. Thinking that perhaps she had not received it, Maree had tried again. Once more there was no communication from Sadie. Having been told where Sadie lived she decided to go there in person; and on one of her walks in the cool morning, she arrived at her gate. The servant who came to the door told her that the memsahib was not in, although Maree was sure she had seen a fleeting glimpse of a dress through the shutters, the outline of which looked like Sadie's round figure.

Curious, she had spoken to Frank about it. Frank had witnessed the snub from English colonials before and patiently explained to her that things were not much different in India than they were in England. The conversation about this had not been held in England, as perhaps it should have been. Being Indian, it was hard to be thought of as a gentleman, however educated you were, he told her.

He had been lucky and his appointment had been made by a broad-minded employer; but most often, you would be passed over even if you were the best candidate. An Anglo-Indian was revered as a hard worker but an Indian with an English education was different. He was a threat to the colonials.

# Thirty-Six

## *1926 Kyd Street, Calcutta*

Maree's renewed pleasure in life and her attention to Max pleased Frank enormously. As he worked to extricate himself from Meugens Peat, who were amalgamating with Marwick and Mitchell and in Frank's view becoming more and more chaotic and less connected to Bengal and the independence movement, Frank decided to find a house with a garden, somewhere Max could play without a hot walk to the *maidan*. Putting out feelers, he had been told that one of the floors of number 11 Kyd Street had become available. This tree-lined street was not far from Temple Chambers. He sent Maree in a carriage to see if she liked it. She took Nataline with her – a giggly outing for the two of them while Max was at school. It was a square white building sitting in a large tree-shaded garden. The ground floor was occupied by a Mr and Mrs Parker and the top floor by an Anglo-Indian family with three children of varying heights peering through the banisters at the new arrivals. Maree and Nataline walked around the spacious hollow-sounding rooms with huge shuttered windows looking out onto the canopy of neem trees.

Maree spun around on her toes, revelling in the space. She and Nataline went from room to room placing furniture in their minds and wondering if curtains would be needed. They peered down into the garden where some outdoor chairs sat invitingly in the cool shadow of the tall hedge.

As they left, the carriage took them down the street where it joined the Esplanade; beyond that the seductive green of the *maidan* beckoned.

"Perfect. Max will love how close the *maidan* is when he's tired of the garden!" The move was approved and within a few weeks the family was ensconced. Maree delighted in the garden, and she invited the families from Frank's office for tea. It was served outside, the servants having dragged a table down the stairs, covering it with a white linen tablecloth. Maree felt like a real lady. She talked little to the families, some of whose English was halting, as her Hindi was very limited, but smiled at them all and patted the children as they came to stare with their big brown eyes at this white woman.

The next guests to their new home were Nataline and Vishnu who came for a candlelight dinner in the garden, the upstairs family staring from the top floor windows as they supped in the golden glow, the servants ferrying dishes from their flat to the table. It was a success. Maree was happier than she had ever been.

A few months later it was with glee that she informed Frank that she was once more carrying a child. The tiny trickles of fear which she felt were overcome as she looked up at Frank's beaming face while his hands cupped around her belly.

"It's time," he said. "We will have another child, this time a beautiful girl; you wait and see. I am so happy."

She was unsure how she would break the news to Nataline – Nataline, who had shared her innermost sadness and insecurities with her. Nataline who would never be able to carry a child; and she, who had been blessed for the third time. In the event Nataline, ever watchful, noticed how Maree carried herself, how she, too, unconsciously touched her stomach as she talked to her, how her face softened. She knew. As they were parading around the *maidan*, arms around each other's waists, Nataline stopped and put both arms around Maree.

"Congratulations," she said, looking into her face; "I'm so happy for you. Can I be godmother?"

"Oh, Nataline, I didn't know how to tell you. I was worried you'd be upset."

"Of course not, you silly goose. It's wonderful news! Does Frank know yet?"

Maree was lounging on the couch some weeks later, feeling rather nauseous, when Nataline came to visit. Maree opened her eyes to look at her friend. She looked pale and washed away. As they talked, her usual vivacious manner was flat and she often stopped mid-sentence to look away, swallow and bite her lip. Between the two of them there were a lot of silences.

"What is it?" Maree asked, after waiting too long for Nataline to disclose of her own accord. "You seem rather peaky, too. We're a fine pair, aren't we?"

"I'm fine, really, but I've stayed long enough. I have some things to do."

Maree mentioned to Frank that evening that Nataline had seemed out of sorts.

"I guess she has a lot on her mind. Did she say anything about Vishnu? Perhaps they are having problems. You never know, do you; hard to tell." And with that she put it out of her mind. When, a few days later, Nataline's bearer came around to the house to ask Maree to visit her memsahib, she sent a message back saying she would try to come the next day as she was still feeling rather sick and was resting.

As it happened, it was not until the following week that Maree felt well enough to venture out of the house. To assuage her guilt she had the gardener make up a bouquet of roses and rhododendrons to take to her friend.

Nataline's servant answered the door. Maree handed her the flowers to be put into a vase. Maree poked her nose into the sitting room. Nataline was not seated in her favourite chair. She called for one of the other servant girls to lead her to the memsahib's room.

Nataline lay on her bed in the gloom, shutters closed.

"Whatever's the matter?" asked Maree. "Has something happened? Are you not well? Is Vishnu all right?"

Nataline's voice was faint, like dry grass whispering. Maree pulled up a chair, eased her stomach and sat close to the bed, leaning towards her friend. She asked the servant to fetch some water for the two of them and then strained to hear what Nataline was saying.

"It's not catching, you'll be okay," she heard. "I... I'm not well." She stopped and swallowed hard, licking her lips. "The doctor said I could get better, but I just don't think so. I feel so weak."

"What is it, then?" Maree asked, her frown increasing as she hesitated to get too close.

"I keep bleeding," she said, "you know, down there; it just won't stop. The doctor is not sure why."

"Oh, you poor thing! What can I do? Do you need some towels? Some water? Where is that girl?" Maree jumped up and shouted down the hallway. She stood at the end of the bed, then walked over to the windows where she opened one of the shutters. Nataline squinted and turned her head away as the bright sunlight burst into the room.

"That'll make you feel better," Maree said. "It's too gloomy in here, and stuffy. Do you have a fan? I'll fan you."

She bustled around the room searching for the fan, turning over clothes on the chair and looking on the dressing table, and then gasped when she saw blood-soaked towels on the floor by the side of the bed.

"Where is that girl?" she said again and, her voice louder now, shouted the few words of Hindi she knew, *"Jaldi karna!"* She felt faint and put her hand on the door jam as the tide of sickness rose up her body and swept all the way into her head and fingers.

The girl arrived and dithered in the hallway, not knowing what she should do.

"See to the memsahib; send the bearer for the doctor. I'll be okay. I'll just go and sit down."

The doctor was walking out of the bedroom as Vishnu and Frank came charging into the house together. Frank skidded to a halt as he saw Maree in the sitting room, her head in her hands. He went to her and knelt down, his hands around her knees.

"Are you all right? What has happened? The bearer just said I must come." He pushed his glasses back on his nose with his index finger. He raised her chin and saw the despair in her eyes.

A few minutes later, the doctor and Vishnu, deep in soft conversation, came into the room. Upon seeing Frank and Maree they faltered; a strained expression crossed Vishnu's face.

"I think you should take Maree home," he said. "There's nothing you can do here. The doctor has given Nataline a sleeping draught."

Frank nodded and hoisted Maree up by her elbows. He recognised this catatonic state. He worried for the health of the baby. He worried about her mood. He could only hope that Nataline would recover, for purely selfish reasons.

But Nataline did not recover; the loss of blood had made her extremely weak and when she contracted pneumonia it was just too much for her body to bear. Maree visited one more time. When she had woken up that morning, a cool breeze had been drifting over her pillow; and she determined to rise out of the darkness which yet again had enveloped her. Frank was not sure that she should visit; he said it might upset her, he didn't want her to hurt the baby. But a resolve had been there from the moment she opened her eyes and watched the muslin curtains dancing. They were speaking to her: dance while you can.

She sat by Nataline's bedside. Her friend was chalky-grey, her long hair in sweaty strands. She seemed so small to Maree. Her buxom friend had been reduced to this tiny person, shrunk in on herself, her chest rising in staccato gasps, lapsing in and out of consciousness. Maree's veil of tears shielded her from the sad picture. Like in a blurred photograph, Nataline still looked beautiful, her features softened in sepia.

Nataline was buried in the Portuguese Burial Ground at Boithakhana. Frank and Maree stood at the graveside, Frank supporting Maree, scared she would faint or worse still collapse into the grave. Her stomach was protruding and the fetid air of the graveyard was not good for her constitution, he was sure. But she insisted on attending. Vishnu stood tall and sombre, his best black suit alleviated by a pale pink rose from Nataline's favourite rose bush in her garden. He plucked it from his buttonhole and threw it on top of her coffin. It landed with a soft 'thwack' scattering some of the petals, the sound of which caused him to start and look around at his friends gathered there. His eyes stared as if he did not know where he was or why he was standing there. A quizzical look passed over his face and then it collapsed in grief as the realisation of it all hit him. To those there who had been so surprised at his containment, it was a relief that he might now begin to grieve. His brother turned him away from the grave and they walked hesitantly down the rows between the imposing headstones and marble chests of Portuguese gone before her. Vishnu was rueful that he could not return her to Goa to lie in the Souza family plot. In anguish, he turned to his brother.

"I can't leave her here; she wants her family. She'll be lonely."

His brother soothed him like a small child, stroking his arm; and not relinquishing his hold, he was able to guide him through the painted blue gates of the cemetery.

# Thirty-Seven

The last few months of the pregnancy were gruelling for Maree. Her discomfort increased with the temperature. Physically the doctor pronounced her to be in fine health, both she and the new girl child she was sure she would give birth to. Her mood, however, hardly lifted beyond a soft hello or goodbye to Frank. The servants hovered around her, bringing her cool lime soda and opening and closing shutters as she felt the need. Her mind dwelt on the past. She thought about Manchester. She wondered how life would have been had she still lived there. Would Frank be her husband? Would she be living in a two up, two down terrace cottage with screaming kids around her ankles? Would she be scrubbing and cleaning the stone steps like the neighbourhood women she had grown up around? Would she already be cold in her grave, wrung out and worn out? Would she have a head filled with cotton wool like Ruby? She thought, however, that her head was no better than Ruby's. Tears leaked. She brushed at them with the fringes of her shawl. She thought of the loss of her friendship with Nataline. She thought about Frank; he was so good to her. Life in India was so different! Would a Tim or a John have been able to give her the things she had now? Here she lay on silk, with servants at her beck and call, jewellery on her wrists and her fingers and around her neck. She had a husband whose business was ever-increasing, becoming more and more prosperous as his relationship with the West Bengal government intensified. She had a chauffeur to drive her around in their new blue Oldsmobile, with the top down on cooler days. She did not have to shop at the market, she did not have to cook, and certainly never needed to lift a duster or cloth to clean. What was her malaise about, then? Round and round went the thoughts, chasing each other, sometimes faster until she thought she might have the answer but slowing down and escaping her before that elusive conclusion was reached.

Trying to shake off her despondence, she walked with Rani and Max to the *maidan*. Max jumped up and down in delight at the troops as they completed their daily parade, their buckles shiny and their red plumes nodding. She smiled at him but the spectre of Ernest who should have stood beside Max, a head taller, wavered in the dust and her smile soon became tears, which alarmed both Max and Rani.

Max reached up to take her hand in his small one and his smiling face was full of worry as he asked his mother what the matter was and why she was sad. Maree, unable to lift him in her arms, bent over to plant a kiss on the top of his head.

"I'm fine," she said, "just some dust in my eyes." Rani knew better than to comment and drew Max's attention to two other little boys playing with a ball under the welcome shade of a neem tree.

Frank was busy but not too busy to notice how Maree seemed once more to be sinking under her emotions. He suggested a trip to the botanical gardens.

"Let's take Max boating. It's a long time since we've done that. What do you think?"

Maree rallied and asked Danuk to prepare a picnic for them to take.

"Do hurry, Danuk," she ordered, "we don't want to be there in the heat of the afternoon."

The driver loaded the picnic hamper into the back of their car, swung open the door for Maree, tipped his cap at Frank and asked where they were going.

The outing was a success, Frank thought, although only he and Max went in the boat, Maree saying how tired she was and that she thought it better to lounge on the picnic blanket in the shade. She waved at the two of them in the boat, Max waving back and excitedly jumping up. She scrabbled to her feet as Frank told Max to sit down while the boat rocked dangerously from side to side, with Max wobbling in the middle. Again, the thought arose that she should be there to protect him; she was such an awful mother. Then Max sat, the boat was still and Frank continued rowing around the lake. She sighed and wondered whether with the new baby she would be any different. As she lay back down, she wondered if she should try to remove herself from the children. To be indifferent to them. To think of them as Frank's children, she being just the birth mother. Would that help her to cope? She did not know.

It was the thirteenth day of over thirty degrees when in early July she woke from her morning nap with a cramping sensation in her lower belly. Surely not her time, she thought; the doctor had suggested, by best guess, the middle of July. The cramping passed and with a wet cloth on her forehead she dozed off again. She dreamed of being on the ship once more, voyaging out to India, a mixture of anticipation and fear being the overwhelming emotion. She felt the water underneath her rocking and splashing over her legs, surprisingly warm, trickling. As she woke, the trickling continued and she found herself lying in water that had pooled in the leather creases of the couch. Dorothy Parker – who had taken to calling upon Maree, climbing up the stairs to the first floor every morning after her chai – found her there, panting and confused. The servant girl was dispatched to find Frank at the office and Dorothy took it upon herself to make Maree comfortable. She took off Maree's dripping scarf and her slip and laid her on the clean bed.

"Wipe up this sofa," she called out, "and bring me some towels and water. It is the memsahib's time."

The doctor and Frank were slow to come as the servant girl had not rushed and had got distracted by the seller at a stall of mangoes on the corner of Old Post Office Street before remembering it was the sahib she was to summon.

The birth was uncomplicated. A baby girl, almost out as the doctor arrived.

"Well done, Mrs Parker," he said. "I could use you as my nurse!"

"I practised as a midwife in England," she answered stiffly. "I could have managed this all on my own, thank you."

As Maree smiled up at Frank, the tiny girl in her arms, she said, "Can we call her Patience? Paciencia was Nataline's middle name. If she can't be a godmother, at least we can always remember her."

"What a lovely idea," Dorothy said, "and if the position of godmother is available, I would love to be considered. Now all of you, out of here; you too, Doctor, and I'll clean and tidy her up."

Frank, Doctor Chandra and Mr Parker sat outside in the garden, smoking companionably until late into the night. A star shot across the sky as they stared up at the vastness.

"One star lost, a new one born in my house," sighed Frank. "Life as we know it, here and now in our universe."

Frank held his black leather-covered *Bhagavad Gita* in his hands that night. Turning to one of his favourite quotations, he read,

*Blessed is human birth. Even the dwellers in heaven desire this birth. For true knowledge and pure love may be attained only by a human being.*

Blessed are we, indeed, was his last thought before falling asleep.

# Thirty-Eight

*1930 Kurseong*

Maree held Patience's hand tightly. If she let go, she might lose her resolve to send her away. Images of Patience flashed before her determined self. She saw her dressed in her Pierrot costume last month for a friend's fourth birthday party. She saw her small face break into smiles, her little feet jumping, jumping on her two-year-old legs as Frank brought around the new car for them to see. Max was at school and missed the excitement. She felt her daughter's small body curling into hers as she sat on her lap listening to a bedtime story, her skinny legs scratched from mosquito bites. She even saw her tiny face with that mop of black curls as she lay smiling up at her from her cot. It was no good. Tensions in Calcutta were increasing and the threat of further disturbance had shaken her; and coupled with the ever-present menace of tuberculosis, it was enough for Maree to ask Frank to arrange schooling in the hills for both Max and Patience. Patience, at four years old, was barely old enough, the nuns said; but after a generous donation from Frank they said they would take her and send Sister Esme to Calcutta to accompany the small girl on the train.

Max stood at Maree's side, hopping from foot to foot. He was excited to be starting a new school. He had outgrown St Joseph's day school and was of an age where the adventure of a boarding school with other boys who loved to play cricket all day long was the most exciting thing he could imagine ever to happen to him.

The children's trunks were piled next to Maree. The bearer sat cross-legged, guarding them. Patience, her eyes wide, watched as the steam train pulled into the station. The noise was deafening as it reverberated around the girdered roof. People stood talking while bearers or servants stood sentry around huge piles of luggage; the sounds buzzed around Patience's ears. She had never seen so many people.

"It's a very long journey," her mother explained to her. "You will be sleeping on the train. Isn't that exciting?"

Patience wasn't sure about that but anywhere her mother went was fine with her. She wrapped her other hand around her mother's skirts and buried her face as her mother talked to a tall lady in grey robes who had appeared at her side. She peeped out and the owner of the stern face, with whiskers she was astonished to see, leant over her and prised her hand from her mother's.

"That's enough now," the grey lady said. "Come along. Say goodbye to your mother."

Goodbye? Patience's curls whipped around her face as she shook her head in terror. Goodbye to her mother? Where was her mother going? Max hopped onto the train ahead of them, the bearer loaded the trunks; and as the grey lady swept her off her feet and bundled her in, she bit down hard on the arm around her chest.

"You naughty little girl!" Sister Esme admonished, but she did not let go and pushed Patience down onto a window seat as she tried to squirm away from her grasp. Through the dirty window Patience's last view of her mother was of her back as she rushed away down the platform. Her vision blurred. Her hands slid down the window as the train chuffed out. Sister Esme grabbed her hands and twisted them to face her.

"Just look at them! What a mess! So dirty!" She grabbed a handkerchief out of her robe pocket and spat on it before wiping off the soot. Patience wriggled in her seat, tears making shiny snail tracks down her face.

Sister Esme sat up, back tall and straight, knees tightly clenched, and folded her hands in her lap. "This is how you should sit," she scolded as Patience tried to tuck her shoes underneath her so that she could sit up again and look out of the window.

After a few hours of sitting and squirming, Patience fell asleep, her head drooping, thumb in mouth, feeling the scratchy wool robe against her face as she slipped into her dreams.

When she woke, the nasty grey lady was still there. Where was her mother? She started to wail. Sister Esme opened the black bag on the seat next to her in exasperation.

"Here," she said, "your mother said to give you this." She held a tin of condensed milk in her hands which she proceeded to open so that Patience could hold it to her lips and suck in the familiar sweetness which succeeded in muffling her cries. She sat there again, squeezing her legs together tightly as she now wanted a wee. What should she do? Usually her *ayah* would take her but she didn't want to go with this horrible woman. The wee was hot and its pungency soon reached the beaked nose of Sister Esme, who jumped up, yanked Patience off her seat, threw open the carriage door and hurried her to the bathroom.

"You stupid little girl!" She smacked Patience's legs as she extricated the child from her wet clothing. "What am I supposed to do with these now?" She held up the urine-soaked underwear and pink dress which dripped onto the floor. She muttered to herself that if she'd known she was going to have to accompany a non-toilet-trained child she would not have volunteered. Sister Maureen, who was usually given the job of looking after unaccompanied minors, had a fever which left her sweating and dizzy in her cell; and so Sister Esme, who had fancied a quiet train trip, had offered her services.

Wrapped now in a blanket, Patience slept the night through, curled on the seat while Sister Esme dozed. At Siliguri the train came to a final halt. Sister Esme woke Patience and marched her onto the platform to wait for the narrow-gauge service, nicknamed 'the toy train', which would take them up to Kurseong. Amongst all the children in uniform on the platform Patience spotted Max, laughing with new friends, as he too waited for the tiny train. She jumped up and down and waved at him, but he turned his head away and ignored her; this would not do, a small, dishevelled girl he did not wish to acknowledge. Her disappointment with her brother forgotten, Patience marvelled as the 'toy train' pulled in and once more, Sister Esme hoisted Patience in.

The train, so small and perfectly formed, wended its way up the mountainside. Patience clung onto the ledge of the window which was open to the elements, and watched a man, bowed and crippled, herding three goats, switching them with a stick as they strayed. They passed through the village of Sukna and children wandering by the tracks smiled up at Patience. She could have put out her hand and touched the buildings but Sister Esme pulled her back before she hit her head on a shop awning. Everything seemed to move slowly, as if in a dream.

In front of the train, market vendors were pulling back their wares from the tracks. Patience turned to tell her mother to look. She cast her eyes about the carriage but in a burst of sadness remembered she was not there. Her eyes glistened but she turned her attention onto the piles of fruit; and the smell of the chapatis being made in the tiny shadowed shops made her tummy grumble. Sister Esme pulled out some naan bread she had bought and Patience nibbled on it contentedly. The loops of the tracks and views out of the window forgotten, she concentrated on the food in her hand.

Wiping her hands on her skirt, she was scolded by Sister Esme who, pulling at the hair on her chin, told her again what a naughty little girl she was. Was she naughty? She had never been told that before. Where was her *ayah*? Her *ayah* who loved and cuddled her, unlike this block of stone sitting next to her. Where was her mother? She had a vision of her mother cuddling her after her bath, or reading to her as she sat, clean and shining after being washed, on the best chair in the living room. Distracting herself, she looked out of the window as the tiny train looped back on itself once more and the valley dropped so far away.

"Sit down!" the grey nun reprimanded; and reluctantly she sat back and wondered if there was any more naan for her. She had long finished the sweet condensed milk which would become a staple of the food packages Maree sent to her from Calcutta over her school years.

After so many days, or so it seemed to Patience, the train journey was finally at an end. She walked fast, trying to keep up with the angry nun attached to her, almost yanking her little arm out of its socket.

Another grey bird, more heron-like than the other, appeared in front of her. The nun immediately dropped to her knees, her robes in the dust and the discarded chai cups, her eyes smiling at Patience.

"Oh, you little darling. So young to be away from your Mummy! I'm Sister Maureen and I'll be looking after you at school."

Sister Esme harrumphed. "Well, she's a naughty one, I can tell you. Nothing but trouble, wouldn't sit still, forever wriggling…" the words fading as she recalled the trip, vowing never to accompany a small child to school again.

Patience beamed at Sister Maureen. This was better. Someone who called her darling and didn't tell her off. She placed her small brown hand in the soft white hand of Sister Maureen and skipped along next to her with Sister Esme, still complaining, bringing up the rear.

# Thirty-Nine

Patience's introduction to school was mixed. Being the youngest of all the children, she soon became a mascot, liked by them all. But when she was naughty, as small children invariably are, the older girls thought of ways to upset her.

One day, she acquired a rubber lizard from one of the servant boys who pressed it into her hand hoping to startle her; but she loved it, and after sleeping with it under her pillow for several nights she thought she would share it with one of the other girls, Zara, her favourite. She placed it carefully in Zara's wooden desk where Zara was sure to see it when she opened it to take out her book for lessons the next day.

Far from being pleased, Zara screamed, screamed so loudly and hysterically that it was all she could do to point out what had upset her. What a fuss, Patience thought, and she made her way over to retrieve the lizard from the desk. Sister Maureen realised the lizard belonged to Patience and gently chided her. Zara, however, was not keen to let Patience off so lightly; and at morning breaktime, she and two of her friends lifted Patience up onto the top of a pillar in the garden and ran off. At first Patience did not realise her predicament, and looked around with interest as the playground emptied out and the girls returned to the classroom. It was only later during a roll call that Sister Maureen realised the small child was not in her usual seat.

"Where is Patience?" she asked the tittering girls.

When she brought in the small girl, her hot little hand held in her own, she stood in front of the class and as Patience's tears dried she told the children how unkind they had been. Patience was unable to articulate why she had put the lizard in the desk but she felt troubled that she had been misunderstood and when released, she slunk back to her desk and sat in her chair kicking her heels against the rungs. Zara looked over at her and mouthed the word "sorry". Patience gave her a lopsided smile but she never did trust Zara again; and it wasn't until the next year when a new girl, Monisha, was introduced to her class that she found another friend.

By the end of the first term, Patience had become attached to Sister Maureen, whose kind smile was always there for her. There was such a hole in her heart where her *ayah* had been, her *ayah* who sang lullabies and cuddled her to sleep; a hole where her mother had been, her mother who read bedtime stories and loved to take her walking in the *maidan* in her best clothes. Sister Maureen had a kind heart; she too had been sent to a boarding school when she was not much older than Patience and she remembered the loneliness and confusion of those times. She could vividly recall the older sister, Sister Benedict, who had seemed to delight in being mean and nasty to all the youngest children as if she needed to challenge the limits of their kindness and good nature. When Sister Maureen was leaving the school many years later, Sister Benedict, upon learning of her decision to join the nunnery, advised her to be stern with all the pupils, to make them fear her. She felt very strongly that you should not spare the rod; children needed to be disciplined and should always obey their elders. This was a sentiment which Sister Maureen certainly did not agree with; but it was only now that she began to understand the bitterness and sense of isolation which Sister Benedict must have felt after forty years of living without joy.

Sister Maureen felt sorry for the little Anglo-Indian girl, separated from her mother at such a young age, and endeavoured to give her some degree of love and compassion which she felt she sorely lacked. One of Sister Maureen's favourite pastimes when not on duty was to sit in the rose garden and revel in the various perfumes, her favourite being a pale pink rosa rugosa she remembered from her grandmother's garden in Cornwall. Her grandmother would walk out in the early morning dew with her secateurs and cut a profusion of the heady blooms to put on the kitchen table before breakfast and Maureen would sit waiting for her toast with her nose in the blossoms. Patience, often left to her own devices after her friendship with Zara took such a blow, would pad out in bare feet to the garden and sit on the wooden bench with Sister Maureen. She would tickle her hand until the sister took the small, plump hand in between her own and begin to tell her stories of when she was growing up in Cornwall. Patience was entranced. Her mother had told her about the city of Manchester where she had grown up but this country sounded very different. The brilliant green of the tea plantations, Maureen told her, reminded her of the sweeping green fields of home. The plantations of course were not bounded by neat stone walls and there was a distinct lack of sheep grazing, she told Patience.

"Was it like the *maidan*?" Patience asked. "It's huge and it stretches for ever and ever."

Sister Maureen laughed and her eyes full of unshed tears told of the gentle countryside she so loved. Her vocation, however, had sent her to this faraway hill station, to this school, where girls like Patience needed her.

She swallowed hard and said brightly, "It must be time for dinner. I'm sure I heard the bell. Come on, I'll take you to the dining room. Sister Esme will be wondering where you are."

Patience wrinkled her nose; she would have preferred to stay in the garden with Sister Maureen but she usually did as she was told and so she obediently followed her into the dining hall where the girls were sitting down on long benches waiting to say grace before their meal.

# Forty

Maree sent letters to her daughter and son weekly. Her son responded dutifully and the few scribbled lines set her mind at rest; he was enjoying the school, loving the sports, writing excitedly of new friends. As for those to Patience, she hoped the sisters would read them out, stories of her everyday life in Calcutta without her; but she did not expect any in return. So she was delighted when halfway through the term, an envelope arrived from St Helen's enclosing a picture drawn by Patience. She had drawn herself, a small stick figure with a large tomato head in the middle, with two grey birds on either side of her. As she looked more closely, Maree realised that the beaks were faces and the birds must be the nuns. There was no other colour on the drawing and no joy, no smiling faces on any of the characters. She sighed. She could hardly wait the five weeks left before she could head up the hills to Kurseong to collect her children for the holidays.

The drive was interminable, the slow dirt roads making progress no faster than the train which the driver passed on several occasions. At one stage, they stopped as the 'toy train' crossed in front of them. The driver got out and purchased some chai from a roadside stall for the memsahib who was feeling more and more faint the higher they rose up the Himalayas. It was colder now and the misty clouds dampened even the leather seats of the car. She rolled up the windows and snuggled under the woollen blanket. The chai had revived her and they continued; hairpin bend after sweeping curve, tea plantations through both windows, neat rows filled with brightly clothed workers picking the tips and placing them in the panniers on their backs, until passing the shops lining the tracks at Kurseong they followed the directions they had been given to the school.

As they made their slow way along the driveway, a heady rose perfume sailed through the car windows, rolled down now by Maree in anticipation of seeing her baby girl. The entrance steps were quiet; no children awaited parents. She hopped out of the car as the driver opened it with alacrity. He knew how keen she was to see Patience. As if on a signal, a grey-robed nun came down the steps towards her. She was smiling and trying to twist around to a small child clinging behind her. Maree's heart leapt at the sight of the dark curls and skinny legs.

"Patience!" she said. "Come to Mama!" But the small child did not want to unclasp her hands from the familiar robes. She shook her head and as Maree fell to her knees on the cold stone step the little girl, brown eyes large with alarm, started backing away from her.

Sister Maureen crouched down and spoke softly to Patience who was refusing to lift her head to look at her mother.

"This is your Mama," she whispered in her ear. "She has come to take you home for the holidays. You'll come back soon. Don't worry."

Each word was a sword in Maree's heart. Her own child did not recognise her. Patience did not want to come home. This was now her home. How cruel and thoughtless she had been to leave her here! She should have learnt her lesson when she left Ernest in England. She was a terrible mother.

The driver stood by the car, waiting for the memsahib and her little girl. He snapped his fingers for the bearer squatting by the steps to heave the trunk into the boot. With great reluctance, Patience followed Sister Maureen as she led her to the car. The nun gave her a big hug, which the little girl happily returned. But as she was being placed into the back seat, Patience clung to the nun and wrapped her legs around her waist. Maree stood hopelessly by, wringing her hands, biting her lip. She thought she should have gone to pick Max up first. Maybe Patience would have felt happier coming in the car in that case.

As they drove to Victoria School, Maree tentatively put her hand out to Patience, sliding it along the seat; but Patience, sobbing softly, moved closer to the door and tried to make herself as small as possible. Who was this strange woman? She wanted her tiny bed amongst the other tiny beds in the nursery room of the school.

Maree had begged that Patience be allowed into the school so young but was feeling the repercussions of her decision. Frank had assured her that the culture of the school was favourable to Anglo-Indians but she had not expected Patience's love for her to be supplanted by that of a nun.

The car beeped its horn, its top down as it swept around the grand courtyard of the school. Boys of all ages milled around in groups of twos and threes, swinging around the awning poles, sitting on the balcony or sitting reading singly, patiently awaiting the arrival of their parents. The white walls reflected the mountain sun as it slanted over the building, its windows facing the majesty of Kangchenjunga's peaks. The crisp air and the surrounding greenery calmed Maree; and even Patience sat up on her haunches and looked over the door at the activity in the school. Several other cars drew up at the same time and boys raced to their parents, the more affectionate and less self-conscious throwing their arms around their mothers and doffing their hats to their fathers.

Max looked around for his father, his smile turning to a frown when he couldn't see him.

"He said he would be coming up to fetch me." As old as he was, his lower lip trembled. Maree held out her hand,

"Come, Max. You know he would've come if he could have. But there is good news!" Maree consoled him, telling him that his father was very busy. Busy organising the possible purchase of a house here in Kurseong. Frank had been negotiating with the owner Mrs Lord, as on the death of her husband the estate was being liquidated. Max grinned at this, perked up on seeing Patience peeping over the door, and ran over to give her a kiss. She threw her arms around his neck and Maree felt a frisson of jealousy that her own daughter had not recognised her but was happy enough to see her brother.

"But I see Patience every week, Mother. All the boys with sisters are allowed to go to Dow Hill for an hour to see them and the little girls come up from St Helen's too. That's why she remembers me!"

Max could not stop talking. He chattered about the catapults which had been confiscated just the other day in assembly, about McNally and Johnson who had run away and been found hiding under a seat in the third class compartment of the train at Siliguri Junction. He giggled at the horrified look on his mother's face and decided he had better talk about the cricket matches with Dow Hill School, about the cinema night they had recently started.

"I love school, Mother. It's great. I'm so glad you sent me here; much better than St Xavier's!"

Maree smiled as Patience bounced up and down in her seat as Max kept talking.

"How about we stop in Kurseong at Cochrane's teahouse? Time for tea together before we head back down to Calcutta?" The children both shouted their assent and Maree felt that her little girl was coming back to her.

The clouds lifted as they came back into the village of Kurseong and the teahouse materialised out of the mist, red-roofed with wide balconies perched over the terraced hills falling away below, bright green and ribbed.

More than ten years in India and Maree still could not accustom herself to the bowing of servants as the doorman in his white uniform, sashed bright red with turban tied to match, hurried to open the teahouse door for her. The children didn't even notice.

They knew no different. She was glad they seemed unaware in their cloistered Anglo-Indian life of the strict caste differences and prejudices which made a social life so hard for their mother.

Seated at a window table, Patience swung her small legs as she perched on the edge of a high chair. Max entwined his around the chair legs and continued with the tales of school, enthusiasm written all over his face. Maree mused about how much easier it would be to have a house here in the hills. She would not have to make the interminable journey up and down. They could live here in the summer months and enjoy the coolness, the peace and quiet: such a contrast to the busyness of the city. Perhaps the children could even live at home, or at least be home every weekend. Never having adjusted to the heat in Calcutta, Maree pined for wet days and she thought she might get many in this cloud-covered hill station.

# Forty-One

When Patience was back in Calcutta during the school holidays her father allowed her to sit in the car as he was driven to his Freemason meetings every Thursday. Standing between the two stone pillars which flanked the driveway, carved black lettering denoting the West Bengal Chapter, he waved at her as she looked out of the rear window, little hands waving madly. Turning on his heel he felt pride that his chapter were considering him for Worshipful Master and this was a great honour. When he told Maree, she smiled a wan smile. She was proud of him, that he knew; but the dark mood engulfing her made it difficult for her to summon up the enthusiasm that she knew he craved.

The past few years had seen Frank rise in standing, his accounting company being the one the local West Bengal government turned to for their liquidation cases. His attempt at cornering the market in providing high quality commercial education had fizzled somewhat. Basu, his articled clerk, had done his best to promote it as a school and encourage local clerks to enrol but marketing was not his forte; and as busy as Frank was, it slid to second place in importance. Frank had written a series of articles in the *Commercial Gazette* feeling it his duty to return back to the community some of the opportunities he had been given in Bombay by the Hindu Education Fund, but this had not eventuated. He needed another avenue. His schism with

Meugens Peat was now complete and Frank was making his own successful way in the Calcutta business world.

Frank's chest expanded as they placed the sash over his shoulder. His medals and insignia were pinned to him with great reverence. This was a fraternity he was proud of, one where he was not belittled or thought inferior. Mr Thapa, a solicitor at the law courts, had put his name forward a few years previously. Mr Thapa told him how all the members would each be given a white ball and a black ball. They could choose whether to place one or the other into a secret ballot box. Black indicated unsuitability for joining. Frank was thankful that as a prospective member he did not receive any black balls, so he was told by his friend.

"They were all white, my friend," Mr Thapa whispered to him. "Everyone was putting in a white ball, I am sure!"

He enjoyed the sense of equality; no airs and graces from any of the colonials. He might not gain entry into the country clubs but here he could converse with all on an equal footing. It had been good for business; and in taking part in the charity initiatives, he felt invested in the community.

He rushed out of his office clutching a letter in his hand.

"My dear, this is such an honour! The District Grand Scribe from Bombay chapter has written to me," he beamed. "He has advised me of my election to Worshipful Master. This is so exciting!" His desire to be the leader of this fraternity was realised.

The ceremony was outstanding; the pomp and circumstance suited him so well. To celebrate personally he had big plans.

"Let's have a garden party," he announced to Maree. "The servants will take care of all the food. You only need to look beautiful, as always, my love."

He hoped this might give Maree something to lock onto, a life-raft in her ocean of despair. Bright lights, laughter, friendly company and good food. The children were safe in the hills; he kept assuring her, no harm could come to them there. He was running out of ideas. He cherished her, he loved her, but it never seemed enough.

She returned his love, he was sure, but he felt an empty void in her very essence; there was a part of her he could never reach, a hollow in which she kept the memory of Ernest and to which she attached a sense of unworthiness, of failure and of terror that she might fail both of the other children she had brought into this world. She seemed an observer, afraid to engage with her life. Frank wondered whether her wholeness would ever return. Maybe he would only ever have a tiny part of Maree.

He enlisted the assistance of Dorothy Parker. The plans for the garden party could be her domain. She had become a solicitous friend to Maree, checking daily on her and encouraging her to walk with her. Maree, however, did not confide in Dorothy; she was polite and friendly to her but somehow she mistook her kindness for interference – and never would she trust someone who might leave her as Nataline had. She sat in the window seat staring out at the garden as the evening faded and heard Nataline's laugh, saw Ernest's solemn face. It was all too much to bear and so she closed herself off, surrounding herself with a carapace which even Frank's love could not penetrate.

"You must wear the sari," Frank cried, "the fuchsia one I bought for you in the bazaar. You look so brilliant in it. My Indian princess!"

Maree laughed a frighteningly hollow laugh.

"A princess?" She knew a princess should not be a shell. A princess should be full of joy and laughter.

Frank took the sari out of the camphor chest with such reverence it made Maree smile. He held it close to her and kissed her on the neck. She sighed, leaned back onto him and she was back in the ice palace, the Indian maharina smiling at her in her fuchsia sari. She shook her head and wriggled out of his embrace.

Over the next week, Dorothy bustled up the stairs more and more frequently. Her enthusiasm was infectious and eventually even the saddened Maree was swept up as her plans came to fruition. She enlisted Maree's help with the flowers and the lights; they sat in the garden scribbling an outline for the servants to follow.

"No, not there," Dorothy admonished a servant. "Look, can't you see, they won't look their best there?"

Maree wandered around the garden with clippers in hand, passing them to the gardener when she could not reach the blooms she wished to see in the table decorations. Tables dotted the lawn, white cloths reflecting the sunlight so brightly her eyes were dazzled. Too much time indoors, she realised. As the preparations increased in intensity, Maree felt a seed of excitement blossoming.

Maree and Dorothy stood side by side in the garden. Mr Parker and Frank, both having only lately returned from work, were indoors, changing their clothes. Dorothy was in a splendid ice-blue dress, sashed with turquoise. Maree, as Frank had requested, was in the fuchsia sari, the rich cerise a contrast to her pale skin. At her soft-skinned collar bone lay the Star of India, its diamonds glistening in the party lights, rays of colour making it seem three times as large. Dorothy had exclaimed at its perfection, its beauty, but now was smoothing down perceived wrinkles in the skirt of her dress, her attention on her own shoes, turning them this way and that.

"What do you think, Maree? Are they too garish?" The patent leather gleamed. "New shoes," she sighed, "such a luxury! Frederick saw them when he was in Delhi last month and thought he must buy them for me."

Maree wondered why Dorothy had taken such a liking to her. Sadie, after all, had rejected her totally. She was used to being ignored by the English now. Neither one nor the other, she had complained to Frank. Dorothy, however, was different. She had never shunned her; had welcomed her to the Kyd Street house from her arrival. Admittedly, Frederick was guarded. He spoke greetings but not much more. He stood aloof now, away from the ladies, smoking a cigarette behind one of the hydrangea bushes.

As the partygoers arrived, mostly work colleagues of Frank's together with their wives, the vivid-coloured saris eclipsed the flower arrangements. Frank clapped his hands with glee. "We must have a photo!" he cried.

Frederick Parker jumped up to offer his services. He was delighted to wield the camera. He had no wish to be sitting with all the Indians in a group photo. Frank moved his head clerk Basu to the front row.

"You must sit here in between Maree and myself; and where is your good wife? Come, come, you must sit on the other side."

"This seat is for Dorothy," Maree said, patting the seat beside her, just as she saved a seat for Ruby at school. "She has done most of the work for tonight. Any success is due to her."

"Never mind, then. Sit on the next seat." Frank took Basu's wife by the arm. Frank bossed the crowd, placing people here and there until he was happy with the arrangement. "You can take the photo now, Frederick." His glasses reflected the lights; the shutter was slow; and the end result was far from Frank's expectation, blurred and misty-looking. Faces were turned away or even looking down; and in years to come, he had difficulty remembering who these people were. He could recognise Dorothy, with her strong, long face. And Basu, his faithful clerk, so devoted to him and the company; but of the others, beside Maree of course, he no longer had any idea.

The secret to Dorothy's friendship was revealed later. Although Maree did not herself divulge any secrets or innermost feelings, Dorothy was a chatterer. She told Maree, one day when they were strolling outside to get even the faintest of breezes in that hot sultry air, that she was not Frederick's wife. He had come to India with his wife, Audrey, six years ago. Audrey had not enjoyed the life here – Maree felt a tug of sympathy – and had returned to England four years ago with their two children. Dorothy had been working at the P&O shipping office in Calcutta and she had met Frederick when he was arranging the family's return voyage. She had needed to contact him regarding a change in the shipping schedule and he was attracted to her competence and matter-of-fact way of dealing with the vagaries of Indian bureaucracy.

"He invited me to dinner at the country club," she confided, "and that was the beginning. There was no question of him divorcing Audrey so I took his name and we moved in here together." She went on to explain that, although they were both English, they were not seen as a couple in the colonial social circles and invitations had been granted to him only, so they had decided to be their own company and make their own friends outside of the tight strictures of that society.

# Forty-Two

*'Wayside'* was hidden. The car slowed as it rounded a particularly tight bend on the mountain road out of Kurseong.

"We may have missed it," Frank said to the driver.

"No, sahib," he replied with confidence, "I am having very good directions."

The driver pulled the wheel abruptly to the right and the car headed down a steep, narrow driveway. Sweet-smelling magnolias and lush ferns brushing the car formed a shadowed archway. After fifty yards a closed wooden gate in front of them sported a sign, *'Wayside'*.

"I am being right, sahib," the driver said. "This is the house."

Maree and the children craned their necks to see the house but it was still hidden. The driver tooted and a gardener rushed up the drive and opened the gate. The car swept onto a gravel driveway which led to a wooden garage. Where was the house? To the right, a stone wall hid the back of the house, its wooden facade a dark green blending into the verdant shrubbery.

Maree breathed a sigh of delight as the children tumbled out of the car. Around the side of the house she could see another gardener tending roses. Two servants came out of the side door hurriedly as the driver clapped his hands.

"Very sorry, memsahibs, the car is quiet. We were not hearing it. We thought you might be here this morning. We have lunch ready for you."

Frank apologised for their late arrival. It had been a slow journey up the mountains from Calcutta. Leading the way to the front door, the servants paused as the whole family were drawn to the low brick wall at the bottom of the garden where the hills tumbled down and down into the dark valleys with their rows of camellias in the tea plantations. Mesmerised, they watched as swirling clouds chased each other up and down the gullies.

"It's beautiful, Frank." Maree clasped his arm as, beaming, they walked up the stone steps into the main living room. A fire was lit in the large stone fireplace, casting a warmth even to the bay window seats.

After the family had made a cursory tour of the bedrooms and the bathrooms, the servants sat them down at the dining table and served them freshly made roti and several curries.

"Are you liking the *dhokla* and *aloo tarkari*, memsahibs? They are my specialities," the cook hurried out to ask them.

Frank beamed at him. Wiping his mouth with a napkin he then gestured to the empty dishes the family had left on the table. "Simply delicious," he said.

After lunch, the two children excused themselves and ran outside to explore the garden, while Maree sat curled up in a blanket looking out at the cupola and the formal flowerbeds. Later, after her rest, she and Frank joined the children.

"Look, Mother," Max said, "there is a huge flight of stairs here at the back of the wall. May we go down and see where it leads?"

Frank summoned the old *mali* who had been watching to see if his carefully tended flowerbeds were going to be trampled by these inquisitive children. He was taken with Patience's smile and held her tiny hand in his gnarled one and they both followed Max, who had bounded down two steps at a time, to see the other part of the gardens down the hill.

Frank and Maree could hear the delighted squeals of the

children and the gentle chiding of the gardener. They turned and looked at each other. Frank's stomach unclenched as Maree's spirit soared visibly. In the last few months he had been wondering how long Maree would stay in India. He was terrified of losing her to England. As much as he had adapted to life in Manchester, here, he felt, was his home and where his opportunities lay. He could not bear it if she left. The happenstance of this house becoming available, Mrs Lord's husband having died and left her indebted to the government, was a godsend. He arranged for her to stay until she could settle all her accounts and return to England. He negotiated to have her leave her furniture and linens, as he persuaded her they were not worth shipping home. He had a ready-made home to offer Maree and the children, close to their schools and within a range for his business to allow him to visit as often as he could.

On their return to Calcutta, Maree had time to contemplate the move.

"Oh, Dorothy," she said, "I'll be sorry to leave you and I will miss our talks but I truly think it will be best for me. I so want to be close to the children. What do you think?"

Dorothy, as much as she would miss Maree, felt too that it would be the best thing for her. She felt relief that Maree had something to look forward to. It was hard sometimes, she thought, to be a constant support and optimist.

"I promise I'll come and visit you, Maree. It is lovely up in the hills. A welcome escape from the heat, the dust and the chaos. You're very lucky, Maree, to have such a wonderful husband who has managed to orchestrate this house and move," she sighed.

Patience loved the gardener's children. They spent hours together playing on the grass, arranging flower heads and forming pathways out of small stones, inventing their own worlds. Maree sat in the bay window, watching. Love for Patience welled up inside her but was immediately quashed by the guilt she felt about leaving Ernest behind. She blinked a few times and turned back to her book. Max made special friends with the headmaster's son and the family were frequently invited to the schoolmaster's house for tea. Maree revelled in the feeling of acceptance. She was not restricted as in the colonial strictures of Calcutta. Frank, looking for clients, visited Rajah Bannerjee's tea plantation on the other side of Kurseong. The two of them rode through the manicured rows, admiring the excellence of the tea crop, Rajah showing him the tea drying and packaging machinery he had just purchased as his plantation was expanding with the demand for the high quality Darjeeling tea.

One afternoon, Patience came screaming up the stairs from the bottom garden. It had become her favourite place to play with the gardener's children Soubash and Amala. Maree rushed outside, as did the *ayah* who had been sitting in the cupola flirting with the second gardener. She had been laughing at his jokes, her sari flung around her mouth, her dark eyes smouldering. He had been pretending to weed the roses surrounding the building. But upon hearing Patience's wails she fled to the steps, bangles tinkling on her bare ankles. She held her arms wide as Patience reached the top step, blubbering.

"There's hundreds and thousands of them!" She held up one leg which was covered in black grape-like bodies: leeches clinging off her dusty shins and calves. The *ayah* screeched too while Maree demanded that the gardener remove them from poor Patience. Her little legs bled copiously as they were twisted off one by one and thrown to the peacocks wandering the garden, so thankful for the feast that they stopped scratching the flowerbeds and strutted around the gardener screaming for more. Maree held her hands over her ears. What with Patience crying and the *ayah* and the peacocks screeching, the rest of the kitchen servants came running out to see what all the commotion was. Peace was only restored when the last of the leeches was thrown away and the *ayah* picked up a sobbing Patience, balanced her on her hip and, murmuring soft kisses on her neck, took her inside to bathe her legs.

There were other dangers in this paradisiacal idyll. One day,

Maree was sitting reading in her favourite window seat, surrounded by the plump silk cushions Mrs Lord had had sewn by local village girls. She glanced up to see in horror that Patience was gaily walking along the top of the stone wall as if it were a tightrope, oblivious to the fall on the leeward side. Where was her *ayah*? Throwing down her book, Maree raced outside.

"Patience," Maree gasped in a tight voice, "come down at once; you might fall."

She was about to fail her third child, she was sure. Her heart in her mouth, she motioned to the *ayah* who once again had been whispering sweet nothings to the gardener. She came tripping up to the wall to snatch Patience from her imminent danger as Maree held Patience's gaze. Maree scolded the *ayah* and Patience both.

In general, though, Maree was happy to see the children as often as she did. She was happy to be away from the miasma of disease and ferment in Calcutta. She was happy when Dorothy Parker made the trek up to the hill station and spent a few weeks in her company. It was a good time for her. She enjoyed the preparation and planning for Frank when he came up every other weekend; and on his longer visits they took the car to visit Darjeeling. On one longer stay, they ventured into Sikkim where they viewed a monastery perched high up on the mountainside. Their driver drove them as far as he could along a rocky pathway until they had to get out and walk. The stream gushed along by their sides, its force spinning prayer wheels in tiny wooden huts. The greenery was so verdant that Maree shaded her eyes. Prayer flags fluttered and led them to the two-storey stone building, its red roof glistening with dew. Maree turned and smiled at Frank. She felt the calm and serenity of the place trickling through her. They sat on a rough wooden bench in companionable silence.

# Forty-Three

## *1933 Leaving Kurseong*

After a few years, Maree's creeping sense of despondence rose again to encompass her very soul. The initial delight she had felt in Wayside and its surroundings had been supplanted by her wish to visit her mother and see her sisters. She was lonely. Kurseong had been a wonderful idea: a hill station setting with beautiful schools for her children, a cooler clime, and away from any pestilence in Calcutta. So why was she feeling this way? She could not explain it to herself any better than she had during earlier 'dark days' episodes.

One weekend, Frank came up with the news that the Indian National Congress meeting had been prevented from happening in Calcutta by a very heavy-handed police presence. The Congress had been scheduled to march down the Esplanade just at the end of Kyd Street. Any offshoots of violence, she was sure, would have exploded down their street, might even have caused burnings and lootings of homes. She was glad, then, that she was safe in Kurseong. But its security did not prevent her from longing to return to England and her family. In Kurseong she didn't have the daily company of Dorothy or the familiarity of her walks on the *maidan*. The recent hand of friendship extended to her by a Mrs Chatterjee was in its infancy and her rather gossipy way of talking about other acquaintances did not much endear her to Maree.

Frank had always wished to ride; he fancied the idea of being seated on a horse, long shiny boots and neatly buttoned jacket giving him a commanding presence. In Kurseong he found a horse in need of a paddock and so the bottom of their garden, down the long stone steps, was fenced in; and when he was in residence, as he liked to say, he would take the horse on long rides through the tea plantations and visit his friend Rajah Bannerjee across the valley at the Makaibari plantation. They spent many an hour sampling the latest tea crop served in the most delicate of porcelain cups and discussing Indian life as it was developing, taking a few stumbling steps towards a post-colonial era. They both agreed that it was going to be a difficult time, maybe a violent time, so much in conflict with the tenets of their Hindu religion.

Rajah was the only person in whom Frank confided any family issues. Rajah was in an arranged marriage, as was the custom, and so was unfamiliar with the difficulties that both Frank and Maree were having. When he mentioned Maree's desire to leave and go to England, Rajah leant back on his chair, the back legs creaking as the front legs left the ground, his considerable bulk balanced. He suggested that Frank arrange for her to travel back soon for an extended holiday.

"She might get it out of her system," he said. "I hear life in Manchester is not the best. At the least she will be grateful and probably miss you and the family so very much that she will change her booking and come back as soon as possible."

Frank noted the 'probably' and was not convinced and opened his mouth to speak; but he realised with the lack of any other plan to tackle his wife's unhappiness that he needed to look into the possibility of a voyage when he returned to Calcutta.

Making a detour, Frank rode into the market. He had seen some Tibetan blankets that he wished to buy. Some for the house would be good; it was cold in winter, and at this time even the fires did not reach the far corners of the rooms. He would wrap Maree in one, the blue striped one he particularly liked. The owner of the stall came up to the horse as he was leaving, blankets tucked into a saddlebag.

"Please, sahib, will you buy more? I am sending the money to my family."

Responsibilities of a 'sahib', he thought; and taking out some more notes he handed them down to the seller who selected three more blankets and passed them up to him. He had been concerned that the gardener's family who lived in a small shed at the back of the property were too cold. He knew they were used to the misty, damp atmosphere, but that didn't stop the cough that the old father had. He had seen him crouched over a small fire, with his arms wrapped around himself, releasing himself every so often to poke the twigs with a small stick. He knew with the festival of Makar Sankranti commencing in a few days that the blankets might indeed prove useful as the family took their holy dips in the freezing mountain streams.

Frank planned Maree's voyage for the beginning of April. She hoped that the stunning white orchids for which Kurseong was named would be in bloom before she left.

"Its original name, Karsan Rup," Mrs Chatterjee told her, "meant Land of White Orchids." So far the sight of the blooms had eluded her but this year she had been promised by one of Mrs Chatterjee's friends, whom she had met at the teahouse, that they would escort her to the best viewing place in March when they were at their best. The group of ladies who met every Tuesday at the Elgin hotel in Darjeeling were happy to include her in their weekly tea outing. They usually travelled up in their cars but occasionally took the 'toy train' right to the top of the town where they only had a few steps to the hotel. There, the doorman would open the wrought iron gates and usher the gaggling group inside. Maree was beginning to forge a life for herself away from the stuffy colonial exclusion she had experienced in Calcutta.

Her new friends made her reconsider if she had made the right decision to return to England for three months. She had been taken to Eagle's Crag, where they looked back down to the hillside town. It was an awe-inspiring view, the snowy peaks of Mount Katchenjunga in all their glory contrasting with the moss-green tea fields. Maree breathed in the mountain air, so clear and clean. How had she ever lived in Calcutta, or even Manchester?

"Look, you can almost see Dow Hill; and there's the school behind it where Patience will go when she leaves St Helen's!"

She could make out the smiling faces of the women as they collected tea down below, calling to each other, babies cocooned in front of them, panniers on their backs. She visualised the market, full of fresh produce. These things she would miss.

Max and Patience had had their last weekend at home with their mother. Maree spent every second with them, hugging, kissing and squeezing them at every opportunity until Max took to hiding in the gardener's shed and only appeared at teatime when called by the *ayah*. Twelve years old was far too old to be smothered by his mother; and what would his friends say if they saw him? The gardener's youngest son, Soubash, had clapped his hands over his giggling mouth when, crouching behind a camellia bush, he had seen Maree bestowing kisses on her son's ungrateful cheek. Max saw him laughing out of the corner of one eye and vowed to make him pay for his insolence. He called Soubash into the shed on the pretence of asking him to play. Later, when Max was summoned by the *ayah*, he exited the shed, pulling down his jacket. A chastened Soubash emerged behind him, adjusting dusty trousers and shirt, tear stains on his dirty face. Max's eyes glistened and he smoothed his unkempt hair, and grinned as only a victor does.

# Forty-Four

Frank secured a passage for Maree on the *SS Mulbera*, as things stood, he was not able to pay for a first class ticket but Dorothy assured him that the second class on the *Mulbera*, a British India Line ship, was nearly as good as the first class on a P&O. It was a small ship with only seventy-eight second class passengers and eighty first class. It had the added bonus, Frank told Maree gleefully, of having had the newly-married Duke and Duchess of York sail in her to East Africa in 1924.

He accompanied Maree down to the dock and saw her on board. She was to travel in a shared cabin. Maree cried upon Frank's departure, her nose cherry-coloured as she wondered again if this was the right thing to be doing. To leave her children and her husband: what was she thinking?

Her cabin companion, a middle-aged teacher returning to the Lake District, was a quiet and respectful person. She washed herself early in the morning and went on deck, rain or shine, heat or cold to sit in a deckchair and read her bible. She murmured her prayers, petitioning for a safe journey.

Maree felt numb, but by the time the ship sailed into Madras harbour, she rallied and began to look forward to seeing her Lancashire family again.

After picking up several passengers the ship continued on

to Port Said. It was as she remembered: oppressive and hot. The ship felt becalmed as it approached the red towering cliffs. Her companion, the redoubtable Miss Penny, stood next to her at the rail as they were escorted through the Suez Canal. They stood silent, taking in the majesty of the desert. It had been many years since Miss Penny had travelled out to India and at that stage of her life, as an adventurous young teacher, she had concentrated on her mission to bring the English language to the infidels in India. She would have liked to have been a missionary, she confided, but at that time there was no mission going out and she was desperate to escape from her authoritarian father and ineffectual mother; and a journey to a far-flung place was exactly what she needed. She told Maree all this one evening when they were both sitting in their cabin, feeling rather seasick as they entered the Bay of Biscay on the homeward stretch.

Maree enjoyed the journey free of any encumbrances and she was happy sitting in the women's sitting room on the long bench seats, watching the comings and goings of all the other passengers. The sitting room was at the stern of the ship and the windows looked on to the wake of the ship carving its way through the oceans, its white road flouncing behind. Being a smaller ship, the journey this time took thirty days instead of twenty-one; and being in second class she saw no sign of the luxuries the Duke and Duchess must have experienced. Food, though, was as usual plentiful, and for her it was wonderful to be able to eat English food again which now seemed foreign and unusual to her. She thought of how her mother would welcome her with a warming Lancashire hotpot; she had expressed this desire in a letter. And how she would enjoy a strong brew at any time of day without thinking of the sweat dripping down her back and her forehead.

She thought about wearing her felt hat, putting on gloves and walking in her stout shoes along the lanes near Chorlton. She hugged herself when she thought of talking to Ruby, her oldest friend. She thought of her sisters. To Nell and to Alice she had disclosed her intention of visiting Ernest's grave in the Southern Cemetery. Nell had written to her that she went every other week to put flowers on his small plot. She said she had told him that his mother was coming and she was sure he had heard. She had felt chills down her spine and tingling in her fingers, which surely meant he was around. Maree was anxious about the graveyard visit but she knew she owed it to the small child. Her firstborn son, whose solemn face she never stopped seeing in her dreams, appeared even on the face of Max in some of his expressions and always in the deep dark eyes of Patience.

After Tangier, the next and last port was London. She hoped that Flo and her husband Bert would come to meet her as they had promised. She had travelled halfway around the world on her own but she would love company for the last leg. Flo had tried to persuade her mother to accompany them but her mother said she was too old for the journey down to London. She was excited to see her youngest daughter but would wait for her here in Chorlton – her daughter for whom she had held such high hopes; the daughter who had dreamed of being a princess.

"Things not going so well in India for her, then?" a neighbour had sniffed when she heard of Maree's return. "Never thought she should of married a darkie," she said maliciously.

Mrs Crymble gasped and turned away, vowing never to speak to her again. She was aware of the growing concern that Indians were causing riots both at home and in India and the threat of violence in the rising Nationalist movement made the headlines of the newspapers which she perused as she stood in line at the tobacconists. But, she thought, Maree and Frank wouldn't be caught up in all that.

"It was such an interminable journey," Maree said to her sister after they had finally found each other in the swirling melee of the incoming passengers and welcoming families. She tried to explain. "Every voyage is different. My first journey was so exciting; so many things to see and do, so strange and unusual that it passed so quickly. And of course I couldn't wait to see Frank." She paused to draw breath, Flo laughing as she squeezed Maree's arm looped in hers. Bert walked behind, a suitcase in either hand. Maree turned to make sure he was following before continuing.

"The voyage coming back with Ernest passed in a blur. All I could think about was how ill he was and how much we hoped Doctor Lingard in Birmingham would be able to cure him. The journey after I left him was ghastly. I hated leaving him behind and I felt it was a real voyage of sadness; but running around after Max made it pass quicker than I had imagined." Flo opened her mouth to comment but Maree continued, "This time, on my own, I had so much time to think, to read and just to sit and stare." She laughed. "Yes, me being quiet, how strange! I think I've changed since I've been to India. What do you think? I worry about you and the others all the time; letters take so long to reach me. I keep thinking if something awful happened, say to Mother, I wouldn't even know until it was just too late. I suppose you could send a telegram, but still, it would all be over."

Maree continued in this way on the whole train journey while Flo just nodded and patted her arm. Bert spent most of the journey in the passageway outside the carriage, smoking out of the window. Occasionally he would turn back to look at Flo who just inclined her head and raised her eyebrows as if to say *she's still talking, don't come in yet*. He didn't want to. He liked Maree, or at least what he knew of her; but this garrulous person didn't seem to be the same Maree he remembered.

Green fields gave way to soot-grimed suburbs, grey and unwashed, as the train travelled through the outskirts of Manchester. Maree looked with curiosity at the houses, the rain-soaked people scurrying around in raincoats or carrying dark umbrellas. Was this still home?

She was confused. Already she missed the colourful blooms in her garden, the brightness the continual sun shed over everything.

They pulled up into the cavernous main station and everything was so ordered and quiet; such a contrast to Sealdah; only the newspaper vendors shouting headlines which echoed from the roofs as they left the station to walk to the bus stop. The chatter and bustle of Calcutta, the slow plodding of animals was replaced by the hissing of passing vehicles as the tyres threw up dirty splashes of puddle water.

Her sense of dislocation feeling ever more intense, she was grateful for the stolidity and firmness of her sister and her husband. Maree's eyes took on a vacant stare as if she were unable to take it all in. Her anticipation got the better of her and the unconscious tears leaking from her eyes were beginning to concern Flo.

"Come on, Maree," she said. "Let's get you home. Mother can't wait to see you."

Maree nodded assent and wiped her eyes with her woollen sleeve pulled up tight into her fist, a habit left over from childhood.

Her reunion with her mother was not as she had envisioned. The beautiful 'princess' coming home to lord it over her friends and family was not her intention. But as Maree walked down her street she saw the awe in her neighbours' eyes. They moved a little apart from her, stepping off the pavement to let her pass, whispering to each other as she walked on, her smiles unnoticed. One of her neighbour's daughters even bobbed a curtsy when she caught sight of Maree as Flo led her up the steps to their mother's house.

Mrs Crymble threw open the door. The tears glistened in her eyes as she beheld her daughter. She had expected Maree to be brown from the sun but her face remained pale. Her mother, disconcerted by the pain in her eyes, vowed to cosset her in her own abrupt manner until some joy was returned to her. She knew the pain caused by a child's early death. She felt the emptiness in her heart for her own dear baby Arthur, even after all these years. She narrowed her eyes. Was that the full extent of Maree's sadness? She was not sure. But she determined to support her and chivvy some confidences from her as she had not had the opportunity to do for so many years.

Agnes pushed up the sleeves of her cardigan, undid her pinny and wrapped her arms briefly around Maree before patting her arm and saying, "Well, the kettle's on; best we have a brew."

Maree had forgotten how the kettle was always on in her mother's kitchen, its comforting whistle alerting all to time for tea.

Bert, cigarette dangling from his lips, dragged Maree's cases up the front step and dropped them with a thud in the hallway.

"A brew, did you say, Mrs C? Phew, I need one after that!" He gestured towards the suitcases. "I suppose you'll be wanting me to carry them upstairs in a bit? I'll have my cuppa first."

"Thank you, Flo, and you too, Bert, for coming to meet me. I don't think I could've done the last bit without you."

Maree sank into a chair at the kitchen table, tracing the gouges and cuts in the wood with her finger. Her head felt like cotton wool. Drenched as she was in the warmth and fug of the kitchen she lay her head down on the familiar scratched surface. The chatter and murmur of voices did nothing but soothe her into a deep slumber. Flo shook her shoulder gently and leaned in to say goodbye when she and Bert made ready to leave. Maree smiled but did not open her eyes.

Night began to fall. Mrs Crymble bustled around preparing dinner; and still Maree slept.

"Come on my girl, you're exhausted. Let's get you upstairs and into bed. If you're awake later I'll bring you up some dinner."

The next few days passed in a sleep haze. As Maree had indeed imagined, there was Lancashire hotpot for dinner, and numerous strong brews brought up on a tray. She woke and tottered to the bathroom but otherwise slept a deep sleep. After a few days of bed rest she felt well enough to visit Ruby.

Ruby, like herself, was nearing forty and every year had scored a line in her face. Careworn was the first word that came to Maree. Ruby was delighted to see her and seemingly unconscious of how she might appear to Maree. She chattered away gaily, tending to baby number four, while swishing a toddler around her skirts, her older two at school.

"So many years since we last saw each other! How many is it? Ten? No, eleven maybe; but you were here and then you were gone. It was such a sad time for you. Tell me about your darling children; how are they? What are they doing while you're here? Who's looking after them?"

The questions kept coming and as best she could, Maree fielded them, exaggerating her life in India, her happiness and her friendships. She would never be disloyal to Frank. She would never voice her doubts about having travelled halfway around the world to marry him. She would never tell Ruby that in her secret dreams she wondered whether she could have become a princess here in Manchester, even in Chorlton, where she felt so at home. Her dissembling tired her and after only about half an hour, she told Ruby that she had to go; she was meeting Alice in Manchester.

# Forty-Five

*My dearest Frank*

*It's difficult to explain what it is like to be 'home'. To have my family around me, caring for me and chattering away. It's not the same in India. I know I have you to look after me and of course the servants make daily life so easy for me but I miss Ruby. I know I'm a silly goose and tomorrow I may feel different but I don't know how long I can go on living in India. Please understand.*

*I miss the children of course, but as they are at school I would only have seen them at the end of term. It was a real wrench when I saw Ruby's children as their little faces beamed at me upon return from the local school. They come home every day! Did you know they're at the same school Ruby and I went to? So long ago!*

*In the eleven years since you and I were here (I won't dwell on the sadness of that time) Chorlton has really grown. Mother's house, of course, stays the same, nothing in there has ever changed in my whole lifetime! I slept in my bed in Flo's and my bedroom and everything was still there, the small basket I made when I was about eleven was on my dressing table and the paper hearts Ruby and I had made one Valentine's Day were still stuck behind the door, edges curling, but Lord knows how they stay up there! Well, anyway, I was telling you about Chorlton; Nell and I took a walk around for old times' sake. We wandered along Chorlton Brook and then we found ourselves in Chorltonville. My, there are some nice homes there. Maybe when we come back we could live there? I can see your face as you read this. You're probably groaning too, I know, I know, your business is doing so well, how could you leave it?*

*I'll write again next week to tell you what I am doing. I think Flo and I are going to Blackpool. So cold at the moment but the fresh sea air should do me good.*
*Your loving wife,*
*Maree*


*My dearest Frank*

*You would not believe the fun Flo and I had at Blackpool. We thought we were young girls again! We walked everywhere and laughed ourselves silly. The wind was so strong it nearly blew us both away, the walk along the pier was quite dangerous, I thought. We saw the wind snatch an old gentleman's hat away and we watched it bob on the tide, under the pillars. He hobbled as fast as he could to the other side of the pier to see where it had gone and if he could rescue it but it had sunk never to be seen again, unless of course it washed up soggy and out of shape onto the pebbles or became a home for crabs at the bottom of the sea.*

*Do you know we walked the whole length of the promenade and back one day. Five and a half miles! I don't think I've ever walked so far in my life. I couldn't do it in Calcutta, I'd die of the heat. I think we kept walking so we didn't get cold. I did come here once when I was little but I don't remember it being so big and busy. We saw a few double decker buses turn up at the tower; I think it was workers from the Huntley factory. They spilled out with their cardboard suitcases and were very excited. Must have been their annual outing.*

*Flo's Bert arranged a nice boarding house for us on the front. Nothing too fancy, but clean and comfortable for our stay. The landlady said we should climb to the top of the tower but all those steps, I don't think I'm up to it. More than five hundred. I think we can take a lift.*

*The famous illuminations aren't on till September. Maybe we can go when you come over. I do hope you can get some time to come and we can travel back together.*
*Your loving Maree*

*My darling Frank*

*I had forgotten how much I love an English summer. Everything is so green, not dusty at all. Of course, there is a lot of rain, my new raincoat is certainly getting a workout. I'm feeling much better in myself but missing you a lot. I'm glad you were able to get up to Kurseong to see the children, although Max is hardly a child, he tells me he is a young man now. Almost thirteen and so grown up. I'm glad Patience is reading well. She is such a little monkey I wondered whether she would ever sit still enough to do any learning. Does she miss me? I won't ask whether Max does because he would say he didn't even if he did.*

*Mam and I are going up north to stay with Alice for a few days. She is not feeling too well so we said we'd go and cheer her up. Her daughter Helen is causing her concern I think. Sixteen and working at a doctor's office and thinking she knows everything. Thinking back, I was not much older when I first met you! I knew everything too!*

*I'm glad your cough is better, you did worry me, you know I always think the worst and that it's tuberculosis. I don't suppose I'll ever change that, you know. Poor Ernest. I went to his grave the other day, I hadn't had the heart or the courage up until now. Nell said she'd come with me but I braved it myself. It was so strange to stand in front and read the writing which we had asked to be put on the headstone. I felt quite hollowed out and I cried for a good long time. I found some pink roses, you know, like the ones Vishnu put on Nataline's grave, and placed them in the vase there. I spoke to Ernest, you know, I told him that I knew I should never have left him. Of course he didn't answer, but I did feel at peace to have finally told him.*

*It must be so hot now in Calcutta. I'm sure poor Dorothy must be fainting away. Is she going to go up to Darjeeling? Did you offer her the Wayside house? That, I do miss.*

*How is Basu going? When do his articles of clerkship finish? Is it next year? He seems to have been with you so long, it must be soon? Would you be able to leave the business in his capable hands?*

*I do look forward to seeing you again. I miss you as much as I love it here!*
*Yours,*
*Maree*

# Forty-Six

*My darling*

    *I was so disappointed to hear that you're not going to be able to come to England this year. Somehow I supposed you would not want to live without me any more and that you and the children would come sailing into the sunset to see me. Ah, well, dreams. What happens now? I suppose it's up to me. It feels so familiar being here, going to Boggart Hole, the trees have grown so much since we first walked in there, walking by the Mersey, picnicking on its banks. Do you remember that time we took some of Mam's sandwiches and you spread out your scarf for me to sit on? How chivalrous, I thought, and then, then you kissed me for the first time. It felt quite scandalous, sitting there where anyone could have seen us. We were so in love. That lady pushing the pram along the path, pretending we weren't even there. She couldn't bring herself to say good afternoon. A bit like Sadie. Such a good friend on the ship but once we were in India I could no longer be one of her social circle. It's alienating, isn't it? I've broached this subject before but I do worry about the children. We have each other. What if they never have a future in India? I've seen how they treat Anglo-Indians; yes, they love to employ them, such hard workers, they say, but always last in line for promotion. What would happen to Max? And Patience? She would have to marry another Anglo-Indian, no choice, not like I had…*

    *How are things in Calcutta at the moment? You didn't mention. Before I came over to England you said you were concerned about the unrest in India, the rise of Nationalism, the civil disturbances happening everywhere. You said*

*Gandhi was a man of peace, a religious man but he couldn't control everyone and those salt marches, I know, I know, a few years ago now, but all those people marching, marching. Yes, they said they were peaceful, but the British, yes, my people, they didn't think so and beat them and imprisoned them. What if, as he gets older, Max gets caught up in all this? You've said not to bother myself with the politics, it will all work out. But in these days, I do think. I have had months to think about life and our life and all that it means. I know I'm not a very clever person. I know I worry about a lot of things.*

*So here I am in Chorlton and there you are in Calcutta. What are we going to do? The summer has been glorious and as August is now here everyone is taking off to the seaside. I'm going with Maud and George to North Wales, it's quite the thing to do these days. I know you don't know George very much but he is a funny man. He is always telling jokes and making us laugh. I am so looking forward to going. Doris, you remember me saying, the third daughter, is coming with us. She is a lovely young lady, so polite and quite beautiful. If Patience turns out like her I will be very happy!*

*My thoughts and my love are with you.*
*Your ever-loving wife,*
*Maree*


*Darling*
*I just wanted to let you know that I received your telegram with the ship details for me. Such a good idea for it to land in Bombay. I know how much you cherish the opportunity to spend time with your sister. So, you'll stay with Jasleen for about a week before I get there, is that right? It's a long train journey for you but of course you'll have me with you on the way back. Just a few weeks left with Mam and the sisters, then. At least when I arrive towards the end of October it should be cooler. You say that the children are very anxious about me and wonder if I am ever coming back. They must wonder if they still have a mother. I'd forgotten how hurt I was when Patience didn't recognise me when I first picked her up from school; you remember.*

*I agree; we must or rather you must set up a strong business, one which will survive on its own and that we can return to if we wish or – as your fervent hope – one that Max can take over in due course. If he is his own man, then he*

*will not be slighted or pushed out. You talk about leaving him a legacy. What
a wonderful idea.*

*I am so happy that we will be working towards returning here soon.
Meanwhile I will enjoy the last few weeks of my time here and look forward to
cupping my hands around your lovely face and planting kisses everywhere I can.
In haste,*
*Maree*

# Forty-Seven

Even after all these years, Maree felt uncomfortable in the presence of Jasleen. It was obvious to her, if not to Frank, that Jasleen thought that Frank could have married better. She thought he had the opportunity as such a prized scholar to have had his pick of the unmarried ladies in Manchester. What was so special about her? It was written all over Jasleen's face. Her viewpoint had softened somewhat with the births of the children whom she smothered with gifts whenever she came to Calcutta to visit, which wasn't often. It was expensive for her to bring her servants and her cook, but she would not travel without them. She could not trust Maree's servants to dress her as she liked and certainly did not trust the cook to prepare dishes to her high Brahmin standards. She had chastised Frank for letting his standards slip, for not adhering to the strict religious regime. He had laughed and said that he was very happy with their food; he was happy with the amalgamation of recipes, of cooking styles; a bit like their marriage, he added.

Maree was glad that her stay would only be for a few days. She too, now actually in India, was so desirous of seeing the children that she felt she would burst if it was further delayed. She had bid a tearful farewell to her sisters who stood lined up on the platform, oldest to youngest, this time – uncanny how they formed themselves this way – and her mother who stood to the side, stoic, awaiting her few minutes with her youngest daughter. How hard it had been bringing up five girls; but with one residing so far away she felt the strength of their number, the comfort one provided when another was caught up in her own family dramas. Agnes was feeling her age, seventy-four now, and although she had never allowed any illnesses, her pace had slowed, her ankles becoming thicker and stiff; she noticed that she was becoming forgetful and worst of all, it seemed imperative to her body that she have an afternoon lie-down.

Agnes had spoken often to her youngest in the last few months about the possibility of her returning to Manchester, to be there to help in her old age and – if she were honest    with herself – to hope that she and Frank might contribute to her financial assistance. Nell and John had been good to her in the past but the shop was struggling, the depression in Manchester still having effects on the buying power of the locals. They had changed their lines; they now stocked more practical items after enjoying some years of fanciful purchasing by their clients; but turnover was the lowest they had ever experienced. They had been unable now to help her with her rent for some months and she knew she would have to ask Alice, whose husband Percy was a Yorkshireman through and through. Never put his hand in his pocket if he could help it and kept Alice on a very tight rein in her spending. He doled out her allowance, counting it out into her purse weekly. That and no more. She must learn to live within her means. He meanwhile thought nothing of spending the same amount in their local, tossing back pint after pint until he came home slurring and mean. Alice knew the signs and kept quiet. Once she had made the mistake of commenting about his intoxicated condition and earned a black eye which prevented her weekly visit to her mother. She could not let her see that. Alice, being the firstborn, wanted to set an example to her sisters; she did not wish to be pitied. It was no wonder that her daughter, Helen, was yearning to be out of the house. She knew her father's moods and had at the earliest opportunity left school and found work at the new doctor's surgery. Doctor Reed was married with two young children, but he soon made it clear to Helen that he would prefer to spend time with her. Being a doctor on call gave him a good excuse to be out of the house at the weekends. The dalliance soon became a full-blown scandal with Percy throwing her, aged seventeen, out of the house. Doctor Reed and Helen set up home together. Her mother would see her weekly without telling Percy, as his anger at his daughter making them the laughing stock of the town would have been shelled out to her. He refused to speak again to his only daughter. A decision which haunted him, since when Alice died an early death, he was on his own, a miserable drunkard.

Agnes looked into her daughter's eyes, holding her by her elbows, gripped her tightly and lightly shook her. Maree's eyes glinted behind the glasses which she now wore; she bit her lip and attempted a smile. Agnes had seen a lightening in her daughter but there were still dark shadows behind the grey of her eyes. Time, she knew, would never heal the loss. She did not know what else to say to comfort her. She said the first thing that came to mind: "Come back soon," and the threatened tears spilled down Maree's cheeks.

"Oh, Mam, now you've gone and upset her," Nell admonished. "Let's get you on the train, Maree, before it decides to go without you."

They had just managed to get her settled in her seat when the whistle blew and they all pushed and shoved out of the carriage, blowing her kisses as they left.

Agnes stood waving as the train pulled out; would she see Maree again? She found it hard to imagine the journey – she, who in all her life had only travelled as far as Blackpool. She dropped her hand and stood staring at the rear carriage as it grew ever smaller and then disappeared, swallowed between factories and slum houses. Alice and Flo each took an arm and kept her close as if their presence would make up for the absence of Maree.

"Don't worry, Mam, she'll be back soon. It'll be two shakes of a lamb's tail, in a flash even! She'll be back in Manchester with her children and Frank too, if I'm not mistaken."

Maree leant out of the window, waving madly at her mother, hoping it would not be the last time she saw her. She had aged so much in the last eleven years. She had gone from being an efficient, brusque person into a rather slower-moving one; one who considered every word as if dragging it up from the muddle of her mind instead of the sharp comments that used to spring so readily from her lips.

Her sisters, her lovely sisters: she chewed the inside of her mouth as she wondered how, as she too had grown older, she would manage without them around her. It had taken this visit for her to recognise how the loss of her mother's small baby boy had mirrored her own. The bond they felt now was immeasurable. She caught back a sob before it embarrassed her, the train carriage being full. She wiped her eyes under her glasses with her forefinger, looking away from any prying eyes.

In Frank's presence Maree threw off the preoccupied air surrounding her which she had gained on the outward journey. For his sake, she threw her arms around him. She showered him with kisses. She linked her arm in his, whenever she could bear the heat. The heat! How it drained her, how it sapped her energy. Even in these cooler days a fire rose in her, expanded in her chest, followed up her neck and exploded in her face, sweat trickling down the back of her neck, under her hair and into her eyes. She was constantly dabbing her face. How did Frank not feel it? How was Jasleen so cool and calm? The more clothes she took off the worse she seemed to feel. Her skin glowed constantly and the effort of moving around made it worse.

She looked forward to the train journey up to Delhi and then changing trains to Calcutta, where once again she could sit quietly, fanning herself, no movement, no thought, just with the end result of seeing her children. She worried whether she would be able to make the journey up into the hills after this. Perhaps the driver would have to be dispatched to fetch them from school and bring them down to Calcutta. No, she thought, she did not wish to stay there any longer than needed. She would catch her breath, acclimatise. She would be happy to see Dorothy but then they would need to go. Every day they spent with Jasleen was one more day before she could hold those sweet children in her arms.

Jasleen had taken to walking around her garden as the sun was setting, its golden rays having lost their daytime strength, with Frank on her arm, chatting to him, expressing her concerns about Maree.

"I know you think I don't like Maree, but I do. Over the years I've realised that you love her dearly and she is the mother of your beautiful children, so I too must love her. For your sake, Frank."

Frank squeezed her hand. She had long ago abandoned the notion of telling him she was his mother. Sometimes she forgot that fact herself. It was such a long time ago. She would always care for him deeply as a mother whether he knew the truth or not; she knew that.

"I am worried about her, Frank," she continued. "She is different this time. You must be careful; her mind is elsewhere, in England I am presuming. I think, as much as it pains me, that you must be considering going back there or she might fade away completely."

Frank confided that he too had consulted her doctor before she left and he had said that she must go, she was in a depressed state and it would do her no good to remain in that condition. Frank sighed; his hopes of expanding his company must wait. He said he was working on how he could leave it, generating income for him if they returned to England.

V

# Forty-Eight

## *1935 Voyage to London*

Patience ran from one side of the ship to the other. The excitement was immense. She had never been to England. What was it like? Would she like her grandmother? Her aunties? Whole families she had never even known existed! Max, at thirteen years old, was sulking. The niche he had created for himself at school was being snatched from him. He didn't relish the difficulty of fitting into another school, in another country. Patience's ebullience annoyed him. What did she know about life in England? He, of course, didn't remember his first visit as a baby but he told himself that he knew all about England. He had read about it and heard about it and what he knew he did not like. It was far too wet and cold, for one thing. English boys at his school had told him about the hazing, about dunking heads in toilets, about the bullying and the caning. Not to say that he didn't have experience of some of that at Victoria but that was his own school, his known milieu.

Frank could not stop smiling. It was all worth it. The Maree he knew from so long ago had returned. She was almost gay. Chattering and laughing, her mood was infectious. She was relaxed and her anxiety lessened. Over the last year he had acquired the East India Railway as a client and their steady stream of work was more than enough to enable him to purchase passage in first class on the British India ship the *Domala*. Their first class cabin was spacious with two sleeping cabins and a sitting room with a work desk for Frank. Patience explored every nook and cranny, marvelling at how the furniture was attached, how she could climb up and look out of the porthole. She, at eight years old, was looked after by the ship. The children were shepherded to activities and to the restaurant for special meal times. Patience did not mind being separated from her parents during the day; she had friends to play with. Flossie, who took great glee in telling her she was nine years old and as such Patience must do what she told her to, became her shipmate. Flossie's golden curls and Patience's dark ones were constantly seen almost entwined, as they crouched on deck immersed in some game or the other. Patience and Flossie did, however, take time to look at the unknown desert, the vast expanse of it as they passed through the Suez Canal. They pointed and giggled at camels, made up adventure stories about travelling through the desert wrapped in sheets against the sand, finding golden treasures buried by the oases and taking them back to England to buy a big house and live together forever.

"I will always be your best friend. Hold my little finger and we will wish it so," Flossie said. Patience was delighted to have a forever best friend. She looked up to Flossie with adoration; but when they docked in London and Flossie strode from the ship with her parents and nary a backward glance, Patience was heartbroken. Maree put her arm around her and kissed the top of her head.

"Never mind, my darling. I am sure you'll find another best friend soon."

Frank and Max walked behind them; for a moment Frank looked around searching for a bearer to carry their luggage but it had been brought onto the dock for them by the ship's staff and they were able to find a porter to put it into the boot of the taxi they were taking to the hotel they were staying at before taking the train to Manchester.

"We're staying in a hotel in London?" Patience's incredulity grew as they pulled up outside the Victoria Hotel near to Euston station. She had never stayed in a hotel and Frank had booked a suite of rooms for them. The young man in a brown uniform at the front desk sniffed as he took Frank's money. Frank had changed rupees for pounds before they left Calcutta but was surprised at how much less he could buy for his pound than the last time they were here. He was unsure whether Mr Robinson, for that was on a name plate on the desk, was suffering from a cold or whether he disapproved of the family. Maree smiled at him but it was not reciprocated. He handed over the key to the luggage porter who placed their suitcases on the trolley. Maree glanced at the cases, shabby and old, and thought that perhaps they should have purchased some new ones before they sailed home. She hoped that all the precious items they had had packed into tea chests would arrive safely in a few weeks.

Patience wanted to run up the stairs but her mother called her back to go in the lift together to the fourth floor. As the creaking lift gates closed upon the family, Maree distinctly heard Mr Robinson say to the porter, "Can you smell curry? I can. Shouldn't be allowed in here!"

Maree set her mouth, clutched her handbag in front of her and decided to let the comment float around unheard, as Frank was busy chastising Patience who insisted upon pressing every button in the lift. He managed to catch hold of her wrist just as she was about to press the alarm button.

"Patience, I know you're excited but please, just leave the buttons alone." Patience's fingers itched but, pouting, she clasped her hands behind her back before leaning over and pulling up her white socks which after the journey she thought needed a good wash by her *ayah*. Suddenly the sheer immensity of the change caused her to gasp and tears began to form in her eyes as she realised she had left her *ayah* behind. Max stood leaning against the back of the lift, arms crossed, one leg over the other, feigning total indifference to his family's emotions. He yawned as his mother turned to look to see if he too had heard the comment made by the man at the desk; but he was too busy playing the sophisticated teenager, in a grey suit slightly too large for his thin frame.

The metal grill doors shut with a clang and Maree thought back to the lift at Temple Chambers, how it had hardly ever worked and if it did, made a grinding sound as if it would soon drop with a metallic clang to the ground floor. As they rose, she cast a glance at Frank who with shoulders pulled back was staring as the floors passed by. She remembered running downstairs with Patience one day in Calcutta when a severe earth tremor hit and she was convinced they would land in a pile of rubble. One of the towers of the law courts had wobbled so much that it fell with an almighty crash as they made their way out of the building in a crush of workers and clerks, narrowly escaping being hit by flying bricks. Her heart had been beating so fast she thought it was the sign of more tremors and she ran so quickly that the small Patience seemed to be skimming the pavement, to the *maidan* where they stood, quivering, until Frank found them an hour later.

Now, in the Victoria Hotel, the floors passed them by as they stood together as if in a family photo, each a captive of their own thoughts. Maree chewed her lip until she tasted that metallic tang. Frank stood up straight, shoulders back, one hand on Patience's shoulder. Patience's eyes sparkled with unshed tears. Max's stomach was knotted and he felt sick but he would never admit to any sense of fear. His anger at being removed from his school in the hills had not diminished and he wondered how he could persuade his parents to send him back. Maybe he could behave really badly at his new school, even be expelled. That might work.

Just as they opened the lift gates, the bellboy (a misnomer for one so old and bowed) arrived with their luggage, having come up in the service lift. He sniffed and stood to one side as Frank opened the suite door. He dumped the bags unceremoniously inside the hallway and turned on his heel without stopping to hold out his hand for a tip.

"He was in a hurry," said Frank. "I was just going to search around for some change for him."

Maree's eagle eye had spotted the old man's disdain but felt that it were better for Frank not to notice that perhaps this hotel was not the right one for them. Best they stayed in their suite until their train the following morning. She didn't feel she could stand for any more slights, intentional or otherwise. She took out a hatpin, dropped her hat onto the hallway stand and floated to the first bedroom, where she fell upon the bed, her shoes dangling over the edge as the children began squabbling about which bed they should sleep in: one bed close to the window or the other close to the small desk. Frank picked up the *Daily Telegraph* newspaper left on the hall table, sat down on the sofa and before reading more than a paragraph about the preparations for George V's Silver Jubilee celebrations his head nodded and the squabbles faded away.

Patience ran out of the room to complain to either of her parents but on finding them both asleep she returned to her room, finger on lips, whereupon both she and Max jumped onto their beds, deciding in this way which one was which; and they opened their books to read. Such model children, Max thought; this wasn't a good beginning to his plan for being returned to his beloved school.

# Forty-Nine

However much Maree had hoped for a smooth transition into English life, it was not to be so. The first few weeks back in Chorlton were not easy. Having decided to stay at her mother's house, the crowded conditions soon proved too much for a family used to a spacious apartment and servants to wait on them hand and foot. Agnes was so slow now and the very effort of pushing herself out of her armchair to pour herself a cuppa tired her for several hours. Maree, unused to cooking, cleaning and looking after her family by herself, quickly became disgruntled. Frank was out most of the days looking for work opportunities to bolster their limited income sent over every month from India. Each day she turned her face eagerly as he opened the front door, a blast of cold wind rushing down the hall, his headshake telling all. He was reconnecting with earlier colleagues and reestablishing acquaintances from both his university days and his working life. He followed leads with no success.

Sadly, Arthur Piggott had died the year before. Frank went by himself to see Arthur's wife Frida, now a frail, shrunken version of herself.

"Frank, it is so wonderful to see you again. I never thought I would. I'm so sorry Arthur didn't live to see this day. You, such a prosperous gentleman, with a wife and children! I must say…"

Frida, who had never had much opportunity to talk when her husband was alive, kept talking as Frank sat and nodded, occasionally managing to interject a few words as he heard about Halvor, now managing the company as Arthur had hoped; about Halvor's wife and family; and then – Frida continued almost without drawing breath – about Hettie and Gertie.

"Hettie was so sweet on you, you know. She was heartbroken when you sailed off to India. I think she thought you would come back to her, but I knew your heart was elsewhere. Friends don't always become lovers, do they?"

Frank blushed, smoothed his hair, took off his glasses and polished them on his handkerchief as he recalled the last conversation he had had with Hettie. He did not think he had led her to believe they would ever be more than friends but obviously his heartfelt invitation to her to come out and visit India had been misinterpreted.

He cleared his throat as he thought of Hettie's last letter, to which he had not responded. He had guessed at her feelings and thought that if he replied she might think that they were reciprocated.

"I'm sorry, Mrs Piggott. I am glad that Hettie is happy and yes, you're right, friends are sometimes just that, friends."

The awkwardness Frank felt dissipated as Mrs Piggott continued describing Gertie and the work she was now doing with the poor people in Manchester. He had a little smile to himself as he thought of how now she would be so familiar with 'Oriental gentlemen'!

He endeavoured to take his leave of Frida with the promise of visiting again with all the family, but Mrs Piggott would not let him go without making a telephone call to Halvor. She teetered out to the hallway, leaning on a wooden cane with an exquisite carved ivory handle, refusing Frank's assistance as he hovered attempting to place his hand under her elbow. She shook him off and dialled.

"You will never guess who is here, Halvor; and no, you cannot be too busy. I'm sending him over right now." Frank could not hear the words of the reply but he made out Halvor's gruff tones coming from the receiver.

"What, you have a meeting in an hour? Well, put it off; you will be pleased, I know you will. Yes, dear, I will tell him."

She turned to him with a triumphant smile, rocking slightly on her tottering legs; she put out a hand to steady herself as she said, "He is expecting you. Well, not *you*, as he still doesn't know who I am sending! But he's expecting someone to visit at eleven-thirty so you had better hurry along if you don't want to miss him."

As Frank made his way by tram to the office, his stomach churned. He reminisced about the first visit to see Arthur at the Piggott and Co. office. How callow he had been, how fresh, how optimistic about work, life and all that it entailed. He still thought of himself as an optimistic person but losing a child and sometimes a wife to the depths of depression had made him realise that life was not always what you wanted it to be. Would he like to be offered a position back at Piggott and Co? Would it be an immense step backwards? How could he, a chartered accountant who had run his own successful business dealing with the Bengal government, possibly fit into a small suburban accounting firm here in Manchester? He didn't think that life for Indians had changed that much. Even his extensive qualifications and experience did not guarantee acceptance.

The incredulous face of Sam as he entered the office sent a warm trickle of friendship down his back. The incredulity soon turned to effusive welcome as he shook Frank's hand with great gusto.

"I can't believe it!" he finally managed to get out. "I didn't know you were back. Are you here on a visit? For good? How are your family? Where are you staying?" Frank chuckled to see that Sam had now adopted the questioning monologue that Arthur was so famous for.

He glanced around to see Halvor standing at his desk in what had been his father's office, talking on the phone. He would have recognised his blond looks anywhere but the face showed signs of age as, he supposed ruefully, must his own. Other clerks nodded to him politely.

Halvor's eyebrows raised as he spotted Frank and he gesticulated to the phone and made faces and gestures to show that he would wind up the call as soon as possible.

Frank was happy to stand chatting to Sam, who told him he was now a partner but that the business was not the same since old Mr Piggott died. It was obvious he didn't want to say too much but he intimated that the business was struggling. No positions vacant, then, thought Frank, who found himself relieved at this.

Frank and Halvor had a cordial conversation, Halvor aware of how high a regard his father had held Frank in but a little aloof as he boasted to him how well the business was doing – while making it very clear that there would be no position here, if that's what Frank was here for.

"Oh, no, Halvor. I am certainly looking to reacquaint myself with my Manchester cohort but my company in Calcutta is doing very well without me and I do hope to return to it in the fullness of time. I'm happy to hear of any opportunities, though, perhaps something I can do part-time. I don't relish sitting around every day while my wife decides where we are going to live."

"I'll certainly let you know if I hear of anything."

Halvor stood. The meeting was over. Frank had the distinct impression that Halvor would never contact him and, as always, was only being polite in memory of his father.

He remembered the first time he had been introduced to Halvor. He had returned to the Piggott house with Hettie after one of their 'walks and talks' as they called them, all the while jousting with each other about the part played by England in India.

Halvor was in the drawing room, his voice raised in conversation with his father. Frank mouthed that he should go but Hettie pulled him by the hand and strode into the room.

"Stop, you two. Halvor, it is good to see you again." She gave him a kiss on his cheek and turned to bring Frank forward, introducing him as the new *wunderkind* at the office. Halvor's frosty look did not endear him to Frank; and although he grasped his outstretched hand politely enough, he soon switched his gaze to his father and then left the room, saying he would continue the conversation later. His footsteps echoed down the stairwell.

Hettie had put an arm around her father's waist.

"Don't worry, Papa, he is always like that when he comes home from university. High and mighty, thinks he knows it all. One day he'll find out that he doesn't." Her father stroked his forehead wearily and sighed.

"I know, I know, but what if he's always like this? How will I be able to work with him in the office? It'll be like two bears constantly standing on their hind legs growling at each other, neither willing to step down."

He sank into the chair behind him. Frank opened his mouth to sympathise but Hettie shook her head.

"Come, Frank, let's go and see mother and get a cup of tea. I think Father needs a little peace and quiet."

It seemed such a long time ago and Frank felt he was another person entirely. But it did nothing to subdue his memory and quell his sense of unease when Halvor did not even raise his eyes as Frank opened the door and left.

Sam's beaming face greeted him as he shut the door behind him, resisting the urge to slam it. He faced Sam, his eyebrows raised.

"Didn't go so well?" Sam enquired.

Frank shook his head and shrugged. "You know what he's like. As well as could be expected. His mother has always expected us to be friends but it never was and never will be."

Sam reached out and touched Frank on the arm.

"Well," he said, "I'll keep in touch and if I hear anything at all about possible work, I'll let you know. Must keep your wife happy."

# Fifty

It was nearly a month later when the phone rang at Brooklands, the new home that Frank had found in Sale. Maree had cajoled him into negotiating to buy it, which had used up most of the money he had been able to bring out of India; so he felt more and more acutely the need for a cash flow from within the United Kingdom.

It was Sam.

"Hello, Frank. How are you? Have you found any work yet? I was talking to Matthew Brown at Beck, Vogel and Wynett and he happened to mention that the accountant who was dealing with the Stoke Potteries account has had a heart attack and they are unsure as to whether he will be able to continue. Do you remember Stoke Potteries, Frank? Difficult clients by all accounts."

"I don't think I knew much about them, Sam," Frank replied.

"It's just a possibility, but may be worth following up," said Sam.

Frank took down the phone number and address of the accountancy firm and said that he would call them on Monday.

He turned to Maree, who was busy arranging lilies in a vase on the hall table. She took a stem between her fingers and raised the flower to her nose, her eyebrows raised.

"That was Sam. Could be useful; I'm not sure. He said there's a possibility of work with Beck, Vogel and Wynett. I don't know whether they will hire me but I will give them Halvor as a reference,

I'm sure he will sing my praises. Anything to avoid giving me any work at Piggott's!"

"Mmm, that sounds promising, Frank," Maree said, but gave him little more encouragement. Instead, she said, "What do you think we should do with Patience? She isn't liking the local school."

Frank didn't answer; he was working out his approach to Beck, Vogel and Wynett.

Early on Monday morning Frank put in a call to the firm. He knew it was a busy time and possibly disadvantageous to him but he was keen and wanted to be first in, if there were such a thing.

He introduced himself and explained that he wished to speak to Walter Beck. The prim voice of the secretary advised him that he would need to call back later in the day when Mr Beck might be able to spend a few minutes on the phone to him. He tried to make an appointment but Miss Blenkinsop, for that was her name, informed him he would need to speak to Mr Beck directly in the afternoon.

Frank came off the phone and immediately set an alarm on the old wind-up clock on the hall table. He was nothing if not determined.

It was not difficult, as it happened, to gain an appointment for Wednesday afternoon. Frank spent the next few days finding out as much as he could about the clients, Stoke Potteries. He could not divulge that he knew about this hard-to-please company and what they might need in an accountant, but he should be able to inveigle some of the information he had gleaned into his interview to persuade Walter Beck that he would be the man for the job.

It did not go to plan. Walter Beck was an arrogant man who believed in colonial superiority. He greeted Frank with, "And what do you want?"

When Frank explained he retorted, "No. We have no work and no availability. I bid you good day."

Although Frank could have disputed the veracity of his words he thought better of it. He had a solution, one he had thought of before but had judged that going to the accountancy firm first might make it more legitimate. Upon arriving home, he stretched the phone cord into the front room and shut the door so that Maree might not overhear his conversation. He felt it was the right thing to do but Maree might not.

His hunch about having a direct conversation with Stoke Potteries turned out to be correct; and within a few minutes he had ascertained that they were in fact looking to change their accountant and were indeed no longer happy with Beck, Vogel and Wynett. Frank's proposal that he work solely for them impressed them and they arranged a meeting for the following week.

Frank was not a vengeful person but he rubbed his hands together and smiled to himself when he realised that he had the better of Walter Beck. His footsteps tapped down the corridor as he went in search of Maree to tell her the good news.

After a successful meeting with Stoke Potteries, Frank became their official accountant. He negotiated a contract which would allow him to go to Stoke-on-Trent for several days a week.

"Did you know, Maree, I've found some information on how Josiah Wedgwood used to arrange his accounting? It's very interesting; perhaps I could adopt it."

"That's all very well," replied Maree, "but have you given any thought to what we are to do with Patience? She is coming home crying nearly every day. Or haven't you noticed?"

"What, dear? Patience, you say? What's the matter with her?"

Maree sighed. "I told you how unhappy she was. You just don't listen. The other children are calling her 'wog' and refusing to play with her, telling her she doesn't belong here, to go home."

"But she's English too; how can they be so unkind? Our beautiful Patience. Maybe we should look at another school."

"That's what I've been trying to tell you but you've been so wrapped up in finding work you haven't done anything about it."

Frank bit his lip. Maree was so used to him organising everything that it would never enter her head that she herself could look at a solution or make some enquiries into possible schools for Patience.

"I'll look right into it, Maree. We cannot have our lovely Pet being unhappy. I shall call the school right away and talk to them about this. It doesn't sound right, It's not right, no, certainly not right."

The headmaster at Brooklands Primary School was glad to be rid of what he thought of as a troublesome little Indian girl and was keen to give Frank a recommendation for Oaklands Preparatory School.

"I think Oaklands will be far more suitable for your daughter, Mr Tarmaster. They cater for the more unusual children, certainly. I can't be held responsible for how my pupils think of her. After all, she and you are foreigners, you know."

Again, Frank bit his lip as, unsmiling, he left the headmaster's office.

"Maree, I've sorted it all out. It's because she is such a special girl that they cannot cope there and Mr Snide's given me a recommendation for Oaklands Preparatory School. It will be expensive, I think, but nothing's too good for our Patience. I'm just glad Max is happy at his school, contrary to all expectations!"

Maree breathed a sigh of relief. She sat on the sofa, closed her eyes and placed her fingers on her forehead.

"Please bring me a cup of tea, Frank. I feel quite lightheaded with all the worry."

Between arranging Patience's schooling and the commencement of his new job, Frank was quite run off his feet for the next few weeks and it was only when an acquaintance brought to his attention the problems in India that he stopped to consider what possible independence might do to his firm in Calcutta. He rushed off a letter to his trusted clerk Basu to whom he had entrusted the ongoing care-taking of Tarmaster and Co. He wanted to find out if he had any hope of maintaining ownership of the company as a foreign resident if independence came. He asked if Max would be able to come and take over in a few years. He thought about returning to Calcutta, to ride out any transition period, but realised he could not leave Maree in Manchester if they had no income and two children to send to school. He could not imagine her running a household on her own and knew that her mother Agnes was too old to help and all her sisters had their own lives and families to look after.

He frowned over a news report in the *Manchester Guardian* which raised the spectre of war again in Europe in the not too distant future. Times were indeed difficult and he felt grateful for the signed contract with Stoke Potteries. Heaven knows, though, what they would be required to manufacture if war indeed broke out. It was all too much to bear thinking about and Frank turned to immersing himself in his *Bhagavad Gita* every night in the hope of finding answers. Maree began another slide into depression while Frank looked on in despair.

# Fifty-One

The possibility of relocating to a holiday home that Frank had found in Rhyl bucked Maree up to the point that she named the house Dilkush, an Indian pastry she had been particularly fond of in Calcutta. It was her sweet place, a place of comfort, a small manageable home within easy reach of the beach and the fresh sea-air walks she so enjoyed.

"I feel so alive when I'm near the sea," she said to Frank.

Frank enjoyed his life between Manchester and Stoke. The move to Rhyl didn't fit in with his plans but he went along with it for Maree's sake; he couldn't bear the thought of her falling into another deep depression. He would make any sacrifice to see her happy again.

Besides, the threat of the war approaching their bit of England came closer and closer. He had tried to preempt this by building an air raid shelter in the house at Brooklands. Patience was furious as it meant digging up the fishpond which she considered to be hers. Maree consoled her: "It will be like a Wendy house, Patience, just you wait and see. We will have beds and blankets and even a small kitchen to cook in. It will be fun!" Patience pulled a face. She was not convinced that this would make up for losing her fishpond.

Maree's moving campaign continued and when bombs shook the shelter and dislodged all the plates and bowls Maree begged Frank to agree to the relocation. Patience added her persuasive powers, as with the pond gone, she would be happy to move to be near the sea.

He was worried for his children. Max, having just started attending university in Manchester, decided to continue living in the house in Brooklands. Despite Frank's reservations Max assured him he would be careful. He would be able to continue studying and he could do his bit by helping as an air raid warden. It was, however, a good move for Patience. Now attending Rhyl Grammar School, she seemed to be making friends and enjoying her extended holiday, as she put it.

Maree began to relax. She thought she might even invite Flo to come and stay. That would be a treat for her. Flo had told her during their last conversation that Bert expected everything to be done for him when he got home and his idea of a good weekend was for her to wait on him hand and foot. She was tired, she said. Philip, their son, grown up, was now thinking of joining the Air Force, doing his bit for the war effort. The thought of that gangly, spotty youth she had last seen, sullen and uncommunicative, entering the armed forces, seemed unfathomable.

Maree thought about Frank and how he had always provided for her. How he had arranged their life. How he had taken all worries out of her hands and how he still cherished her. She hugged her arms around herself. She was lucky. She really did have the life of a princess. Why did she ever feel depressed? It was really beyond her. Life was good. She shook her head and took out her fountain pen to write to Flo.

As Flo put down her overnight bag, Maree felt a shimmering dark shadow drop from her shoulders and flee out of the door. She smiled and hugged her sister tightly.

"It's so good to see you, Flo. Come in, come in; I'll get us a cup of tea and you can help me unpack some of this hideous pottery Frank keeps bringing back from Stoke."

As they unpacked the box in the lounge, in front of a very welcome fire, they took turns in grimacing at the Toby jugs as they appeared out of the wrapping paper. Maree sat back on her heels and laughed as Flo's expression mirrored a particularly ugly one.

"He's so proud of these," Maree said. "I haven't the heart to tell him I don't like them. The pottery gives him discounted seconds, I think, and you know Frank: doesn't like to miss out on what he thinks is a bargain!"

"Ooh, what's this one?" At the bottom of the box Maree unwrapped a tall china figurine of a lady wearing a rust-coloured dress with a white ruffled petticoat on show and clutching her bonnet as if on a windy day, her scarf fleeing her arm.

"My," said Maree, "her hat reminds me of something I would've made, oh so long ago. She, now, is beautiful. I will put her in pride of place. Perhaps Frank will bring me more like this if I praise it highly and put it right here on the mantelpiece!"

Maree tucked Flo's arm under her right elbow and clasped her cold hand.

"Why aren't you wearing gloves, Flo? It's right parky out."

Flo shrugged and pushed her other hand into her coat pocket. She did not have the courage yet to tell Maree how difficult things were at home. Bert always liked to pretend they were doing so well but she was given little for the housekeeping, and new suits for Bert came before warm gloves for her. The wartime shortages made it even harder for her to save any money for things she needed.

"Look," Flo cried out, "they still have entertainment on the pier; let's go! It reminds me of when you came back from India that time. Remember? We went to Blackpool."

Of course Maree remembered. It had been a dark time for her. The stay in England with her family had slowly brought her out of the shadows and she had revelled in the time she had had with her sisters.

"Tell me more about India, Maree," Flo said. "It's so grey and cold here. Tell me about the heat and the colours."

Maree sighed. It certainly was a different world. She closed her eyes and conjured up the oppressiveness of the heat. She felt a rush of warmth rise from her toes to her hairline and she took off her blue felt hat to fan herself.

She laughed. "Can you believe it? I really felt the heat, then. It's just like that, you have to fan yourself all the time and of course in the monsoon season, although the temperature is a little lower, the humidity is worse and you feel like you're swimming through water. No, nothing like the sea spray we're feeling right now!"

They both squealed as they rushed out of the way of the next wave approaching the breakwall.

Maree kept talking. She told Flo about her social life. How she and Frank had been shunned. She told her how she found Nataline, how she was in a similar situation, how she felt like a sister, and how sad it had been when she died and how she felt as though she had no one to talk to. Flo said that she felt like that all of the time and there was a deep sadness in her pale blue eyes. Maree's glance flicked up and she grasped Flo's hand again, rubbed it and held it lightly against her cheek.

"I've never thought to ask, have I? I'm always too wrapped up in myself and Frank to even consider what life has been like for you with Bert. I always thought that he was such a kind man when we were young. I never realised he could be mean to you. I thought how generous he was to arrange that bed and breakfast place for us in Blackpool."

Flo snorted. "He never gave me any housekeeping money for two weeks after that! He said I should never have gone. He's like that. Loving and generous one minute and cutting and mean the next. I never know where I stand, really."

Maree turned her gaze to Flo. Had she ever tried to find out anything about her sisters' lives? Flo brushed away a tear.

"Ooh, this wind's cold," she said. "It's making my eyes water.""Let's go and find a tea shop," said Maree. "Do let me treat you. It sounds as though you could do with a cream bun or two!"

Flo clasped both her hands around her teacup and didn't care that it was not ladylike. Her hands were warm now and she leaned forward to whisper more about her life to Maree.

"You know," she said quietly, "I felt so guilty when Ernest died. I really thought that Philip would die too. I felt I deserved that to happen; I think it was because of Bert. He always told me what a dreadful mother I was and that an accident would happen to Philip because I smothered him too much and he needed to be toughened up, not mollycoddled."

Maree could not stop the tears welling. She swallowed, passed a hand across her forehead and without looking directly at Flo she said, "Mam could be really mean sometimes, you know. She said it should have been Philip who died. That I was the best daughter and I shouldn't have had a child's death to deal with. It shouldn't have happened to me."

Why had she blurted that out? Her cheeks burned. She was as mean as her mother. It should have remained her secret. Their mother would probably never remember saying this. Her memory was often blank these days and the girls were forever reminding her of events past.

Maree sat back in her chair and looked directly at Flo, who was still staring open-mouthed at this revelation.

"I'm so sorry, Flo. That's the worst thing I've ever said. I don't think that, at all. I hate the idea of having a favourite child. That was mean of me to even tell you. Please forgive me."

At least you don't have to choose between children, she stopped herself from saying. What was wrong with her? Her mind was dragging up bitterness and acrimony but it was through no fault of poor Flo's. Was this part of her depression, she wondered? An urge to put others down? She was supposed to be regaling Flo with memories of glorious India and her privileged life there. Was it so privileged, she wondered? The slights she had received made her a fairly solitary person, Nataline being the only one she had shared her thoughts with. Nataline, who had been her staunch backbone when she returned to India after leaving Ernest, and when he had died all on his own in the sanatorium. What a dreadful mother *she* had been.

"Forget I ever said that." She glanced over at Flo who was determinedly eating her cream bun, her face set. She had so looked forward to Flo's visit. Why was she spoiling it?

"I'll tell you more about India, if you like," and she was pleased to see that perhaps Flo was shaking off her earlier comments as she nodded her head in agreement.

"I'd like that," she said. However, her voice was tight and somewhat strained and Maree knew she might never be able to make it up to Flo, her nearest and dearest sister.

The rest of Flo's visit was overlaid with a gauze of tension, almost invisible, but not quite. Maree made an effort to be affectionate to Flo, even when least warranted. Frank noticed the strange atmosphere and asked what was wrong but Maree could not bring herself to tell him. She said that Flo was missing Bert.

In early January Maree received a phone call from Maud. Philip had been reported missing presumed dead whilst flying over Bermuda. Maree dropped the phone and crumpled to the floor. Guilt, guilt. She was so guilty. When Frank came home he returned the beeping handset to its cradle and picked Maree up off the floor where she had been sitting since the early afternoon, pale and shaky.

"Whatever is the matter?" Frank asked urgently as he held her against him. "You can hardly stand; you're shaking. What has happened? Is it Max? Patience? What, then?"

"Do you remember when Flo stayed here last autumn?"

"Of course. Is it Flo? What's happened to her?"

"No, no, not Flo. It's Philip; he's dead. All because of me and what I said."

"What did you say? How could anything you say cause him to die?"

It was a painful conversation but Maree managed to tell Frank about the comment from her mother that she had relayed to Flo. How unthinking she had been, how mean; and now it had all come true. It was all her fault.

"I'm sure your mother can't have meant it. Why would she wish a grandson dead? Well, one over the other? What an abhorrent thing to think, even if it were about Ernest! And for you to then tell Flo!"

"I know, I know; it was so foolish of me. I don't know why I repeated it. I still don't know to this day and now, now..." She burst into tears again and held onto Frank as a drowning person to a life-raft. His hands, soft and reassuring, stroked her back and with a thumb he wiped away the tears as they coursed down her face.

"Come now, come," he said, "this is not your fault. This damned war, it causes so much sorrow and pain."

# Fifty-Two

Neither Philip, nor his plane, nor any of his co-pilots were ever found. His death cast an urgency over Maree and Frank's plans. War was affecting them directly; an unwelcome intruder into their family.

Frank was sitting in the living room reading the paper and looked up at Maree who was fiddling with some knitting, a hobby she had recently decided to take up. More often than not she threw it down in exasperation but she was persevering, determined to make a jumper that Patience would wear.

"I think I'll put some of our furniture from Brooklands into a warehouse," said Frank suddenly. "I would hate to lose any of the knick-knacks we brought back from India, wouldn't you?"

Maree nodded in agreement, counting her stitches loudly in an effort to concentrate. It was no good; she could not manage both things. She put the blue wool down in her lap and looked over her glasses at Frank.

"I just wish we didn't have to go to Manchester at all, Frank. I think we should get Mam to come and stay with us here. I'm really worried about the bombs."

Frank shook his paper and agreed that it would be better if he didn't have to go at all but that he would go once more to persuade Max to return for the time being, together with his mother-in-law, and to put the furniture into storage.

Agnes was only too pleased to come to stay with Maree. She

confided that she had become anxious in her old age and the nightly bombing threats were certainly too much for her old bones. Maree thought it was probably too much for her heart, too, but said nothing. The hurtful words she had blurted out to Flo hung between mother and daughter. Of course, Agnes was oblivious; it was Maree who felt tense with her mother around.

Max would not be persuaded to come home to the holiday house and he stayed on in Manchester, studying as best he could alongside his volunteer work as an air raid warden, a position he took very seriously and gave as the reason for not returning. Max enjoyed the frisson of excitement of being involved in something bigger than himself. He felt he had grown into an adult during this time and although he would not admit it to his parents had no intention of ever returning to the family home.

In his cursory phone calls to his mother, he said that he had met someone and she was becoming very special to him. Maree, of course, was full of curiosity but Max divulged nothing other than that she too was studying accountancy and her name was Doris. And with that Maree had to be content.

Frank had been driving a circuitous route to Stoke, avoiding the metropolis of Manchester as best he could for his own safety but to please Maree too. She chided him before every journey.

"Don't go through Manchester, Frank, it's far too dangerous; you know I can't sleep if I know that's where you're going. I have enough to make me worry with Max refusing to come home; not to mention my sisters, especially Nell with the shop; you know she could be targeted…"

"I think that's highly unlikely, Maree. They don't live in the thick of things, they're not near an industrial area or anywhere that could be thought of as a threat to the Hun," Frank said.

"And what about Ruby? And her family? I think we should ask them to come and stay too," Maree continued.

"That's such a kind thought, but could you really cope with all those children and your own, here? The house isn't that big, you know; it's not Brooklands," Frank said; and Maree, realising the truth of his words, dropped the subject.

Frank returned from Stoke one day with another box of pottery. Maree sighed as she looked around the small house for somewhere to store it before she could find a more permanent position for the pieces to be on show as she knew Frank wanted.

She managed a small smile. "What have you got this time, Frank?"

"Look at this lovely lady, Maree. The old balloon seller. Isn't she wonderful?"

Maree had to admit that she was indeed a much lovelier piece than any of the Toby jugs which seemed to be breeding on the top of the pelmet, up to which she had clambered on a stepladder to place them out of her line of sight. Frank, however, admired them every time he entered the lounge.

She turned the piece in her hands: brightly-coloured balloons looking like shiny gobstoppers; a kindly face, lined but smiling, under a flower-bedecked bonnet. She smiled inwardly, pondering her awareness that she was drawn to any figurine in a bonnet – and knowing the answer why.

"Here, I'll put her here on the dresser. I think we'll have to bring down the china display cabinet at this rate; I have no more room! It's as much as I can do to keep this silver clean."

Frank's chest visibly puffed. He loved the silver tea sets, the biscuit barrel and the beautiful miniature table and chairs with a tiny tea set on top of the fine filigree work. It was a masterpiece that his sister had had made for Patience. His thoughts flew back to his sister. It had been such a blow to him that she had died so soon after they had arrived back in England. His face creased with memories of her: she, who had supported him throughout his whole life and his career; she who had never lost faith in him and had managed to negotiate his scholarships through the Hindu Education Fund. It had meant so much to him that upon hearing of her demise through a curt telegram sent by Jarod he immediately sent some money to the fund in her honour. He had received a kind note from the secretary and the address at the top, Angre's Wadi, took him back, rewinding the years at top speed, to the journey he used to take to the fund's office. The foetid smells, the pale sacred cow with the knowing lash-fringed brown eyes wandering the alleys looking for offerings, the shrine for Hanuman that he raced by with a quick *Namaste*; it was all still there, tucked away, a private world that he rarely visited.

Maree was saying something and he blinked rapidly as his mouth formed an affectionate smile. She was his world. She always had been, ever since the first time he had glimpsed her through the shop window, pale and innocent with her life before her, examining ribbons for a customer.

"Yes, dear, you're right. I should arrange to get that china cabinet sent back as soon as possible for you. I can't see that we will be going back to Brooklands any time soon. This dreaded conflict seems to be getting worse, not better. The peace we were promised seems even further away."

"Don't talk about it! My stomach is in knots as it is!"

The phone rang and Frank went into the hall to answer it. A few minutes later he returned. His face had aged. It was Maree's turn to ask what was the matter.

"It's Max on the phone, Maree. You'd better speak to him."


"How could he do this to us?" Maree sat on the sofa, twisting her rings around her fingers, pulling at them, removing them and replacing them.

"It's what young men do, I'm afraid. He thinks he should fight for his adopted country. Well, you know, it's not his birthplace, is it?"

The balloon seller looked at them from the dresser. Even she seemed to have lost her smile.

"I'd go to Manchester tomorrow if it would help," said Frank sadly, "but he knew that; that's why he didn't discuss it. He just signed up and then informed us."

"I can't lose another son, I really can't... I don't know what I would do..."

Frank did know. He knew she would sink back into that black abyss from which, this time, she might never emerge.

# Fifty-Three

"He'll be training for a while. If it's any consolation, joining the Navy might be the safest of the Forces."

Frank kept his fury at Max to himself. He didn't want to further inflame Maree's grief; he needed to support her. He decided that he would go to Manchester anyway to see if he could pull any strings to persuade Max out of this foolish notion he had. He didn't want his dreams of Max taking over the company in Calcutta going up in smoke, together with Max, of course. How could he be feeling selfish at this time? It was certainly with mixed emotions that he decided to travel to Manchester with the small amount of petrol he had left for the car.

As Maree was too engrossed in the news from Max, she felt no trepidation as Frank set out. The bombing of Manchester had become somewhat sporadic and so thoughts of Max were foremost in her mind, rather than danger to Frank or to her home. Yes, Frank must go. He must persuade Max to resign, say it was a mistake. Could he do that? She feared not, but it was worth a try. How could her beautiful boy be putting himself at risk? He should never have stayed in Manchester. Surely, he must have developed a taste for danger with his volunteering. When he called he mentioned the smell of the burning buildings, the adrenaline rush as he and other volunteers put out fires and moved rubble to find those still alive. He said he liked the warden's uniform, being part of a group, a common cause. She should have noticed the signs. If only she had been more observant and not wrapped up in her own much safer life in Rhyl. The Heinkels wouldn't bother bombing Rhyl; nothing but a pier and entertainment.

She awoke in the night, sure she could hear the whine of aircraft even though knowing that it wasn't likely; but she wrapped herself up in a grey knitted shawl she had just completed, dropped stitches and all, and raced in to rouse her sleepy mother.

"Mam, come with me. Hurry up; I think there's bombers. We'll go to the shelter."

Maree's urgency and the memory of burning buildings were enough for Agnes to hurriedly draw on warm clothes over her nightdress and hobble after Maree into the back garden where the shelter was located.

It was a false alarm; and after about thirty minutes Maree realised that she had not heard any bombers or bombs. It was all in her imagination. And besides, wouldn't she have heard an air raid siren if that were the case? She couldn't stop shaking, though. Agnes held her close as they sat with their backs against the tin, soothing and shushing her as if she were a small child afraid of the dark.

"It's all right, ducks, you're safe. Mam is here."

After a while Maree felt restored enough to stand and she pulled her mother up with some difficulty.

"Where's Frank? He should be here. And where's Patience?" her mother enquired.

Maree realised with a frightening certainty that she had forgotten all about Patience. How could she do that? She raced inside and up the stairs into Patience's room where she lay fast asleep, her black tousled curls on the white pillowslip as she smiled at some dream and licked and smacked her lips. Maree's heart was pounding from both the exertion and the fear. She must never tell Frank: his darling girl left behind while his wife cowered in the shelter with her own mother's protective arms around her. She tiptoed towards Patience and gently put out her hand to pat her and to reassure herself that Patience was actually there and none the worse for being forgotten. She was indeed a terrible mother.

But there were bombs that night over Manchester. The phone call when it came was none less than she deserved. She said that to her mother afterwards. How could I have been so complacent? He was all the world to me. Her thoughts jumbled. Max was alive; she felt grateful. Both he and Patience were alive. She would be fine. Would she? Max said that the warehouse had received a direct hit. Her husband, her loving husband must have died along with the china cabinet and the other fine furniture he had stored in the warehouse. He was going to get the cabinet for her and then... and then... It was hard for the thought to crystallise: while she was cowering in the shelter, a victim of her whims, her husband was being crushed, blown up, mutilated by the very bomb she feared. A stray V bomb from an antiquated Heinkel had steered its way along the streets of Northenden and found the very warehouse where Frank must have been arranging the loading of the cabinet into a small truck.

"No one left, madam, I'm sorry to say," said the warden as he stood in front of the barrier preventing Maree from entering the bombsite.

It was cold. She wrapped her fur around her, Max propping her up.

"Come, Mother, there's no point looking; you can't see anything. It's all gone."

Maree was ice. Guilt. Her life was guilt. If she hadn't agreed to Frank coming to Manchester, this wouldn't have happened. She turned her head sharply and stared at Max. No, it was his fault. He shouldn't have signed up. Frank was coming to talk to him, to persuade him to rescind his decision. The words wouldn't come. She swallowed down the anger.

Maree sat stiffly looking out of the car window, withdrawn into herself, as Max drove her back to Brooklands. The gateman raised the boom as they turned into the road. Maree looked up through the tree branches cowering over them. How blue was the sky. She wound down the window and felt the soft air rush through her hair.

Suddenly, Max braked. The car halted at the driveway entrance. Shaken out of her reverie, Maree's gaze followed Max's. Frank's car was parked in front of the house. She opened the door and fell out onto her knees.

"What? What? What does it mean?" she pleaded with Max who had run around the car to pick her up.

"Frank! Frank!" She screamed at him as he made his way down the front steps, wondering why the car had stopped at the gate.

"What's the matter? What's happened?" Frank asked as Maree rushed into his arms, her legs buckling under her.

"Father, Father! How are you here? I don't understand!" Max clamoured.

"What do you mean? I was summoned to Stoke about some government contract, so I thought I'd go there before sorting out the warehouse and you." Frank raised his eyebrows while looking over his glasses.

Maree was feebly banging her fists against him, sobbing so hard that she couldn't explain. Max began to speak, the words stumbling incoherently out of his mouth.

"We thought you'd been bombed. Last night… the warehouse… everything gone…"

Max dissolved, the shock of his father appearing finally breaking the outer strength he had shown in comforting his mother.

# Fifty-Four

*1957 Old Colwyn, North Wales*

Maree looked in the mirror. She tucked her fur coat tightly around her; her mink hat was cocked at a jaunty angle. But Maree did not feel jaunty. Why on earth did Frank think that standing for council was a good idea? She knew the answers. They had had the discussion more times than she could remember. These usually took place in bed.

Maree would prop herself up on her elbow and look at Frank lying back on the pillow, as he perused the latest Tory policies.

"I don't know if I want to be a politician's wife. I don't like being in the limelight."

"My dear." He turned to her with a somewhat condescending smile. "It's only local politics! The local council. I just think it's time for the Tories. 'Life's better with the Conservatives' just about sums it up. Don't you remember what it was like under Attlee and Labour? We were really struggling as a country. I think it's the right thing to do."

"I don't really care who's in power, Frank, but I do care about us and our family. Do you really think being on the council will help us?"

"It's not about us, Maree. This is about the community and

what's best for us all. I really think it's time I gave more to this country that's been so good to me over the last twenty years."

Maree lay on her back, her arms crossed over her chest covering the fine lace nightie. She sighed. This was an argument she was never going to win.

And so after the blue silk scarf was tied to her satisfaction, she tried to fix the blue ribbon to her lapel. The fur was thick and she pulled back her finger in annoyance and stuck it in her mouth.

"Frank, please come and help me. I've already pricked my finger." She examined the tiny bead of blood on her finger and knew this would not suffice as an excuse for not attending the vote count.

As she waited for Frank to come into the dressing room, she sucked her finger thoughtfully. All that campaigning, all that attending public events. What if it were for nought? She knew Frank would be heartbroken. He had set his sights on public office in his adopted country. Max had warned him about the anti-immigrant vote but Frank didn't feel like an immigrant.

"Don't be silly, Max. I'm well known in the district. I was educated in Manchester, I qualified and worked here. I've been Lodge Master, part of Rotary and now I'm retired I think it's time to do this."

Standing on the stage in the local council school in Old Colwyn, Maree's face was drawn with tension; the count was in. She braved a glance at Frank who was standing with the other candidates, his shoulders back, his hands clasped, his shoes glowing like freshly-opened horse chestnuts.

At the back of the hall a chair scraped across the floor. A short stocky man made his way down the centre aisle, his face determined, his hat between his hands. He blinked furiously, and from his twisted mouth he began shouting.

"Bloody Tories. They don't help me, or any other working man!" He lifted up one hand and with an accusing finger at Frank, said,

"And you, you wog, what do you know about us miners? Come here, take our jobs, marry our women…" He got no further. Two men grabbed him underneath his armpits and, kicking and shouting, he was manhandled backwards up the aisle. He spat in the face of one of the officials,

"You're as bad as he is. Bloody wog; go back to your own country!"

Maree's gasp was loud. Her face was white as she turned to Frank, who had stepped backwards with a strange look on his face. His mouth was open but no words would come. Pain was coursing down his arm; he clutched his chest and stumbled back again, landing heavily on the floor.

He choked, and turned up his frightened face to Maree, his dark eyes losing their focus as he muttered, "I'm not a wog, I'm a professional…"

Maree shushed him, holding his hand tightly in hers.

"I know you are. Frank, you can't leave me. Please don't leave me. What will I do without you? Frank… Frank…"

Her tears fell freely as she was lifted to her feet by the surrounding candidates and well-wishers who stood back in silence as two St John's ambulance men rushed forward to administer to Frank. After a few minutes, the older one shook his head; Maree's knees buckled underneath her. She collapsed.

Maree was standing at the graveside. An icy wind made her gasp and Max tightened his grip on her arm. She turned her eyes up to his and he saw the questions in her gaze. Max's wife Lucy stood behind them, fussing at the boys in their best jackets, their knees red and chapped in the March cold.

It was unbearable that Patience had been unable to be here for the funeral. The telegram from New York, the fog preventing their departure. It was too much. Frank would sort it out. She felt better and turned to tell him so. The empty space to her left and the vision of the dirt piled in front of her sliced through her like a knife as she thought of the leadenness of a world without Frank.

"Take me home, Max," she whispered. "I can't stay here any more."

Max shouldered his way through the mourners who looked quizzically at the sight of the mother and son leaving before the end of the service. Lucy shrugged, and with a slight raising of her eyebrows smiled nervously at those brave enough to meet her gaze.

Maree stumbled on the gravel, even with Max's arm now around her waist. He was sure she was going to fall. She might even wail. She looked so distraught; he needed to take her away from here.

"He won't like it here," she said. "Why did you insist on a grave? He wanted to be cremated," she sobbed.

"Lucy thought it best," he said. "She organised it all for you. Remember? So you didn't have to be troubled by it."

"Frank will be troubled," she hissed, "or have you forgotten he was a Hindu? How could you do this?"

She felt in her pocket for the *Bhagavad Gita*, its smooth leather surface comforting. She pulled it out and held it tightly against her chest and then tucked it between the black buttons of her wool coat.

"What are you doing, Mother?" Max asked. "I thought we were going to put that in Father's coffin. Why do you have it?"

Maree's eyes glittered.

"This is all I have left of him! Lucy has taken away all his clothes, all his books and papers. She won't have this!"

"Mother," Max sighed, "she is only thinking of you. She didn't want you to have to sort all his things out."

"But I wanted to!" Maree sobbed. "I wanted to hold his jackets, to feel the scratchy wool on my skin, I wanted to read his letters, I wanted everything of his! Now I have nothing but this book."

VI

# Fifty-Five

*1971 Colwyn Bay*

"Don't leave me here! Please, don't leave me!" Maree's pleas echoed down the corridor. Patience's pace increased and the cries grew fainter. The mixed smell of urine and bleach arose from the carpeted hallway and she felt sick with it all. It was a dull place; brown carpets and pale green walls mucky with handprints and whatever else she was scared to think.

Max had had enough of dealing with his mother. He had told Patience she needed to come over from her cushy life in the Caribbean. Lucy suggested that Maree go into a nursing home. The initial niggle of guilt he had felt had been quashed by Lucy, as she had insisted on it. She threatened to leave him unless he did so. She would not remain in the family home. Max sighed and had to tell his mother of the decision.

"It's all for the best, Mother. You know you've never been good at taking care of yourself. And now you're just not eating. I can't be looking after you all the time and Lucy is just too busy with the boys." Maree looked up from the sofa where she was sitting, two stale biscuits set out on a patterned china tea plate.

"I can't leave here, Max. Frank won't know where I've gone," she said.

"Oh, Mother," he sighed, as his gaze took in the shrine to his father. A hand-coloured photo of Frank in his Masonic regalia looked out at him from its gilded frame. In front was his black leather *Bhagavad Gita*, creased corners and thumbed pages. Other photos of the family, hand-painted, crowded the small table. At the back stood a small urn which she pretended contained the mortal remains of his father as he had wished. He shuddered. It was time for his mother to vacate this morbid place.

Lucy took charge of the dismantling of her mother-in-law's home. Her no-nonsense attitude made short work of the ornaments, the chests, the furniture, the precious collected belongings from India; keeping a few for Max and the boys, a small chest for Patience for whenever she deigned to come; and the rest of the things, well, they were disposed of. That was her way. When Max came back from a selling trip to South Wales his mother's house was empty. He walked around the rooms wordlessly, his face registering the absences. The shadowed walls outlining where the china cabinets stood; the pelmet where the Toby jugs had frowned down at him; the dents in the pressed-down carpet from the sofa his mother had sat upon alone for far too many years; a rectangle of darker carpet where the Indian carpet had been laid. Memories, it was all memories. And where was his mother now? In some miserable, sad nursing home, the only one Lucy said they could afford for her.

Patience arrived exhausted from her trip across the Atlantic full of intentions to remove her mother, to care for her. But where could she take her? It was impossible, of course. She could not take her back to her life in the Caribbean. She could not stay here away from her own family. She spent the visiting hours in Maree's room. Maree's face brightened as she saw her daughter come through the door. Patience shied from the unkempt woman she barely recognised, shrivelled and sad. Her mother was seated on a chair which should have been replaced long ago, its flowered upholstery stained and frayed, the wooden armrests scratched and pale with wear and the desperation of previous residents. Maree held out a hand whose nails badly needed filing, Patience noted. She was a terrible daughter.

Guilt was replaced by anger. Anger she felt at the institution, at the nurses, at her brother, transformed itself into action. She wet a threadbare grey flannel with warm water at the small chipped basin and washed her mother's hands and face with care. She filed her nails, she shampooed her hair, she tenderly brushed the fine grey strands and curled them around cheap pink plastic rollers. The beatific smile on her mother's face as she worked her fingers through her hair, the unfurling of her body as she leaned back against her daughter, elicited a sob from Patience which involuntarily burst out as tears trickled down her face. Her mother didn't notice.

"Where's my sari?" her mother asked. In the corner of the room sat a small camphor wood chest. Patience wiped her face and rifled through the contents. In the bottom drawer of the chest she spotted the bright fabric edged with gold thread embroidery, as brilliant as the day Frank had bought it in the bazaar. She brought out the fuchsia sari, one piece of clothing that had escaped Lucy's ruthless dispersal of her mother's precious belongings. A sari she had seen her mother wear on only a few occasions. A treasured possession which remained with her.

"Put this on, Mother," Patience said, as she wrapped the voluminous yards around her mother's waist and across her shoulders. "Tell me the story, Mother. Tell me about this wonderful sari."

Radiant; a princess. Maree stared into the mirror. She could hear the swish of the ice-skates, feel Ruby next to her, see the beautiful Indian maharani seated up in the box overlooking the rink resplendent in her glistening sari, jewels winking around her neck and from her ears. She blinked. Frank stood just behind her, draping the fine silk over her shoulder. He leaned down and gave her a kiss on her bare skin. She smiled, smiled up at him.

# ACKNOWLEDGEMENTS

My maternal grandparents, to whom I owe my inspiration for this novel which draws in part from stories my mother told me, together with snippets of information gleaned from the following, *A Rising Man* by Abir Mukherjee, *The Milliner's Apprentice* by Hazel Wheeler and *Every-day Life in South India* by Kuppusvami.

www.ingramcontent.com/pod-product-compliance
Lightning Source LLC
Chambersburg PA
CBHW070546120726
47909CB00007B/2254